E. Alexeev

Gakko Academy

Share the adventure!

Alexeev

Book Two

Magic Dome Books

Gakko Academy
Book # 2
Copyright © Evgeny Alexeev 2024
Cover Art © Linni 2024
Cover Design: Vladimir Manyukhin
English translation copyright © Benjamin Patrick Miller 2024
Published by Magic Dome Books, 2024
ISBN: 978-80-7693-472-6
All Rights Reserved

This book is entirely a work of fiction.
Any correlation with real people or events
is coincidental.

Table Of Contents:

Chapter 1. No Place like Home 1

Chapter 2. Adult Games? 15

Chapter 3. Conclusion 29

Chapter 4. Total Dominance 43

Chapter 5. Party Interrupted 57

Chapter 6. An Alarming Meeting 71

Chapter 7. Hiro's Strategy 85

Chapter 8. Yoshiko Sakurawa 99

Chapter 9. Harbinger of War! 112

Chapter 10. Allies 126

Chapter 11. The Fight 140

Chapter 12. The Night Club 154

Chapter 13. The Duel 168

Chapter 14. The Outcome of the Duel 181

Chapter 15. Old Secrets 196

Chapter 16. Eika 209

Chapter 17. "Shadow".................................... 222

Chapter 18. Listen to Your Gut 236

Chapter 19. The Test 249

Chapter 20. Unintended Result 262

Chapter 21. Not Enough? 276

Chapter 22. An Intense Lunch Break.............. 290

Chapter 23. The Lunch Break Continues 304

Chapter 24. Getting Ready for the Duels 318

Chapter 25. The Duel 332

Epilogue 352

Chapter 1
No Place like Home

I WORE MYSELF OUT working on the armor, literally clenching my teeth. I was suffering from an intense deficit of Psy energy, and so, frankly speaking, God knows if I was getting anything out of my long stay in the hospital or not. It was useful in some way, though. I had no training, no escapades with women, and no more mutilation of my body at the goddamn Gakko Academy. But I was getting practically no Psy from all this comfort. And so the rate of my tattooing was nothing at all.

Even so, it was more than likely that I would get beaten up once again at that odd educational institute, and then I would be right back in the hospital. Even though it may have been a short time, I still took advantage of it. Afterward, in addition to doing the tattoo of armor, I would finish setting up the runes of strength and speed. That didn't take too much Psy, just a whole bunch of time and mental effort. Well, there was the advantage of being in the hospital.

The business could have been improved by Kiyoko, and my girlfriend, never one to disappoint, often visited me right after school. It just was that my mom or Yuki Ueno would always show up right behind her around that time. There were only a few times we managed to be alone together, but some of those times I wasn't able to move my body, and by the time I could have done something, a nurse or some other visitor would always get in the way. What a mess!

Then, when the doctors came to the conclusion that I could be moved and continue my healing process at home, they took me to the Tanaka Clan estate. That is when I made the decision to no longer take my time with those procedures. There was a risk, of course, that I would be beaten up at school, but the threat from the senior nurse was no less dangerous. That needle-shooting hand with its fatal tricks could tear me apart in a single go much harder than any school hooligan. What kind of place was this? There were dangers all around me!

True... But it was good to be home. Fewer shots, more food. There was only one thing missing, and I guess you can figure out what it was. Eika had been promoted, and no one else was allowed onto the estate. My mom made it clear that she wasn't against the idea of Kiyoko visiting, but the matter was complicated by a whole host of archaic customs and ancient pacts. As though it was not proper. If a young girl were to visit the castle of another clan... well, then she would have to get married immediately.

And it didn't even matter that I was okay with that, that I had suffered so much that I was ready to submit to slavery. It had not been settled by our family, but the Takadas. **In general, as soon as Kiyoko so much as brought up the topic, life would show her and me too a big old middle finger, and then we would just have to hope things wouldn't go tits up.**

But while at home I once again my great strides in my healing, and within two days, literally, Matvey Nikolaevich and his team of crafty wolfhounds had started training me again.

Apparently, they had taken my beating as a personal affront, and since they could not get involved with the fighters in a conflict directly, they took all that anger out on me. There was no way to tell if that was punishment for a lesson badly-learned, or if they were trying to make sure I wouldn't get so messed up next time. Whatever the case, I was now training three time as hard. They didn't even give me time for sleep, those bastards!

I had personal training in the morning. Of

course, now you couldn't even call it personal anymore. The warrior Yakut personally attended to my fervor in strengthening my body. If he wasn't sure of something, he stepped in with a simple solution, without any of the complex punishments there. He just doubled the amount of exercises I had to do, the goddamn maniac. Considering the current number of sets was already at the limit of the powers of my rune of regeneration, I was really going to exceed it now. Shit! I would get to the first level of the tattoos of strength and speed like this. Or those monsters would kick me there. To hell with this training!

The Taekwondo trainer wasn't trying to kick me anywhere. He just thought that I already had a rune of strength and speed, at least forty of the final level. How else could you explain his demand that I jump ten feet in the air and hit two boards held up in the sky by a special apparatus? Or that I break ten boards in half by hitting them all with my head, one after the other?

And the goddamn Jiu-Jitsu trainer? How are you supposed to get a lock on a heel flying straight into your face? You think that's a figure of speech? No bullshit, that crazy guy from Brazil would kick me hard in the head. If I managed to get the lock, he would say, "Great job, we will keep training later." If I messed up, my tender nose would once again be forced to make out with the dirty, calloused, and extraordinarily stinky foot of my Jiu-Jitsu instructor.

And freestyle wrestling? You think they taught me some interesting holds, or how to rise up from parterre, so I could romp around with Kiyoko better in bed later? Hell no! They thought I was an idiot, incapable of the higher arts of fighting. So, as a warm-up, they made me throw a 200-pound mannequin filled with sand 300 times in a row.

My muscles were so sore that I couldn't even lift my hand up to my face to wipe away sweat. And that was when that pervert, pardon my French, took me to a tire tread, taken from what seemed like it must have been the Mars Rover, which had appeared in the dojo from God knows where. It was crazy heavy. For the first fifteen minutes I just circled it, groaning, and trying to get a grip on the heavy piece of crap.

According to my trainer, I was supposed to throw that massive piece of rubber from the entrance of the gym to the end, ten times in a row. Jesus, I even tried to use a mop as a lever. At that time the trainer was talking to someone on the telephone, and I had decided to at least move the heavy tread even a little bit. What actually happened was that the mop broke in half, and I, like a real idiot, stood in front of my trainer, staring at the two sticks in my hands in disbelief. And I was supposed to throw this thing from one end of the gym to the other?

"Genji, you will do this," he said softly.

"Trainer, couldn't you teach me wrestling, some holds or throws or anything?" I asked, pitifully.

"No point," the teacher snapped.

"Why not?" I kept whining.

"Because nothing useful will come of it now. It would be 'pearls before swine.' Got it?" He shouted.

"Eh... Trainer, I still don't understand," I shrugged stupidly.

"You complete idiot," the fighter gave me his unflattering assessment. "Right now anyone could lay you out on the tatami and put their pearls on your ungifted face with no problem. You are nothing, you are worth nothing! Now grab that stupid tire and drag it to the other end of the gym!"

To hell with this training. Now they're even threatening me with balls on my face, the perverts!

But in the evening I got what made it worth it to deal the sufferings of the day. Two hours of personal training with Matvey Nikolaevich. He didn't show me any cool moves, in fact he didn't show me anything at all. The Yakut taught me how to think. How to think before a fight, during it, and after. And he taught me how to use my meager arsenal.

"Genji, your main tactic is to work in stages. Wide sweep kicks, low kicks, kicks in the groin, kicks to the inside of the thigh. If you can get to their knees, so much the better. The body is harder, you can only get to it with a side kick. The kick is simple, but not very effective, unfortunately. You have to work on it a lot in order to do any real damage with it. But if you can manage that, it will be a powerful weapon!"

"Teacher, can I work the body with punches?"

"It's too dangerous, since it's not an equivalent exchange. Only do it if you are sure that you can close the distance and then get out of the line of attack. A few short hits to the liver, all around the body, but once again, only if you have no other option, and you can't keep your distance." The trainer gave me, as always, short and effective recommendations.

"Understood. Thank you for your instruction, Matvey Nikolaevich. But why am I considered to be no good at fighting?" I was still stewing about the "pearls before swine."

"You have to understand, Genji... You see how the grapplers train? Holding on to each other, pushing with their shoulders, grabbing their arms?"

"Yes, teacher."

"Well, here it is. That won't work for you. If one of the gifted can grab you like that, then the whole fight is over. He will squeeze you until he breaks your bones and rips your muscles apart, since your physical strength is at completely different levels. Just imagine that you have your opponent in an armbar. What do you think will happen if he is much stronger than you?" Matvey Nikolaevich asked.

"I won't be able to put enough pressure, and he'll get his arm out," I answered immediately.

"Yes. And if you don't let go quickly enough, he will pull you towards his face. What will you do then?" My trainer gave me another riddle. That was how he coached me, always making me imagine different situations and find the best response.

"Headbutt him across the nose?" I said, somewhat doubtful.

"That would work, especially in a street fight. But if the wizard manages to get their forehead out instead of their nose, they you will just mess yourself up. Wizards have an energy shield around them, so it would be like hitting your head against a concrete wall. Of course, you might break through it, but more often than not you're just hurting yourself more," explained the teacher. He had put everything in a comprehensible way.

"So then, what should I do?"

"What you were already doing. Wide throws, deflection, using the inertia of his body. Grab him like he's not a powerful wizard, since his weight and physical properties as an object remain the same. So you have to use it, even though some of the gifted believe themselves to be immovable walls," the Yakut said, chuckling, remembering something from his own life.

"What about pressure points?" Those lessons had been like a breath of fresh air for me. Of course, I could have gotten there myself, but only with my meager experience, a done deal.

"Then everything is more difficult. You can only go for those ones where a wizard won't be able to use their strength, like the sole of the foot, that's a great option, or the finger, or you can use a hook, like you did in your last fight, not a bad choice. Give them a good pull in the earhole or the nostrils or the mouth. Or, what about this?" At that the trainer, unexpectedly having bent his finger into a hook and not giving a single shit about my skin and muscles, jammed it right under my ribs.

"Ah! Hey... Instructor, let go!" I yowled, dismayed. It wasn't just painful, but somehow extremely unpleasant, and I would have paid any price to get away from that hook. But there was no escape...

"There you go! You see how you have to train your fingers? Otherwise they'll have you like a little girl..."

They kept hitting me more and more new exercises. Oftentimes I hadn't even begun to think that I might have the muscles that Matvey Nikolaevich was forcing me to work out. A simple push-up could be turned into a sophisticated torture or an acrobatic trick, depending on your point of view. For example, once they gave me a wooden stick, about three feet long, and made me do my push-ups on it. But the trick was that I had to put an end at an angle to the floor, meaning I had only one point of support and had to do my push-ups using a "gun grip". It was like some sort of local challenge.

Or they would have me hold me arms in the arm with some weight attached. Add to that the pull-up bar, the parallel bars... Soon I would have no need to do my tattoos. Either they would kill me with all this training, or the locals had found something more effective than Psy. Jesus! This much exercise wasn't possible for anybody but cyborgs.

Somersaults, insane jumps, wallruns, gymnastic exercises on furniture... they taught me how to run away from wizards, how to keep my distance in confined spaces, unexpected ones, unlikely ones. It wasn't just about speed, which I still couldn't compare with wizards in, but how to get down from raised areas, practically crawling, and vice versa, how to jump up where they wouldn't expect you.

And we continued working with objects separately too. I personally asked that they fill my gaps in using pieces of cloth, like clothing and towels... And of course there was the standard work with sticks, with blunt objects, spun around to become wide-ranging weapons, piercing and cutting. Goddamn, they even gave almost a whole week for working with the pen! It turned out that when I was in Professor Jackson's lair, I nearly had access to a high-caliber machine gun, but my dumb ass didn't know how to use it right.

In addition to my studies on tactics, I also personally took to studying strategy. It was one thing to learn what to do in a fight, and a completely different one to learn how to escape one or to take it on your own terms. Every other time before I had been forced to defend myself, and always at a disadvantage in numbers. That would lead to nothing good. It was vitally important for me to change the conflicts from fights of one against all into fights of us versus them.

Setting out all the students of Gakko Academy along with their interrelationships was simply unfeasible. That would be hundreds of fighters, along with their families, friends, and enemies. But getting a broader overview of the main gangs would be worth the effort. I have been needing to stop acting willy-nilly for a while, get my shit together by learning exactly where I need to exert pressure, and where it would be good to concede some ground. It was time for me to make my own moves, no longer waiting for them to come out of the woodwork.

I got the basic information from Genji's memory. They boy had been dreaming of taking over Gakko Academy, in some way hoping to duplicate his father's feat of putting together a decently-powerful criminal syndicate made of orphans. His thinking was just too blunt, unrefined. His mind was filled to the brim with fights, duels, and other nonsense. But there was also information about allies, internal connections, the fine details of mutual relationships… It was sparse, though.

I had a magnetic whiteboard brought to my room. They put it right on the wall, and I, armed with colorful magnets, markers, and photographs that I had printed earlier, set about drawing up an outline of relationships. I started with my own class, then on to the whole second year, and then all of the school gangs.

It was imperative for me to draw out my class in as much detail as possible. Their parents, brothers, sisters, relatives, clans, and if I could find the information, even the companies where they worked. I paid special attention to situations where relatives studied in the same school, like with Kiyoko and Akira, or if there were children of the servants of the same clan or the workers of the same company. That let me make additional connections and explained many of the reasons for hostility or friendship.

Well, the easiest link to make was just me and Kiyoko. We were a couple, which meant that Akira Takada and her circle wouldn't give me a hard time. At least as long as there was love and understanding between me and my girlfriend. Or the connection between Makise and Rokero, although I didn't have to worry too much about that, since Makise was hardly ever at school. Okay, now imagine a whole set of connections like that, throughout my class, my year, and the whole school. It was work enough for a whole analytical department!

I would somehow have to find the information, consider it, confirm it... There were social media sites in this world and they would have a ton of it. Some of the school gangs even kept lists of their members there, and on individual accounts people would put up pictures with other people, they would like their friends and troll their enemies. Even some fights started on those sites. A treasure trove of information, but who was going to find it and organize it all?

But I made use of that work right there, on the spot. Yeah, for sure, my classmates had become the center of my attention, laser-focused. I knew very little about the adolescents I had spent most of my time with last year. I was even talking with my parents less often. Genji didn't pay much attention to details, but that was all in his memory, and now it was coming up to the surface under the influence of the rune of concentration.

Well, Ichiro Hattori had set up some kind of club for smart kids, better known at school as the "Nerd House". But shit, he had more boys and girls in his club than any other gang. And now all those dorks were seriously improving their physical strength and speed. There were a lot of them, united by common interests, and moreover, they had been picked on mercilessly all last year by monsters like me and Hideo Takayama. So they would now be cheering each other on, possibly to some terrible revenge.

It might sound funny, but you could make an army of them. What's more, they were the only organization in the second-year that featured students from all four classes, and not because of family ties, but because of their real shared problems, interests, and goals. Sheesh, they even went to the café every Friday! One of the nerds had put a picture on the site with the whole group in it.

So, after looking through all my classmates, I had found a completely different side of them. But the most surprising thing was waiting for me once I got to the tight-knit Kato Brothers group.

Chapter 2

Adult Games?

FOR OBVIOUS REASONS, I paid special attention to Takeshi and Ryuen Kato. I mean, I had ended up in the hospital because of those guys. Everything started out normally. Two brothers and four assistants, the group that had done me in with their bats, and the two girls who hadn't taken part in the conflict. However, I wasn't ruling out the possibility that one of them had been keeping people out from the pool and the other one had been blocking the hallway. Yeah, that's probably what happened.

I knew their names quite well, now I just had a tedious social media analysis ahead of me. Their friends, their families, their pictures. I came to their parents, the brothers', and going through their workplaces and colleagues, I made a fairly unsettling discovery. The Kato brothers were supported by their father, the founder and sole owner of the Kato financial and industrial group.

The children of his co-workers were in our class and supported Ryuen and Takeshi. But I had suspected that for a long time, and the fact was no great discovery. But a thorough analysis of their pictures, meeting places, and all the people that showed up on holidays led to an unexpected discovery. Ryuen had had his picture taken a couple of times with a young, sporty-looking woman. A brunette, not my type, honestly not very pretty at all. But there was something about that girl... Some sort of natural magnetism, the aura of a predator... She was dangerous.

Just what was an adult woman, well put together as far as I could tell, need with a youngster like Ryuen? Was she a predator hunting after the heir to the Kato Group? Hmm... It didn't seem likely. I began a dedicated search. I went through a mountain of photos that Kato and his company had put online and found not just that one woman, but four adults that showed up now and again around the teenagers.

I immediately removed relatives and parents from consideration. These were definitely outsiders. I dug deep into this group of young people. And here it was, clear and concise: a Kato corporation project group. Here the four managers are opening a factory in a neighboring prefecture, here they are representing a start-up in a technological park building, and here they are in their own office.

They had not made a great secret of their activities, engaging in the fairly public lifestyle of young, talented, promising middle-managers. So there was a good number of pictures of their office too. Of course, they were carefully airbrushed, without any extraneous detail. But in one of them, a part of a whiteboard, accidentally left in the picture, caught my eye. For anybody else, that tiny scrap of information wouldn't have raised any suspicions. Almost no text at all, just lines leading who knows where. But I had the exact same outline, so I was interested in it.

My little investigation had yielded fair results. I was not fighting with the Kato brothers at Gakko Academy, but rather with the might of their father's organization. Okay, those guys, like my trainers, were not formally interfering, but where do you draw the line? Training a child is a sacred right, and it's not like they were teaching me to fight a specific enemy, collecting all the information about him beforehand and mapping out all his problems and weak points. All of my classmates are trained like that, not to mention other kids too.

But here there were third parties clearly gathering information about students, analyzing it, developing tactics and strategies, and then directly coaching kids. Sure, they didn't send their own warriors after me, but they meticulously planned an attack on me in the showers, setting up the roles, resources, and time. What else could that be besides a direct threat on a student by adults? So now we have a completely new weight class, meaning we need to make completely different decisions. I needed to figure out as quickly as possible how many soldiers were in my personal army.

I found my father in his office. Luckily, he was alone and could spare a minute for me.

"Dad, hey. Could you tell me how I can interact with the soldiers in my unit and how many there are?"

"Son, do I understand that you want their help to solve a problem you are having at school?" asked my father, staring at me intently.

"Yes, dad." I wanted to explain myself, but my father spoke first. He was the big boss, after all, and he loved to pummel his subordinates and his only son with facts and moral instruction.

"Genji, you must understand that that is not the best solution to your problems. Imagine if the Tanaka Clan helped their son today, and then the Takada Clan responded in kind tomorrow. A war between adults leads to nothing good. The weak young become strong because of their parents, while the strong ones might end up destroyed. Is a school dispute worth those losses?"

I let my father talk in peace, since what he was saying was exactly right.

"Dad, what if adults from the Kato

Corporation have already started working against me?" I said, shocking my father with the news.

"What? How do you know that?" My father was already on his feet, like a tiger ready to pounce.

"Dad, I did some research on the Kato brothers' social media. They shared some pictures with a few people—"

"Hold up! I don't understand. Do you have anything more obvious?" My father's question was reasonable. My words must have sounded like so much gibberish to him.

"I have an outline in my room. Come with me and I'll show you. Then it will all make sense." I said, excited about it. It would have been really hard to explain my conclusions in words. I felt like I knew exactly how right I was, but I couldn't prove it.

For the next half hour my father and I went through the outline on my whiteboard. The leader of the clan went through the photographs with a fine-toothed comb, looking over the profiles of the suspects and comparing them to the pictures of workers on the Kato Group corporate website. The bit of the board in the project managers' office was magnified as much as possible, making it easy to read two names, the names of Gakko Academy students.

"Hmm... Yeah, it's all clear now, but it's still not easy to prove." My father was leaning his chin against his hand. "On the other hand, we are not a court that has to study the evidence or prove anything..."

"So, can I get the Tanaka Clan's people involved?" I had decided to make things a bit clearer. It was, for me, a matter of life and death, metaphorically speaking. Who knew what those so-called consultants would advise their charges to do next? I barely escaped with my life last time.

"I don't think it a good idea for you to get involved. It is a fact that those people planned and then tried to put into action an attempt on the life of the Tanaka Clan heir. Either from a lack of professionalism, or deliberately... The only thing keeping me from a swift declaration of war is the fact that Kato Group has never gotten in our clan's way before. However, that does not in any way absolve their guilt here," explained my father.

That was shocking to hear. Did he really mean to say that heads might start rolling just because of a school fight?

But how was he supposed to see it? To him it certainly would look like an attempt on my life. Adults had pushed adolescents to kill an ungifted. On top of that, they planned for the victim possibly escaping and used cricket bats to stop it. What else could that be but an assassination attempt hidden under the guise of a normal school fight?

"So what now?" I asked my father,

considering my chances of participating in this issue in a different light.

"You're going to stay home until we can figure out if it is okay for you to go to school. On top of that we can hide how quickly you are recovering," my father said, decisively.

I had nothing else to do but train and call Kiyoko in the evenings. Of course, a phone call is a poor replacement for physical touch. And considering how worn out we were by our training and studies... Well, I had precious little contact with the female sex, might as well be barking at the moon.

*   *   *

"Darling, what is going on with our son?" Hena Tanaka had finally found a moment alone with her ever-busy husband and asked him the question about the one thing she cared about more than Goro in this world.

"That idiot, Satoshi Kato, gave his two sons a whole project group to help them to seize power in Gakko Academy." Goro was stating facts.

"Yes, but we also hire trainers for our son," Hena said, rationally.

"That is true, but there is a fine line between the two. Our trainers prepare Genji in body and mind for his ordeals, but they do not use their arms and legs for him, and they do not think for him. They can give him tips and strategies for duels, they can hone his skills to a fine point, but Genji himself decides when and where to use them. But it seems to be different with Kato. The decision to kill our son and the means used by the attackers were, I am sure, decided by the managers of the Kato Group." This was the leader of Clan Tanaka's explanation.

"Darling, that would be quite hard to prove. If you were to suggest to Genji in a private conversation that he should lie in wait for Kato's sons, then would you not also be considered an accomplice?"

Hena always acted as a critic of Goro's impulsive ideas, to act as a counterbalance, leading to well-considered decisions.

"I understand that this would not be convincing for Satoshi. And we are not so much stronger than Kato Group for me to start flying off the handle. But we can't leave it as it is. Sooner or later the group will get to our son, at best putting him once again in the hospital, and at worst, killing him," Goro concluded.

"So what did you do?" Hena demanded. She knew that Goro had never been so despondent to just come to her for advice, meaning he had taken action already.

"All four were being watched. Normal managers are nowhere near as well protected as the heirs of Kato's manufacturing empire, meaning we have managed to set up in their living areas and their favorite bars and clubs.

Book Two

Our military wing was able to kidnap all the members of the project group today. Everything was done professional, leaving as little trace as possible. I believe we will have at least 24 hours to get our evidence and present it to Satoshi Kato."

"Goro, do you remember how I told you to go easier on our prisoners? Well, forget that! No mercy for those assholes who tried to kill my only son!"

The seizure of the four office workers went off without a hitch. The big man could have put up some resistance, having been a dueling champion and a passing wizard, but the kidnapping team had exhaustive information about the site, and the powerful bandits, not holding anything back, just knocked him down with a two-ton vehicle.

Such an intense yet inelegant method excluded the possibility of any duels, fights, or even noise. The alleyway was empty, the car was stolen, and the unconscious body was instantly loaded into the back and taken who knows where. Any random witnesses could easily assume that an accident had happened, and the kind-hearted driver had simply taken the victim to the hospital himself without waiting for an ambulance.

The blonde was abducted from a stairwell, where the cameras had been smashed in advance and all the lights broken. The region where that hottie lived could hardly be called high-class, so such things had happened before. The girl had just had a knife of frightening efficacy pressed against her face, and, fearful of losing her greatest asset, she obediently followed her kidnappers.

The feisty brunette was caught in a bar. A skeezy boy from the Tanaka band spent the whole night picking the young girl up, and once he had gotten her in the mood with alcohol and dances that were barely acceptable in polite society, he suggested they go together and hook up. The brunette, who had not had sex in a long time, was drunk on lust, took the bait immediately.

Of course, not everything was left up to the irresistible charm and sex appeal of the young lover. The experienced criminal wasn't taking any chances. He had put some miracle-working powder into the brunette's drink, the kind that would drive even the most frigid woman on Earth up the wall. He had even put aphrodisiacs of local manufacture onto his fingers in advance. There's no telling what did the trick in the end, but the poor girl simply had no chance. Of course, she was never taken to bed...

The auburn-haired one was taken last, as he was the leader of the group. But the boy seemed to be quite smart, immediately surrendering upon seeing the barrel of a gun. It's always like that with the smart ones. They try to plan for everything and so end up scared by the simplest threats against their lives.

All four were captured on Friday, right after work.

Nobody was waiting for any of the managers at home. All four were single, non-local, since no others were chosen for the project group. Only loners, unburdened with families and friends, could handle that much work. They had about two days until they were back at work, and their parents, even if they couldn't call them, wouldn't raise the alarm so quickly. So Goro Tanaka would have at least 24 hours to interrogate his captives in detail.

The managers were not soldiers, and they didn't have the training of advance scouts, so they didn't hold out long before they cleared their consciences. This, by the way, is one of the weak points of a corporation. Not being clan members, the hired employees are not ready to die for a common goal and value their lives much more highly than what is to them the ephemeral acquisition of honor and glory for the clan.

Hired experts are good for peaceful work, best when they are educated, experienced in working with different companies or even countries. They have no boss over them to impede their progress. But when worst came to worst, when an enemy was threatening to break their balls or permanently scar up their beautiful face, they always crack.

The work was made easier by the fact that there were four managers. The captives were taken to different rooms and a game as old as time began. The Tanaka Clan had a number of good guesses, and all they had to do was present them as facts obtained from their colleagues in the other rooms, and suddenly the truth would come out. And well, if you let a little blood, threatened to break their fragile little fingers with a hammer or pull out their nails with pliers... Information flows like water.

The Kato Group had made a few strategic errors. The project managers had not received independent financing for their work with Takeshi and Ryuen, with some of their operations paid for directly with company cards, which was comfortable and easy to report. That was how the detective agency hired by them to collect information on the generals and captains of the school gangs was found.

There turned out to be some janitors and security guards who had given information in exchange for small amounts of money, and who could have provided some insignificant support if necessary. That help, such as a shout or holding back unwanted participants, could fundamentally alter the landscape of a school conflict. Those people were on retainer, and the payment came from the Kato Group account. Major breach of protocol.

But there was more to come. The fat one had

obtained a floor plan and photographs of the shower and personally coached Ryuen and Takeshi in their merciless revenge on Genji. That was not military training, but training for a cold-blooded killing, simply using the heirs of Satoshi Kato instead of a gun. The auburn-haired one and another trainer had taught the boys how to use their bats. A scale model of the changing room was made at the corporations training grounds, where the two monsters had learned how to properly beat the Tanaka Clan heir with sticks.

On top of that, many things had been documented. The project group had to justify the money they spent, so the blonde and the brunette never failed to take pictures and videos. The material was carefully collected and meticulously filed away. Some of it could not be obtained, since it was back at the office, but most of it was printed out from the personal e-mails and cloud files of the managers.

All in all, a picture was formed of a deliberate series of attempts on the life of Genji Tanaka. Two attempts had already occurred, and a third had been planned, using the upperclassmen whose parents were dependent on Kato Group. Their instructions about how to do the most damage possible to him, the weapons that were planned, and the methods for their use, all of that left Genji little to no chance of survival, and only his incredible ingenuity and luck had saved his life over and over.

Maybe the managers never even considered that their actions could be interpreted that way, but any outside party, considering the facts of the case, would come to the obvious conclusion. Now the leader of the Tanaka Clan had something to show Satoshi Kato.

Chapter 3

Conclusion

THE REQUEST FOR A CONFAB from the leader of the Tanaka Clan was completely unexpected for Satoshi Kato. The activities of the financial/industrial group and the interests of the criminal clan never overlapped. Different regions, different areas of influence. The Kato Group was engaged in the legal production of various goods, metalworking, and their associated financial services, banking and insurance activities.

The Tanakas were basically running a racket, with small-scale wholesale, real estate, and contraband. It would be theoretically possible for them to overlap in contraband. Some of the components used by the Kato Group had to be imported without going through customs, or otherwise they wouldn't be able to stay competitive on the market. But here too, Satoshi Kato had other criminal partners, completely unconnected to the Tanakas.

In such a situation, there was simply no way to guess why the leader of a criminal syndicate would need to request a meeting with the founder of a legal, above-board company. The thought that it may have something to do with the disagreements between Satoshi's children and Tanaka's offspring had occurred to him, but Kato brushed it aside. It was too insignificant, in his opinion, and what would they even have to say? About fights between three teenagers? It was ridiculous to waste time even thinking about it.

Then what did Goro Tanaka want? Had he possibly decided to risk everything and attempt a takeover over the Kato family business? Unlikely... The criminal syndicate, of course, was no slouch, and, judging from what he had heard, they were fairly strong, but they would have to carefully weigh the pros and cons of getting into a fight with the Kato corporation. The company had recently successfully fended off the efforts of one of the aristocratic clans, and that was not just about getting protection money from shopkeepers.

Perhaps the issue was about the activities of Kato's microcredit organization? Some sort of criminal scheme? Did the Tanakas want to launder some money or find something out about one of their clients? That was entirely possible. Criminals often asked them to clarify the solvency of this or that victim or to check the finances of a company. Racketeers often did not take a fixed sum from businessmen, but rather a substantial percentage of their profits. And how did you establish that? Through the bank, of course.

Having come to that rather logical conclusion, Satoshi began preparing himself for the conversation. Fundamentally, he should refuse Tanaka. Letting out bank secrets had a bad effect on business. Who would trust a bank with their money, if it could be known to criminals the next day? On the other hand, it all depended on how important the client was. If Tanaka had decided to put pressure on a small shop owner, then who gave a damn, he would just give him the information.

Then the criminal clan would be indebted to Satoshi Kato. And if the client were more important? Well, then he would have to refuse. Just business. And those in business had to understand one another. Secure in his conclusions, Satoshi calmed down and went to the meeting in a good mood.

However, despite his conclusions about the peaceful nature of their discussion, Kato did not hesitate to take precautions.

They would be having lunch together in a rather popular restaurant with a large number of customers, meaning that there would be no way to use violence to solve problems. On top of that, the founder of the company was always accompanied by five or six bodyguards. They were all wizards at the rank of Sensei, as was Kato himself. In most cases that small army would be enough to deal with any problems, especially in a well-populated and public place. That was all that mattered, just to hold out until the city police showed up, and they could deal with the breakers of the peace.

But the first alarm bell went off when the leader of the Kato Group entered the restaurant. The seasoned warriors experience gaze immediately picked out at least ten gifted warriors arranged around the boss of the Tanaka Clan. On top of that there were also ordinary criminals of the clan in the room. Some of them had come as couples, trying to give off the air that they were just there to eat, but gangsters make for shitty actors. That was alarming. There were simply too many of them for a simple conversation.

But it was too late to back out now, so Satoshi approached the table with his warriors. The bodyguards looked around, trying to find good places for themselves, but no matter where they sat, there were enemies all around. In all likelihood, even Kato's cars had been blocked outside by people from the Tanaka Clan. This was no simple business meeting. It was rather more like an all-out criminal visitation. That kind of thing also made Satoshi angry, and he could fight fire with fire. That was why, to be sure, his company had survived so long and was still independent to this day.

"This does not seem like a friendly conversation!" said Kato, straight off, no hellos, as obstinately as possible.

"You thought I invited you so we could have a nice chat together?" Goro Tanaka smiled sardonically.

"Then we should have met in the woods. We could have worked out our misunderstandings without bothering anyone." Satoshi took another tack, clearly showing his displeasure with the Tanaka Clan.

"Could have been in the woods too. Right now we are going to kidnap you and take you away," responded Tanaka, calmly, making no threats, but no less terrifying for it. And few could doubt that the gangster could not back up his words with actions.

"I don't really feel like being in this annoying situation anymore." Satoshi said, putting his chopsticks to the side and crossing his arms over his chest. Goro, on the other hand, heartily dug into the food set out on his plate.

"Too bad for you. You should be getting all you can out of life. Who knows when it will just... end?" The threat in Tanaka's words was much clearer now, and Kato could not help but respond.

"You called me here to threaten me? Is it war you want? I'm ready for it!" Satoshi left no doubt that he was confident and ready to fight, even though he had fewer numbers and would definitely lose. That did not mean, though, that his opponent would carry an easy victory. Fighters from his corporation were already hurrying on their way, and that could change the situation entirely.

"Don't get all worked up, Kato. If I had wanted to fight you, then your factories and offices would have already long been burned to the ground. And you can be sure that I have good reason for it," Goro said, heavily, like a ponderous mountain. He was capable of exerting pressure and destroying someone with words and glares alone.

"Then voice your concerns and stop beating around the bush. I am ready to take responsibility for myself and my people." Kato was shaking slightly, but he was not giving up. He could also go blow for blow, taking as well as he gave, otherwise he would never have become who he was.

"Good to hear. I am pleased to know that you are ready to answer for the work of your people." Goro chuckled. "You are right. Let us not waste time. This file contains everything that led me to contact you."

At that, the gangster handed over a hefty

folder containing photographs, plans, and pages of evidence. There was a lot of material, and a less well-prepared person might have gotten lost in the mountain of paper, but Kato had seen more. Moreover, the report, as might be expected, had been made in accordance with the standards of his company and organized in a way that was intuitively comprehensible for its founder. What, had one of his workers made it?

The reader was captivated and focused, and Kato was more and more interested the more he read. Shit, his own managers had done this? Goddamn idiots, wasting so many resources on solving Ryuen and Takeshi's school problems? How could they have taken this minor issues so seriously? At the same time he no longer wondered who had made the report. Those deluded fools from the project group had made it themselves, most likely while sitting in the Tanaka Clan's dungeon.

Having acquainted himself with the documents, Satoshi sat still for a while, digesting the information and readying himself for a difficult conversation. During that time, his conversation partner ate one food after another, utterly unfazed. But now his inflammatory behavior and barely contained rage were understandable. Kato himself would be unbelievably angry at anybody who tried to do the unthinkable and take the lives of his children.

"Certainly you don't think that we did this on purpose?" Satoshi said, having collected himself.

"You don't really think it matters to me, do you, whether or not the Kato corporation's people did this on purpose? How would you react if some Tanaka members had accidently crippled your sons?" Goro answered the question with a question, and it was hard to argue with his logic.

"You are right. I recognize that I am at fault and I am ready to take responsibility for my negligence and the actions of my people. However difficult it might be, Satoshi was capable of admitting his wrongs and take his lumps. And it didn't matter that Tanaka had more fighters with him now, since Kato would have no less in a few minutes. It was just that Tanaka had given absolutely logical and well-formed arguments. You had to pay for your mistakes.

"Well then, call off your men. We have blocked them off on a neighboring street. Also, right now Takeshi and Ryuen are guests of the Tanaka Clan, so I would not try to make this into an armed conflict, if I were you," Tanaka, still unfazed, said without missing a beat. "And make no mistake, we have roughed up your people a little. But they are all alive, and their debt to the Kato heirs has been paid in full."

"Was it really necessary to take my sons?" asked Kato, upset at the situation, himself, the careless security officers, his stupid sons, and the exceptionally dimwitted managers of the project group.

"Well, I had no way of knowing whether you would react logically. Maybe you would just come in guns blazing? Then all of this careful military strategy would have been for naught. Then the police would get involved... How will we solve this problem?" Tanaka asked, bringing up the main point of the meeting.

"Hmm..." Somewhat surreptitiously, Satoshi had already begun to set forth a concept he had worked out a little in advance. The founder of a massive corporation could tackle even the most difficult problems. "First off, my sons and their friends will swear an oath of loyalty to Genji Tanaka, not as servants, but as mercenaries, lasting until the end of their school years, with no payment."

"Don't you think they will lack motivation? My heir does not need anyone to be on his side through force." Goro felt it necessary to make this clear.

"The boys will judge it correctly and they will understand. What's more, I have already suggested that they give up. Your son is too tough of a nut to crack. And there is no shame in working for the strong. It will be advantageous for my sons now, and later, in the upper classes, they will be a reliable support for your child." Kato, as always, was clearly laying out the advantages of his decision, hinting at the fact that Genji was not a wizard and the gap in their powers would only grow over time.

"Makes sense," agreed Tanaka, although they both knew that that was meager compensation, not nearly enough to close the issue.

"Are the managers alive?" Kato asked, predictably.

"Alive, whole and hearty." Tanaka allowed himself to jest a little. The tense nature of the conflict had relaxed, since Kato had shown himself a decent man, not afraid to own up to his mistakes.

"I have a business site associated with the project group. Right now it consists of some manufactures who are autonomous of Kato Group and a small mall. I was planning to diversify some of my stock and start building a new, independent company for my sons. The property is all valued at five to six million pounds. I offer all of it to you as compensation for these inconveniences." Satoshi managed to force the words out. It was always hard to part with honest money.

"Hm, yes... one after another," stated Goro Tanaka, cryptically, and offered Satoshi his hand as a gesture of peace.

He was thinking about his son's rapidly expanding holding company. The small chain of laundromats, stores, pharmacies, and other small places had been enlarged by a clinic, an office, and now some manufacturers. Genji would have all the opportunities to build his own completely legal empire. The Tanaka Clan had gotten more from Kato than he expected, but... If he put the life of his son in terms of monetary value, then the payment was a pittance in the face of the possible loss.

* * *

Goro had not been bluffing when he said that Takeshi and Ryuen were guests of the Tanakas. The boys were being held in one of the small restaurants owned by the clan. It had been closed to guests, with only two customers in it now, chewing their basic sandwiches without any appetite, served to them by a soft-hearted waitress.

"How long do you think it will take our father to deal with Tanaka?" Ryuen asked gloomily.

"I don't know, but I'm sure it has to do with us," answered Takeshi, who had spent the entire time analyzing why this might have happened. The younger Kato heir had come to some rather unsettling conclusions.

"You think so? You really think Genji's father is that stupid? To do all this because of a school fight!" Ryuen was always superficial in his thinking, incapable of deep analysis, so he couldn't really get how badly they and their friends had messed up.

"It's not about the fight, it's about who started it," answered Takeshi curtly, side-eying him.

"What do you mean? It was us and the guys from the Kato Group who started it," Ryuen said, annoyed, comprehending nothing.

"And there's the rub. Think a minute, what would happen if some Tanaka gangsters killed us?" Takeshi had taken to simplifying everything.

"Okay, yeah, that wouldn't be good. But those guys didn't come to the fight with us." Ryuen's words, despite being a little petulant, carried a kernel of truth.

"Now it all depends on how they interpret it," Takeshi said, confusing Ryuen.

"So are they going to let us go, or not?" Ryuen asked, returned to the simple issue before them.

"They will," I said to Ryuen, having been eavesdropping on the last part of the conversation before opening the door to the café.

Our dads had come to some agreement and decided that I should take the Kato heirs home myself. Yeah, I wasn't too happy about the idea, but who was I to argue with the joint decision of a business mogul and a criminal mastermind?

On the way to the Kato estate, my classmates were silent, feeling offended, although really I was the one who should have felt that way. But I felt like my father had come to some agreement with the elder Kato, and that couldn't have been that easy. So I had to just be patient and wait, even though I was really wondering what the mighty gangster and the business mogul had in store for those two.

The reality of it surpassed all my expectations. A decent force was waiting for us at the Kato home. In addition to the founder of the company and my father, it seemed like there were colleagues, the parents of my four classmates, and the whole group of project managers, who I had expected. Hmm, the blonde was even better in real life than in pictures...

Dammit, this again. This was definitely from either the local energy or the concoction I had swallowed. There was something off about my reaction to women, and their corresponding desires were also starting to make me question. I used to think I was just that attractive, but now I was starting to be plagued by troubling doubts.

Okay, Fumiko might just be under the influence of her job. There are teachers who lose their virginity to eighteen-year-old boys... Eika might have been working on some long-term plan. I was the son of her boss, after all. Kiyoko had just fallen in love with me... But all of these explanations taken together, even though they were logical, still were somewhat alarming. And now this hot blonde shows up...

Yeah, I got off-topic again. Basically, all of these people, in simple terms, were here to pledge fealty to me. Uh-huh, just like in the Middle Ages. I'm joking, of course. But for my classmates I was basically their lord for the next three years, and the project managers were so on the hook that they may as well be considered slaves, well-paid slaves, but slaves nonetheless. And they were just that at Kato Group, just their master had changed.

I also was given to understand that I had gotten somewhat richer, and my holding company had been enriched with new spheres of activity. Damn, Yoshiko wouldn't be able to deal with all that. But the group of promising managers were now also workers at the holding company, and they would pick up the slack. As for me, the schoolboy Genji Tanaka, all these little additional things were hardly worth worrying about, since now I had more money than I could manage or even spend.

What I was most thrilled about was the outline that the project managers had made, the one describing all the gangs at Gakko Academy. Their work was much more substantial and informative than my own, but then again, they had spent multiple times the amount of money and time that I had. Now direct interference by the adults in the goings-on at the school were banned, but I was allowed to use what they had already acquired. Meaning that I now knew the school better than anyone else, almost certainly.

Chapter 4
Total Dominance

MY POSITION IN THE CLASS had become uncontestable. My six vassals under the leadership of Takeshi and Ryuen Kato, my former friends the Wada twins, Rokero Abe, and Jiro Fukuda, along with Ichiro Hattori and, obviously, my girlfriend Kiyoko made me the unconditional leader of the class. The remaining loners in the class would have to side with me, or they would not survive. Even if one of them managed to get recruited by one of the school gangs, they would still have to spend most of their time in the classroom. Nobody could stay stubborn in that situation for long.

Still, having studied the enormous work of the young Kato Group managers, I had come to the unsettling conclusion that my position had not really improved, but had actually gotten worse. Now, as the leader of the class, I would have to answer for them in front of the school gangs, each of which would want to add this tight-knit group of ten warriors to their own army.

My fights, seen in relief from the opposition of upperclassmen, could be considered meaningless scuffles. The teenagers at Gakko Academy were absolutely fighting for leadership in th school nearly every day. You wouldn't even need a formal reason to start a war. An off-hand comment, a loud laugh at the wrong time... All of a sudden the conflict spirals into a free-for-all war.

I came back to school the next day. I had no intention of breaking my rule of being a little late to my first class. This despite the fact that nobody had ever been at my locker.

Click-clack, click-clack. Behind me I heard the swift tapping of heels, and I turned quickly. Damn. It was not Fukimo, not even some pretty teacher that I could enjoy looking at. No, behind me came the clicking of the heels of the terrible math teacher.

"Genji Tanaka, wait a moment," her voice came suddenly, although I was hoping to make a quick exit.

"Ms. Yasuko, I am late for history," I said, somewhat impolitely trying to extricate myself from this tiresome bitch.

"Don't worry about that. I will inform your history teacher that you were late because of me. I would like to discuss your prior successes in my subject. Are you working with someone at home?" It was like the harpy was reading my thoughts.

God, she has such a harsh look. I never felt such a wild desire for her before, but my sexual desires were so random now. So it was good that I had such a satisfying choice of beautiful womenfolk that I wasn't forced to abandon all good sense.

"Teacher, I studied the subjects by myself. When you're in a cast and you have no access to the internet or TV, then you end up with a ton of time to work on yourself," I answered as honestly as I could, since the feeling of that demon woman reading my mind was still so strong.

"That's odd. It doesn't work like that, Genji. To close such a significant gap is unbelievably difficult to do on your own, and considering your consistent absence from the lessons, it is extraordinarily unlikely..." The bitch had begun to voice her thoughts out loud. "Or you have some special talent."

"Ms. Yasuko, I have no great talents, and I've also recently been hit over the head so many times that I think I've lost all my ability to study." I instinctively began drawing the teacher's unwanted attention away from myself.

"Maybe so, Genji," the bitch said, somewhat perplexed.

To hell with this, I would just fail the next exam! I would have to play a real idiot, otherwise I wouldn't be able to get away with it when this bitch got me in one of her mathematical mazes.

"Ms. Yasuko, may I go?" I reminded the bitch that I was there.

"Fine, go..."

I went into the class, confidently surveying the students. The first thing I saw were the surprised eyes of Kiyoko, shining with warmth. The Kato brothers, pacified, watched me in anticipation of fulfilling their duty, Rokero lowered his head cautiously, Ichiro bowed warmly... Not everyone in the class knew yet why it was so, but they were sure that Genji Tanaka had once again achieved leadership of the second D class. And his rule was now even more stable than it had been last year.

During the break, Kiyoko, who had missed me so much that she wasn't even a little bit shy, attacked me with hugs. Even though that wasn't really what I wanted, it was still quite nice.

With things like that, the class went by extremely fast. Nothing particularly interesting happened all day. The whole class went to lunch together, taking our tables in an orderly fashion, showing we were a unified whole.

I looked at those around me, making plans for the future. Today I had to discuss how we were going to survive with the stalwarts of my future gang. No one was denying that there would be opposition from the upperclassmen, and we had fights ahead of us. And we didn't know whether it would be better to maintain our independence or to join one of those gangs. Neither one guaranteed safety or a lessening of school fights. So we had to choose the lesser of two evils.

I invited the guys to my apartment that evening. We would have to decide how to act in the future together, since it would affect all of us. Getting everyone to agree would be nearly impossible. The more people there are, the more opinions there will be, making it very difficult to come to a unified point of view. Just the most important people would be enough for my council, that is the Kato brothers, the Wada twins, Ichiro Hattori, Kiyoko, and that was all. The rest of my classmates would somehow have to agree with one of them.

I had ordered food and drink to my room in advance. I was planning to have a business meeting and then a little party, as a sort of teambuilding. We decided to walk to the office, since it was only ten minutes by foot, at most. The combined security of the Tanakas, Katos, Takadas, Wadas, and Hattoris guaranteed that everyone would be safe. Only a crazy person would decide to attack the heirs of five different families.

There was an awkward silence amongst the guys at first. I had gotten together a group of too many different kinds of people. The Kato brothers had always been on the outside, making a point not to talk to anybody but their own group. The haughty Wada sisters cared only about Genji and his hangers-on. Ichiro Hattori was a complete outsider, a nerd that the guys even now were watching in puzzlement.

Kiyoko Takada had spent all of last year pretending to be a sweet little angel. One thing was sure. Before she broke through, the fragile girl, skinny as a nail, could barely have shown any physical prowess or anger in a fight, but magic had changed everything. And I decided to work with the fact that many in the second year still overlooked her. The gifted change all the time. Class leaders lose their positions and the upper echelons found new stars. Only the upperclassmen, with the advantage of years, understood what was happening, constantly watching out for potential newcomers to add to their armies.

We quickly reached the office. An elevator had been added to the penthouse, with access from the parking lot right under the building, meaning that the three-story office space was essentially separate, and I would not bother any of the rented properties with my guests. The door with a code lock, the elevator with mirrors and chrome handrails, and here we were, in the small foyer of my cozy little headquarters.

Opulence and space would not surprise the

children of businessmen, military officials, and gangsters, but the guys were looking around with their mouths hanging open. They were not shocked by the richness of the place, done up in the local minimalist style. They were shocked by the fact that their peer had already been giving such expensive real estate. Everyone could calculate how much it cost. I suspected that the parents of the students of class D at Gakko Academy were in for some difficult conversations.

We decided to eat right in the office, where there were comfortable chairs, little tables, and a whiteboard. I ordered food from a nearby restaurant, ramen in boxes, meat with rice and fish and vegetables fried in batter that could all be eaten in in a place that was not all for eating. Also, these teenagers were in no way ready to make some sort of official feast, and to me that kind of tradition was completely unnecessary. On Skayd we had to choke down our pills wherever we could find a convenient place, and nobody cared about eating together.

"Guys, I have brought you here to discuss the future of our class. You all know that we are coming upon a time of conflict. The upperclass gangs are gathering forces, so they will be trying to sow dissension among us, drawing us into an all-out war... I'm not even going to talk about our neighboring schools. That is a problem, but before we start trying to solve it, I need to know. Are you with me?"

"Yes, Genji!" Kiyoko shouted first and immediately blushed.

"Nobody doubts that," said the Wada sisters, unable to keep from making a snide remark. But then they answered my question, "Just like last year, it is the same this year. Genji Tanaka is our boss!"

"You know it!" answered Takeshi for himself and his brother. For now they were my most loyal supporters, although only it was not of their own accord.

"I am with you, Genji," added Ichiro Hattori last, shyly, once again perplexing the others, who believed him, with reason, to be too weak to make that decision. But I saw potential in him for my future army, and I had seen his spirit in the fight with Hideo, and I valued his sharp mind, which was why he was with me.

"Very well," I had taken this role somewhat formally, but it was a necessary expression of loyalty to their new/old class leader. "We have two ways to survive at Gakko Academy. The first is to join one of the school gangs. The second is try and stay independent. Let's discuss which one we should choose."

"Joining one of the upperclass gangs is not that bad an idea. Of course we will have to work for them, but being part of a larger force is safer," said Takeshi first. It made sense. He had planned the same thing with the project group and had no reason to change his mind now.

"On one hand, we will be protected by their authority, but on the other, we will have to take part in their fights. What is more dangerous now, that's hard to say, since the upperclassmen have a lot of unresolved issues," said the Wada twins, unexpectedly well-informed. Well, one of them said, and the other nodded along.

"Akira would take us into her gang, if Genji agreed to it," saying Kiyoko, putting in her two cents.

None of them, except the Kato brothers, had every seriously considered the issue before, so each one was looking at it very superficially.

"Genji, what if, instead of just standing on our own, we try to get stronger by using the other classes?" asked Ichiro Hattori, unexpectedly bold. He had not disappointed me, showing his sharp analytical mind. It was hard to come to that conclusion on your own.

"Oh, hey, Ichiro, what, have you grown a spine?" The Wada sisters were staring at him in disbelief.

"Hah, as if they wouldn't destroy us, and now he wants to fight with the whole school," Ryuen said, showing off his slowness. Takeshi, for his part, justifying his reputation, carefully watched my reaction to the statement.

I wasn't about to waste time. I had studied the Kato corporation project group's materials and come to the same conclusion as Hattori. It had just been easier for me. I had everything prepared for me, while Ichiro, as far as I could tell, was just using the facts that his group of nerds had been able to find.

"So, what do you say, Genji?" asked Takeshi, understanding that I had come to the meeting with my decision already made. It was just valuable to know in advance if everyone else would accept it.

"I prefer Hattori's idea. Let me explain why. First think about our possibilities if we join with one of the school gangs. Kiyoko, will you tell us about Akira Takada? You don't need to spill any of your sister's secrets, just what is known in the school."

"Sure, Genji. Akira is the strongest fighter in the school, and she has chosen her army to match her. They are the fourth-year A class. But over the last year and throughout this year, my sister has managed to subjugate the B class too. Her gang has twenty to thirty fighters, all wizards with a well-developed gift," Kiyoko gave the sales pitch for her sister.

"Yeah, but Takada's army has a major problem. In fighting for supremacy in their year, they have overlooked all the younger classes, and now there are no third-years with Akira. What do you think will happen to us when they graduate?" Ichiro asked pointedly.

"Dammit, I didn't think about that!" Takeshi, who had been planning to align the class with Takada after my destruction, put his head in his hands.

"Yeah, Kato, you have to think before you start breaking bones," the Wada twins rebuked him.

"It's true," I said, taking the role of discussion moderator, "Takada is our best choice, especially for now. Both because of her link to Kiyoko, and for defense... But a year from now we will be destroyed. I know firsthand that a weak leader will always be kicked while he is down! But don't take that personally. I am not at all upset with you."

"Okay, who else then?" asked Takeshi.

"Not Hiro Sasaki, for sure," Ichiro answered for me. The army of the fourth D class was considered to be the weakest one at school.

"I agree," Ryuen gave his support to the nerd.

"Yeah, that is not the way for us to go, joining those weaklings, even if they have joined up with the third D class and seem to want to grab us too," the Wada twins chimed in.

"What's wrong with Hiro?" asked Kiyoko. "He is a strong fighter and could easily take on other classes, but he only holds sway over D class, out of principle!"

"Who really knows? A lot of people think that he's touched in the head," answered Takeshi with his opinion. "It just means he's not the right fit for us."

"Hmm... That just leaves the leader of the

class C army — Osamu Saito?" Ichiro asked himself. You could tell from that that the guy was uncertain on the inside as well.

There were bad rumors about Osamu Saito circulating around the school. He often meddled in the affairs of the weak and had been caught trying to mess with first-years multiple times, in contravention of all the unspoken rules of Gakko Academy. Only Akira Takada and Hiro Sasaki were holding back the baser instincts of that bastard.

"Oh no, we have no business with that psycho," said the Wada sisters, crossing themselves.

"I'm afraid of him." Kiyoko shrank into herself.

And, in truth, that dick had been terrorizing all the pretty girls in the school. Even Akira's protection had not guaranteed Kiyoko's safety completely last year. Perhaps that was why my girlfriend had tried to hide her beauty at school.

"But they're still the most promising gang at school. The fourth-year C class took over two third-year classes — A and C. Next year, if they get enough second-years, they'll be the strongest army in the school!" Takeshi began talking like that, pragmatically, not giving in to his clear inner distaste. But then he said, "But I still don't want to be under Osamu Saito, not for anything!"

"So, what, there's nothing left for us?" Ryuen had seemingly awoken from a nap and was now looking at everyone with eyes wide in shock.

"Well, not necessarily. There is still the third-year B class. They say their leader, Makise Abe, is planning to come back to school." Ichiro Hattori once again showed off how well-informed he was, then hinted at my own victory over Abe, saying, "And now, thanks to our boss, we know why none of the four could knock him off."

"What, the Abe clan prodigy has decided to come back to Gakko?" The twins were shocked, since there would be no shortage of people trying to capture a developing prodigy.

"I heard that Aoki Ketsu himself guaranteed the Abe heir's safety while inside of Gakko Academy," shared Kiyoko.

"Ahh... so we should submit to Makise?" suggested Ryuen, completely crazily out of place, showing how confused he was, for which he got an elbow in the side from his younger brother.

"What is stopping us from taking over the third class?" I decided to shock my classmates with that.

"But Makise—" Takeshi suddenly cut himself off. "Wait! You did it once, and that means you can do it again. But the issue isn't just Makise. The third B class is all tough bastards, that's why they managed to take on the Gakko gangs in the first place!"

"Guys, what you said covers all the answers to our problems," I said. "From Makise and his class we can see an example of how you can stay independent without joining an upperclass gang. It is possible to take over the third B class. I was able to defeat Makise once, which means that you can destroy his army. But to be more assured of victory, we should start by getting all the rest of our peers to join our class!"

Chapter 5

Party Interrupted

AFTER WE DISCUSSED EVERYTHING, I invited the guys up to the roof. A pool party was just the thing to bring us all closer together. I had already shown my classmates the rooms where they could find their swimsuits. Kiyoko changed in my bedroom, which I did on purpose. Maybe today would be the day to be with her. I could hardly wait to be alone with her, but it would be pretty rude to just leave my guests like that. So, after satisfying myself with a long-awaited kiss, I began to play the role of a good host.

Everybody went upstairs in a good mood. Up there were snacks, fruits, drinks, comfortable lounge chairs, and an amazing pool. My classmates were super excited about all the extravagance. They weren't surprised by the pool with a sauna, but by the fact that it had all managed to fit on the roof of a normal five-story building. After partying a little, everyone jumped into the pool. We swam around, sweated in the sauna, and just had fun for a couple of hours. Time flew by.

I didn't just have strategic plans about Gakko Academy that evening. I also had more... worldly intentions with Kiyoko. The penthouse was enormous, and we would find a place to hook up. We, almost entirely shamelessly, were kissing, and having taken the far end of the pool, I taught my beautiful girl how to swim. Sometimes we clung close to each other, sometimes I brazenly caressed her where her swimsuit was open.

The Kato brothers got along well with the Wada twins and also ended up splitting into pairs. Ryuen was playfully splashing around with Suzu in the water, while Takeshi was lying on a lounge chair with Rika, chatting about something. The younger Kato had already allowed himself the liberty of placing his hand on the girl's thick thigh, and Rika was utterly ignoring his forwardness. Only Ichiro was left to his own devices, but that guy seemed to be doing just fine, talking to someone on his phone. Most likely with Tomoko from the second C class, who was the cause of his fight with Hideo Takayama. Well, I was planning to strengthen our group, starting with an alliance with the C class. Hideo kind of owed me one, anyway.

There wasn't too much time left. Soon we would all have to go home, since we had school tomorrow. Without even realizing it, I, intoxicated with the closeness of Kiyoko, had pulled her into my bedroom. It was like I was in a trance, and she was acting no better. It would be naïve to write that all off as just teenage hormones and young love. Something was clearly happening to me, something that let me have an effect on the various women who fell for me.

But I just didn't have the strength to worry about that now. I was dying of desire, and Kiyoko was showing no less passion. We had all but run into the bedroom, and I, without pulling away from her honeyed lips, locked the door. We had just about all our clothes off. Her bra was torn off, flying onto the floor, and the sight that was revealed literally blinded me...

I brought my lips to one of her breasts, grabbing the other and squeezing hard. I quickly put my free hand down her dainty little panties. Kiyoko was just as horny and just as forceful as I was.

And her phone rang. Constantly, insufferably... At first Kiyoko just waved it off, but then the ringtone changed, almost imperceptibly. Coming to her senses immediately, she grabbed the phone and pressed it to her ear.

"Yes, dad, I will be down in a minute," answered Kiyoko while putting her clothes on.

Son of a bitch!

"Did something happen?" I asked as soon as she finished her conversation.

"The Mori clan has declared war on the Takada clan. Genji, I cannot disappoint my father. My place is in the keep of our ancestral castle." Kiyoko had a look of sympathy for letting me down on her face.

"Darling, everything is okay. We have our whole lives ahead of us!" I said to calm her down and started looking for my own phone.

I suddenly had the selfish thought that I shouldn't have brought Kiyoko to my bedroom, where she had changed her clothes and left her phone. If not for that, we might have gone all the way. But, more likely, Takada soldiers would have just broken in and taken the heiress of the clan. Dammit, we should have just left the other guys sooner!

"Thank you for understanding, Genji."

"Let me walk you out."

She got dressed in a minute and we rushed downstairs. I only managed to throw on a t-shirt and the first athletic shorts I found. Then I came back and changed clothes.

At the same time, I informed security about our guest's problem.

My people already knew what was going on, since jeeps carrying Takada clan fighters were already rushing to our office. I had only my normal school car today, with just a driver and one security guard, not a lot. Kiyoko had also come to school with just two bodyguards, but in a couple of minutes there would be about a dozen fighters from her clan here.

Soldiers from my security force were mobilized just in case. There were now about fifteen guys on the second floor, two of whom were at the rank of Sensei, a serious force. I decided to take most of the force and accompany Kiyoko home. There were always cars ready in the parking, army surplus, just monsters on wheels. That kind of help for the Takada heiress would be no problem in these difficult times. We were just about out the door when both our phones started ringing at the same time.

"Sir, do not go. The forces of the Mori clan are gathering around the home," said one of the security guards in a hurry. "Go back upstairs and wait. Two of our people will join you there, while the rest will defend the first floor."

At that moment all the doors and windows started closing over with automatic steel shutters. The three upper floors were not equipped with that system. Dammit, we shouldn't have been so stingy and just got it done! We went back upstairs, running into our alarmed classmates on the way. They were still not dressed, just haphazardly wrapped up in towels.

"What's going on?" Takeshi Kato was the first to ask.

"The Mori clan has declared war on the

Takadas, and it looks like some of their army has come for Kiyoko," I quickly informed my friends.

"Jesus, what a bad time!" The Wada sisters were upset. It looked like they had spent a good time with us.

"What are we going to do?" asked Ichiro Hattori.

"Wait. This is adult business, and I think it will resolve itself fairly quickly. The Mori clan has no reason to attack the possessions of the Tanakas, since they risk getting two enemies instead of one," I said, trying to calm my classmates down.

But I had my doubts. My father and I had tried to make the eleventh unit of the Tanaka clan as independent as possible. We didn't hide Goro's support, but it could always be considered that it was just an ally, not part of the clan. So, since the building and its location were not backed by the Tanakas and were considered somewhat independent of the Oyabuns, the Mori clan could definitely be unaware of the consequences.

On the other hand, it's not like they hadn't seen cars from some of the strongest clans outside of the building. Shit! Of course the drivers had put their cars in the parking garage. There was about enough space there. So the Mori clan would be right to conclude that only the Takada heiress was here. Maybe the girl was just picking up some jewelry... Well, when the owners pushed their alarms, the police would show up immediately.

My worst fears had come true. The stupid Mori clan was attacking the building. We could hear shots coming from the street, and a concerted attack in response from the defenders in the stronghold of the office. What were the attackers expecting? This kind of attack would take a couple of hours, during which time the Takada fighters, at least, would get to the building. Maybe they were trying to lure out Kiyoko's father? We had to do something, and fast.

"Kiyoko, call home and tell them you're in danger. Let them know that the heirs of the Tanaka, Kato, Wada, and Hattori clans are here. They might be trying to draw your father out." I tried to speak as neutrally as possible, since anything we did now might be the wrong thing.

If I was right, this was a fake siege. The father would hurry to save his only daughter, they would seize him on the road, and kill him, and there you go, war over. Then again, if the Takada forces didn't come in time, then we would be overrun. Kiyoko would be taken hostage, and that would also be a loss. What could I do? Her father, most likely, had already been called and was taking measures, but we had to tell him why we were doing what we were doing. The guys would tell their own people. I mean, when all those people from so many clans were coming here, the Mori clan wouldn't be able to do anything but retreat. After I asked them to, my classmates started calling their homes, and I called my dad.

"Dad, the office has been attacked. I think the Mori clan either wants to draw out Kiyoko's dad or to take her hostage. That's a big problem, and the Takada forces might not come in time," I spoke shortly and to the point. Time was of the essence.

"Our people will be there soon. Take care of yourself, son." My father understood everything without needing any more explanation.

I hung up and listened to the sounds coming from below. Something was clearly wrong. The Mori clan had decided to storm the building.

At that time I didn't yet know that they were planning both an ambush on the head of the Takada clan and to take Kiyoko hostage, which is probably what they were doing. In my humble estimation, it would take a fair amount of time for them to deal with the combined Takada and Tanaka forces, sheltered behind steel shutters.

But our enemies had other ideas. There were two explosions. It seemed to me they were using local heavy weapons. Then two gas grenades flew through the broken shutters. The Tanaka forces were holding fast on the first floor and in their base, probably with gas masks, and my guests' drivers and bodyguards were holed up in the parking garage. They were knocked out down there too.

I was watching all of that happen on the security monitors. I had a connection on the screens in my penthouse. For convenience the guys and I had put it on the big screen in the living room. Dammit. The security forces hadn't come up to us, and our enemies getting into the building was sure to be a major issue.

The first thing was to block off the elevator. It only came to the fourth floor. There weren't yet exits for the first three. The fighters on the first floor controlled the stairs, and there were steel doors there as well. But that didn't seem to be much of a deterrent for the Mori guys. Shit, shit, shit... Okay, the most important thing now is to stop any attacks from the elevator shaft. The security forces would have to hold the stairs until my father's guys got here. I didn't have any weapons in the penthouse. If we got out of this, I would bring a whole arsenal. If only I had a plasma gun, or at least a cobalt bazooka, like the underground weapons dealers used to make on Skayd...

But, for lack of anything better, it came down to, once again, using what was at hand. Hmm. My Teacher always used to say that a person was the first weapon, but a person with a needlegun was better than a person with a table knife. I stopped the elevator, but I felt like the Mori fighters would know how to deal with that. I asked my friends to bring some heavy stuff to the shaft, like all kinds of vases, metal stands, and other junk, which I would thank the interior designer for.

I carefully pried open the doors, and, without looking, threw a heavy crystal vase down. My elevator shaft was fairly broad, and there were two ways to come up. The first was along the wall using special tools, and the second was the steel cables. I guessed that the Mori fighters would used the cables, and I was right. My reward was threats, shouts, and swears.

"Hey, you up there! I'm going to cut you into pieces, just let me get up there!" one of my victims screamed.

His body had, it seemed, smashed into the elevator itself, judging from the noise. The intruder hadn't managed to climb up too high. He was shouting loudly, with a voice full of strength and energy. That meant he needed some more! I had four crystal vases, which was too bad. I kind of liked them. The guy went quiet after the third one, so had either hit him a good one, or the Mori fighter had wised up a little. I wouldn't be able to go by his voice anymore. I would have to look and see what was going on.

Although, to hell with that, what if they start shooting in the heat of the moment? The guys at that moment dragged in a massive concrete pot from the greenhouse, without even taking the tree out of it. I think I'll check the shaft after I send the bonsai down it. Oh yeah! They had even started shooting down there. It seemed like they were trying to stop the concrete pot with their bullets. But no such luck! There was a loud smash, the sound of a falling body, and over it all the groan of two hundred pounds of concrete, soil, and tree hitting the elevator and those who had been lying on it.

Yeah, the elevator would have to be replaced. I carefully looked down the shaft. The pot, of course, had not broken through the roof of the elevator, although it should have been able to. The two bodies had softened the blow and spread it over the area. But everything was crushed, bent, and broken. The intruders were definitely knocked out, and somebody seemed to be rustling around inside the elevator, but if they wanted to come up they would have to clean up the bodies of their friends and the pieces of concrete.

But the boys were dragging in some more ammo. I had a shitload of those pots in the greenhouse, enough to fill the shaft up to ten feet.

Just to make sure the guys below didn't come up with something new, we threw a couple more vases down there, breaking the elevator for good. Too bad, I liked that one too. I had even thought about Kiyoko in there and... well, you know. We would have to change it, and put a nice little couch in there too, just in case.

Our enemy had gone mysteriously silent.

But it was clear that our two-hundred-pound arguments and their powerful force were not going to be defeated. It would be hopeless to try and mount an attack in those circumstance, and they definitely didn't have time to think of anything else. In addition to the Tanaka clan fighters, the Katos and the Wadas were on their way here, and Ichiro had even asked the company he worked for to send a special forces unit.

The fight ended for us when we heard the voice of a reserve infantryman, amplified by speakers, coming from the street. The soldier didn't say much, simply telling the Mori clan members to lay down their weapons and come out with their hands up. The severe man didn't start telling them what would happen if they didn't listen, he didn't even start counting. I felt like they were just looking for a reason to start shooting the attackers, so upset were they at the audacity of clan in attacking a bunch of school students.

The locals weren't being sentimental, and taking out kids when attacking an estate was not considered bad form, just nipping the problem of future avengers in the bud, almost a hallowed tradition. But this deliberate hunt for heirs, even at the risk of injuring their classmates... It was not welcome. It was a slippery slope leading to taking schools by storm or setting up snipers outside of educational establishments. The Mori clan was clearly facing some serious consequences.

The adventure was over for us. The adults would handle it from here. We were in no hurry to leave yet, and in any case, we all decided to accompany Kiyoko home. But we hadn't yet been able to relax. The tension was still there.

The Mori fighters did not try to play heroes, giving up with no delay. When they were put in handcuffs and taken to parked cars one by one, we could see a veritable army of our clans. All the nearby streets were filled with armed men and armored jeeps. Legends would start circulating about our party now, you know, it would even be on the news.

I put Kiyoko in her car, and the Wada, Kato, and Hattori convoys accompanied us straight to her house. With such an impressive defense, nobody would dare to attack us. They said that the Takadas took revenge for the attack on a fair number of Mori clan targets. Another war was slowly brewing in the city. I hoped it would stay local.

The Mori clan would probably avoid problems from the randomly attacked clans by buying them off. Nobody had died, and injury and discomfort could be made up for with money. Of course they would get me a new elevator and renovate the façade of the building. Broken windows, busted decorations... Even a little bit for the fact that the heir nearly shat his pants with fear, all of it would be paid for.

I wouldn't be seeing Kiyoko at school any time soon, and I wouldn't be visiting her either, since her estate was now in lockdown...

Chapter 6

An Alarming Meeting

IN THE EVENING, Hena Tanaka, in my parents' wing of the estate, dialed her husband. Unfortunately, the leader of the clan was more and more often out of the house on business. His empire was growing, with ever more business to take care of, and much of it demanded his direct participation. And today, in addition to all that, he now had to deal with the Mori clan. His son had become the unwilling cause of a possible conflict with a fairly strong clan. Hena could not just let that go. She was worried both about her husband, who might be drawn into the upcoming war, and by the fear that Goro might punish Genji...

"Darling, how are things with you?" Hena said as a warm greeting to her husband.

"It is all fine, Hena. Don't worry. I have taken care of everything," the clan leader answered confidently.

"Then the problem with the Mori clan is finished, dear?"

"Yes. The Mori clan is not capable of an altercation with us now. They are embroiled in their war with the Takadas, and they don't need any their enemy to have any extra allies. Also, their men clearly overdid it. So they have compensated us in full, fulfilling all our claims and caprices," said Goro, boasting a little, happy with the extent of the compensation the Mori clan had paid.

"Great! But sweetheart, are you going to punish our son?" Hena asked, with worry in her voice. Her husband, kind-hearted by nature, was sometimes forced to display exceptional cruelty, otherwise he would never have survived the situation they grew up in.

"What for, Hena?" Goro said in surprise, having actually been thinking about how to commend his son for another profitable deal. Lately, all of Genji's scrapes had starting bringing the family significant profit. It might not be the best way to go about it, but you couldn't argue with the results.

"Ahh, well, I thought you were going to blame him for the fight with the Mori clan," Hena said, sighing with relief.

"Pff, you think my son could have predicted

a clan war would start? And that, on top of that, those idiots would attack the estate of a neutral party?" Goro asked, a little flippantly, then added, proud of his son, "The boy acted like a real hero!"

"Yeah? Tell me about it. I couldn't ask him. As soon as he showed up he ran off to train." Hena could not pass up the chance hear her darling son's exploits regaled.

"The Mori clan invaders took the parking garage of Genji's office by storm using gas. So they had to take into account our facilities at that moment. While some of them were blocking the security forces on the first floors, a special forces unit decided to break into the penthouse through the elevator shaft." Goro started telling the story as if it were an action movie or a high-energy thriller.

"No way! What, were they trying to get to the kids?" Always somewhat indifferent to battles, Hena became a real softie when it was about threats to her son.

"Yeah, looks like it. But our son expected the enemy to do that. He and his friends attacked the Mori killers who were climbing up a up with four crystal vases and some concrete pots from the greenhouse, ha!" He couldn't hold back his pride as a father. The legend of the half-dozen schoolkids who had stopped two bad-ass killers from a pretty strong clan using home décor had already been embellished and was making the rounds of the district.

"Amazing! Darling, we have to show our appreciation for the boy somehow. What about something with Eika? Genji certainly liked that serving girl, and she wasn't against it, was she?" Hena was completely in charge of everything at home, and her son's flirting with the servant had not escaped her notice. In fact, she had observed and approved all of it.

"Don't you remember our conditions for service? Even an intimate connection is not supposed to be a problem in the future. I do understand that the boy is growing up and old ties may hold him back." Goro said, coming back to this topic they had gone over in depth a thousand times.

"Tanaka, get to the point! We discussed this long ago and set up red flags everywhere, for all the people working for us." The fire could be heard in Hena's voice, the fire that had once caused many of Goro's former competitors to bow to him and ally with the Tanaka family.

"Hena, Eika failed our tests. She even recognized herself that she was losing control of the situation. She realized that her attraction to Genji was inappropriate to her service duties. You remember her disappearing more than once?" Goro was more well-informed about the issue with Eika, since she had actually been part of the military wing of the clan, while Hena, after the birth of her son, had mainly taken care of civilian matters.

"Yeah, and she said she was going to get an education or move up to the next rank, right?" asked Hena.

"That's right, but we also had her checked by doctors, at her own request. The results were shocking. If not in love with our son, she definitely was experiencing a strong and uncontrollable passion. She knew herself that keeping a bodyguard close to a member of the family in the state would be potentially dangerous," Goro said, unexpectedly.

"Why didn't you tell me about it at the time?" wondered Hena.

"We were not certain in our conclusions. The results shocked all the doctors. Eika was a stable, high-ranking warrior. Those sorts of successes are only possible with an iron will, discipline, and self-control. That was why she was allowed into the inner circle of our security. Nobody ever believed she would have those kinds of problems!" Goro was not hiding his disbelief.

"I understand, dear. You are right. Letting such an emotionally unstable person get so close is not okay. She wouldn't be able to do her duty right, and either jealousy or offense if Genji should refuse her could lead the girl to treachery," Hena said, making logical conclusions.

"And that is why we were forced to send Eika to another territory," summarized Goro.

"And what about the CEO of the holding company? Yoshiko Sakurawa went through a difficult experience with him, and I think she had some feelings for our boy before being hired by the clan. Is that not a potentially dangerous situation?" Hena continued trying to understand.

"Yoshiko has problems. She was raped by Professor Jackson multiple times, during which he left numerous lacerations on her breasts and stomach. Now she has scars not just on her body, but her soul. But we have that situation completely under control," answered Goro.

"Can it be fixed?" Hena asked, empathetically.

"The scars on her body were healed within a week, but the psychological trauma cannot be healed so quickly," her husband responded, shrugging.

"But did you manage to figure out if she experiences the same kind of feelings as Eika for our son?" Hena asked, getting to the point.

"Yes, our investigators, before agreeing to her candidacy as director, were able to suss out that data directly. She also definitely has feelings for Genji, and does not know why either."

"Then we might have a problem. We cannot control his relationships at school. And the administration could manipulate him entirely using that, if they figure something out," Hena said, worried.

"Yes, Ketsu Aoki has too tight a leash over

the school, and the Tanakas don't have nearly that kind of influence there. We don't even have any source of information. But what really worries me now is Genji's relationship with the Takada heiress. Now they seem to have become a potential source of danger," Goro said, showing his discomfort.

"We will just have to hope for the best. Our son has shown an indomitable will and self-control." Hena's pride in her son could be heard in her voice. He had held up fairly well, given all that had happened to him.

* * *

Despite our adventures, nobody cancelled their evening training. I did ten laps around the estate, working up a sweat with pull-ups, dips, push-ups, jumping rope, and flips... Then stretching, the most basic thing. Then I did some training with a punching bag, stuffed full of sand and soft plastic, improving my strength and the power of my punches. Then I moved on to the inflatable punching bag, an exceptional work-out for speed and precision of your punches.

It wouldn't be too bad to work with boxing gloves, but I do that with my trainers, and I had already cancelled my training with them because of my meeting with the core of my army. I would be working out alone. So I went over to the thing attached to the wall that let me practice my knee and elbow strikes. Even though I wasn't supposed to work on clinches and close-quarters, but someday... And with my tattoos of strength and speed I would try to compete with the gifted at short distances.

Tired and satisfied, I headed off to take a quick shower, and then, totally wiped, fell into my bed. A luxurious dinner was already waiting for me in the room, the servants having timed it perfectly to arrive just as I was getting out of the shower. Damn, they do good work. But I would not have been against eating a little later, if Eika were giving me a back rub, or the other way around... Heh... Anyway, in spite of the disappointments, I enjoyed my food. Food was a second source of joy for me in this world.

After getting another mouthgasm from the tuna steak, wild rice, green bean salad, and a massive jug of fruit juice, I got to work on fixing up my rune of concentration. You have to train your brain too. Sure, at this rate I would soon know all of the material from the second year by heart, but, on the other hand, there were quite a few other fields her to develop my mind in.

After reading my textbooks and some related literature, working on my runes came next in the plan. I had to set up the fine framework of the one for armor and continue working on the one for speed, which I had decided to do before the one for strength. The Psy tattoos hadn't been taking up too much of my time, which was because lately I was using energy faster than it could be replenished.

But today, after my romp with Kiyoko, I had noticeably more. Hmm… I had no idea how I was going to deal with this necessity. I just didn't have enough information, and even my rune of concentration wasn't helping. But I knew one thing, which was that sex was clearly helping me, and that certainly wasn't the worst news to get. I would have to experiment with this a little more. Oh, the things I do for science. Tomorrow I would definitely have to get with Fumiko…

I fell asleep while still thinking those thoughts.

* * *

In the morning, as always, I got ready carefully. Going to school was like going to war, and it was the kind of beast that would bear no carelessness. I took my steel ruler, my notebook with its metal cover, one tactical pen in my bag and a second one in the pocket of my jacket, the flail in my sleeve, my shoes… but I didn't take the armor for my arms and legs, since I thought my armor tattoo would work better and would be constantly with me.

But there was a problem. Most of my arsenal was intended for fighting in the classroom, where I would put my ruler on the desk and hold my notebook in my hands. But now everything was basically fine in the classroom, and, when you consider the Kato brothers and my other allies, it would be pretty hard to take me on in the classroom. And all my weapons were either defensive or worked for an ambush. So, by and large, I had to nothing to attack with. Ninety percent of my previous victories were due to my opponents underestimating me and my use of their own energy. Those tactics would not work during a real attack.

But for today I had one more trick, taught me by Matvey Nikolaevich. The Yakut always carried around Chinese meditation balls with him, called Gantan. They were about 1½ to 2 centimeters in diameter, carved from nephrite. The master held them in one hand, constantly rolling them around, changing their places back and forth. I had thought that the balls were to help you focus, and that the stone might somehow be helpful for magic.

But I was wrong. The balls turned out to be for more than just concentration. First of all, they strengthened your hands, since holding two slippery objects of a decent weight and constantly rotating them was another kind of exercise. Secondly, they could also be weapons. If you threw one of those round things at someone's head, and you were skilled enough, you could even kill them, especially if they were ungifted.

So now I always carry them with me, and starting from today, to school too. The ones made of nephrite, or even of steel, would be too light for defensive purposes. If one of those things hit my opponent on the body it wouldn't stop them, and believing that I could hit them right on the head in a fight is kind of ridiculous. I needed something reliable, that would work one hundred percent of the time.

So we made our own set of Gantan. Nothing too expensive, but we thought they should be made of some heavy metals. However, that was both too expensive, and also I didn't really have the strength for that much weight. So, we used lead as a sort of interior filling. The outside was a layer of chrome-plated steel, with lead poured inside, with the opening welded shut and carefully polished down so no trace of the filling process could be seen.

We ended up with two balls, both 2 inches in diameter, weighing about a pound each. Imagine what would happen if one of those balls hit you somewhere on your body. Well, it shouldn't matter where, the hit would have the desired effect. The speed, multiplied by the mass, would do what it was supposed to even if it hit an advanced wizard. And the Gantan wouldn't arouse a lot of suspicion. A lot of people carried around prayer beads, bracelets, even phones that they would fidget with, so the Gantan wouldn't surprise anyone.

I entered the school like a man on a mission, confidently spinning the pair of steel balls in my hand and brazenly gazing around. I decided to quickly check if the always late Fumiko was by the lockers, and then to go to her office. I was ready to give up a class for my sweet teacher. Ha, whatever, I would happily spend the whole week in her arms. Yeah, I know, I'm not acting too deliberately here, but the end of this story has to come, literally and figuratively.

I was riding high on anticipation of meeting the sexiest teacher of all time and space, but I was still maintaining my caution. Gakko Academy was no place to let your guard down. And not for nothing. In the hallway that I could not escape in any way, an upperclassman, with a threatening look on his face, was lounging on a windowsill.

He was tall, nearly as tall as me, and I have already told you that my body was not considered small by local standards, and was still growing. He had fairly long hair, which was in style, but that would be just a liability in a fight. His nose was broken, his knuckles were bruised, his jacket was haphazardly hanging off his shoulders, and he had a tattoo on his neck.

The boy was clearly an athlete, most probably a boxer, the favorite sport of wizards, but possibly he trained in other kinds of one-on-one combat too. The tattoo marked that he belonged to an Oyabun, either a family tattoo or one showing the boy worked for one of the criminal clans. It fit his age and style completely. He was trying to act like a real gangster, just missing a cigarette in his mouth and a bottle of beer, but Ketsu Aoki had forbidden those within Gakko Academy. Outside you could smoke to your heart's content, but in the school it was a big no-no.

Haha, something told me this guy wasn't dicking around here for nothing. Clearly he wasn't waiting around for his girlfriend, but for me specifically.

It was impossible for me not to recognize Hiro Sasaki. He was the leader of a gang which was mainly composed of students from the fourth-year and third-year D classes. He had a strange love for the D classes. As far as I knew, he could have easily crushed the fourth-year B class, run by Akira Takada. And that is to say nothing of the third-year classes. But for some reason, Sasaki had never shown any ambitions toward the A, B, or C classes.

A little strange. However, there were rumors that he had faced three fourth-years when he was in his third year and won. He was a strong fighter, and I had already guessed what he wanted to talk to me about. I had to give Hiro his due. He had come to this meeting with me alone, like a brave leader, confident in his own strength.

"Hey, are you Genji Tanaka?" Sasaki called out.

I didn't show any interest in him, and kept walking, not paying attention to this upperclassman who I was not actually acquainted with.

"Yeah," I said, laconically, and stopped, waiting to see what Sasaki would say.

"Can I have a couple minutes of your time?" he asked, rather politely, which was completely dissimilar to the normal behavior of the leaders of the school when talking to an untested second-year. I would have to respect that and not immediately call bullshit.

"Sorry, I am late for class. Let's talk another time," I answered, purposefully not making trouble, but also not submitting. I wondered if he would get upset immediately, or if he could handle it.

"Let's talk on the way. I only have a few things to say," he suggested flexibly.

"Okay." I was on my guard. This general of Gakko Academy was acting way too out of character.

"You're going to the second floor now, right?" Hiro said, showing how informed he was.

Math class was there, in fact. What was going on? Had he checked my schedule in advance?

"Yes," I said in one word, trying to keep some distance between myself and Sasaki, just in case...

Chapter 7
Hiro's Strategy

WE WALKED DOWN THE HALLWAY seemingly without issue, but my sewer rat instincts told me that I was not in a good place. Hiro was a real wolf, or rather a fighting dog, beaten down by life. He was like I had been on Skayd, much stronger and worse than Genji. And he was crazy, a real psycho. I knew guys like that. So he would not be able to plan out his next moves. Most likely, he didn't even know himself what he would do next. Or was that just a carefully crafted disguise?

"Genji, you have probably heard about my special relationship with D classes. Now I have received some good news, which is that you are the leader of the second-year D class. You must understand what I need from you now. Can you figure it out?" asked Sasaki, clearly hinting at what he wanted.

"I have no idea what you mean." I was playing dumb on purpose. If the guy wanted to say something, I wasn't just about to agree to it.

"How not, Genji? I have heard that you a smart kid and think of everything in advance," Hiro said, purposefully displaying good-naturedness, but also coming closer and closer to me. "I have certainly made it clear to you that my dream is to unite all the D classes under my own banner, you got it?"

"Not entirely." I kept playing dumb.

"Hmm… Genji, I need your class, and so this is very simple. Either you bring it to my gang yourself, or I will do it without you." Sasaki was not angry at all. The psychopath was completely certain of his own strength. That was a bad sign!

"Those are big words, Hiro, but I won't give up so easily," I warned the overly confident jerk.

"Ah, it's too bad we couldn't come to terms without unnecessary action." Sasaki had clearly taken on the role of an elder statesman.

The whole way I had been on my guard, preparing for a fight to break out. My sewer rat instincts were telling me that I had to start it here and now, get the upper hand. But the new gang leader inside me was against that option, telling me I had to stick to the plan, solidify my hold over the second year, and then negotiate with Hiro Sasaki's gang from a position of strength.

It would be best to just wait until Sasaki

graduated, and then there would be only one class left of his gang, who I could negotiate with. All of these ideas were making me take it slow and not intensify the situation. But still... I was too confident in my strength, my string of victories were starting to convince me, and I had put my armor tattoo on... I was starting to feel like I was invincible! Oh, but I would pay for that.

You have to be honest with yourself. All my previous victories had been possible only because my opponent had either underestimated me or because I had surprised them with a new trick. But now a time had come when my enemies were taking me seriously, and were, of their own initiative, taking into account the depressing experiences of those who I had beaten. The situation had become extremely dangerous. A gifted fourth-year, experienced, soberly judging the situation and exceptionally calm... I had already given up the advantage, so Hiro would decide if there would be a fight or not, which meant it would be unexpected for me.

I put some distance between us, as much as I could without looking like I was running away. Hiro did not try to get any closer, which calmed me down a little. Ahead of us was a turn, then stairs, and I would be at the chemistry class. Maybe it would all work out. But suddenly three students came from around the turn, two fourth-years I hardly knew, and... fatass Bo? What was that idiot doing with upperclassmen, especially during a class? Our fatso never missed a lesson, clearly putting success in his studies above his skills in battle. Not that it did him much good in either.

And now it seemed like I had correctly guessed Hiro's devious intentions and understood where he learned which class I was going to. I would not be able to hold my own alone against four other, but I would have to at least ruin their plans a little. In Bo's eyes I could see his joy and a long-harbored desire for revenge. This jealous, miserable failure had clearly been looking for a way to destroy me for a long time, and here it was, in Sasaki.

Everyone knew that he was fantasizing about uniting all the D classes. So this guy, who wished me ill, had got everything right. The only one standing in Sasaki's way was Genji Tanaka, and those two assholes had made an alliance behind my back. I supposed they would beat me up, setting up Bo as the only victor, which would immediately destroy all my authority. But that was still better than Sasaki killing me himself.

If the fourth-year wins, nothing changes. The war would probably continue unabated. But if fatass Bo beat Genji, who was gaining popularity, once again... Then the class would lose its unanimous leader again and would be easy prey for Hiro Sasaki's gang. If I was right, then the most important thing now was to take out this oversized traitor. It was too bad I would have to waste the ace up my sleeve on this, truth be told, not very dangerous fighter.

Hiro went first. Out of the corner of my eye I saw his hand start glowing with energy and speed toward the back of my head. It seemed like he had decided to knock me out, and then let Bo set up the duel. I mean he was giving his ally a head start. But then how was he going to prove that the fatass had actually beaten me?

Oh, here's the answer. I started hearing voices coming from the stairs.

I nearly avoided Hiro's punch, and he, so as not to knock out an ungifted person, just tapped me under the ear. In principle, that should have been more than enough for Genji to lose focus and give Bo a couple of free attacks. Even if some passerby should see that strange glancing blow, they would not consider it too dangerous, and would accept that fatass Bo had done me in one on one. And if the fatty couldn't do it right away, the two fourth-years would correct the results with a couple of rousing hits.

Hiro's hit had, of course, knocked me a little, but my first-level armor and a generous hit of Psy energy lessened the effect quite a bit. Moreover, while pretending to be staggered, I took a few stumbling steps toward fatass Bo and his two companions. Having been warned, most likely, that he needed to attack me right after Sasaki's hit, Bo rushed forward. And he paid for it. No matter what, I had to take the devious fatso out of the equation, so that Hiro could not put his plan for taking the second-year D class into effect.

I had to waste one of my steel balls on that dumbass. The two-pound thing whizzed into the face of that jealous failure, an expression of nauseating happiness right on it. His nose, shining with grease, was crushed by the heavy piece of lead, and only his magic saved him from death. But he was guaranteed to have a broken nose and get knocked out soon anyway.

My simple move had definitely taken the fourth-years by surprise. They started moving backwards so the witnesses they had invited in advance would have no doubt that fatass Bo had won a brilliant victory all on his own. But when they turned the corner, they saw me, standing over that fatty, on the verge of losing consciousness, the frozen Hiro Sasaki, and the two utterly flabbergasted fourth-years.

Hmm... Osamu Saito's boys and some second-years were among the witnesses. That meant Hiro had brought some of his enemies to see this, to have an objective view. Although maybe this was the beginning of an alliance against Akira Takada? It was entirely possible, especially considering that she couldn't come to school until the end of the war with the Mori clan. Two wolves could come to agreement and tear apart Takada's army while she was gone. Butsu, her deputy, was, as far as I could tell, pretty dumb, and would not last against two enemies like that.

But now was not the time for far-reaching thoughts like that. I had to minimize the number of hits I was certainly going to get from this trio of fourth-years.

I didn't spend a long time considering who I would throw my remaining Gantan at. The most dangerous one here was Hiro Sasaki, and maybe my argument, reinforced with lead, would get through to him.

But this was a gifted, close in rank to a Kohai. That's nothing like a newbroken second-year.

The leader of the gang was able to dodge it, and my weapon, instead of hitting his face, slammed into his chest with a loud crack. It broke a couple of his ribs, but it didn't put down my enemy, but rather enraged him. But at least for a few seconds Hiro was no longer a danger to me. No matter how much of a monster he was, after a hit like that he would have to catch his breath. So I turned back to the two guys who had been with fatass Bo.

They were just coming to their senses, clearly having been unable to adapt to the quickly changing circumstances. But now they were ready, and there was two of them. I meet my opponents with my ruler and notebook. With a sharp hit I cooled down the enthusiasm of the left one. He was taller, more muscular, and at first glance, more dangerous. That was a mistake. I should have stopped the one on the right! Smaller in comparison to the other, he deftly struck me in the side. Neither my attempt to block, nor my notebook, thrown away in desperation, saved me from his all-encompassing swing.

I doubled over in pain. Even though my armor had taken the brunt of the damage, but using that technique he could have ripped out my liver, even without magic, and now, having pumped up his power... Ah, it was like taking a sledgehammer to the side. Son of a bitch! The only good thing was that when I bent over after the hit, a cross from the tall guy flew over my head. It seemed like I had really pissed him off with my ruler. A hit is a hit, but I poked him in the eye!

I avoided a couple of attacks from the two fighters, so I was able to counterattack successfully with my ruler, which gave me some time to recover and a hope for survival. Ah! Survival... A kick of tremendous force threw me against the wall. Of course, that did take me out of the zone of attack for the two boxers, but you couldn't call that trip pleasant. Moreover, the place where I got kicked was aching with pain.

Now Hiro Sasaki threw himself into the fight. But what kind of fight was it? They were beating me, practically without resistance, and fatass Bo was no longer a factor. Clearly he was upset due to my Gantan, and surely he would be, it was two pounds of pure pain! And, it seemed like, having lost the chance to punch me, Hiro had started kicking me pretty good. That was rare among wizards, and I would have to take it into account in the future. There was not a lot of magic in their legs, and so it was hard for wizards, but it was enough for me right now.

It was good that he wasn't using his hands, since he couldn't really get his fists to work with his ribs broken by a leaden ball. It was time for tactical decisions. I had no doubt that I was not going to win this. I was holding on now by the skin of my teeth. The first hit had spread the pain into my liver. The rest, even though they were not nearly as effective, still came with the strength that wizards could pack into their swings and jabs, so even the glancing blows were too much for me. If it weren't for the armor tattoo, they would have long since kicked me through the wall. Another thing was that when the boys missed me, they knocked massive pieces of concrete out of it.

So what are going to do? I was going to pass out in the next ten seconds, so I had to get someone for sure, that way the score would be two to one, if you counted Bo, and a tie if you didn't. I had to get through it. My reputation and future were on the line, ha. Hiro would be the best as a sacrifice, but the fourth-years were such monsters that just one successful attack wasn't enough to knock them out, and now the others were coming...

I pulled the oldest trick in the book, a simple one, which was probably why it always worked. I went in a spurt toward the tall one, the one I had treated to my ruler at the beginning of the fight. Those guys bought it, which was logical, thinking I was running off to my classmates for help. If I had rushed toward Hiro, it would have been suspicious. The only thing over there was an exit from the school, and they would be able to beat me twice as hard in the street. Here I at least had a wall to cover my back.

The guys took a few steps back, trying to trap me in. I threw my ruler from my right hand to my left and stabbed it into the skinnier, but much nimbler one. He should have stopped me when he had the chance. The piece of metal, impelled by my hand, surprisingly easily broke through the fourth-year's shirt, skin, and muscle right by his right collarbone. Yes, I did it! It seemed like my little trick with tossing the ruler from one hand to another had had more of an effect on my opponent than I expected.

I let the flail out of the sleeve of my right arm and started swinging it clockwise. Hiro, who had obviously heard that I had smacked Takeshi Kato in the temple with it, threw his hands up to protect his head. That would still hurt, but the head is more important. I didn't think I could hit an opponent in the temple if he was actively moving and protecting himself. So I swung it across his nuts. That kind of attack would certainly give me the victory over Hiro. Sure, Hiro would hold that against me forever, but it's not like we were friends before.

A loud crack informed me that from now on the title of chief ball-breaker would be mine. Damn, judging from Hiro's scream, I had cracked both his nuts with one hit. Do you think his magic will be able to unscramble those eggs? Or was it a done deal once the white mixed with the yolk? I chuckled a little thinking about that. Then I smacked him there with the flail a couple more times, just to be sure.

I had already fallen from the blows raining down on my back. The two fourth-years caught up to me and took out on me all their rage for this bloody battle started by me and my ruler. The one who still had the ruler sticking out of his body seemed to be kicking me, and the tall one, whose eye I nearly put out at the start of the fight, was using all his limbs at once. It was only now, looking around, did I understand why I kept thinking he was going to pause in every situation. It turned out that my first hit had put a deep cut above his eye, and the poor guy kept having to wipe the blood away. It was like I had seen all that and taken it into account, but was only realizing it now.

"Holy shit, that second-year definitely learned some tricks from somebody!" exclaimed one of the fighters of the most promising gang at Gakko Academy.

"Yeah, you can't even tell who trained who. I would put my money on Genji, to be honest. He's clearly ahead," answered a tall, stocky fourth-year.

"Well, yeah…"

"Look what he did here…"

"Shut up all of you!" shout Osamu Saito imperiously to his fighters.

"Mmmm, I think he's hot!" a striking brunette said, in spite of her boss's command.

Her short skirt barely covered her thick round buttocks, and her school uniform had its top three buttons undone, exposing her surprisingly mature breasts to the thirsty gazes of these teenagers. The only person who could get away with ignoring a direct command from the powerful Saito was his blood sister, the third-year Naomi.

* * *

Osamu Saito was having a hard time figuring out why Hiro Sasaki was having such trouble when he had the upper hand entirely. Three fourth-years and one second-year against a single Tanaka? Nobody could doubt the result of that encounter. But he had witnessed a miracle with his own eyes. Saito appraised both his and other people's strengths critically, and he had never considered the leader of the fourth-year D class to be a weakling. What's more, they had tangled with each other numerous times, both one on one and in groups. Neither one of them had ever had a clear advantage over the other.

It looked like another noteworthy power had shown up in Gakko Academy, which would change everything. Entering this alliance with Sasaki against Akira Takada was supposed to have allowed him to take control of this rebellious school. But Genji Tanaka, who had already taken over his own class, might be enough to tip the scales in favor of Akira. And there were rumors going around that her sister, the heiress of the Takada clan, was head over heels for the leader of the second-year D class...

* * *

The security forces, coming on to the scene, were greeted with what was to them a familiar sight. Two second-years and one fourth-year were knocked out on the floor. The fourth-year was curled up oddly in the fetal position, instinctively pressing his knees to his stomach to protect his crotch. The other two fourth-years were still conscious, but one of them had definitely lost a lot of blood and had slid down to a sitting position by the wall. The steel ruler sticking out of him looked pretty bad. The second one was also sitting on the floor, apparently whole, but his whole face was covered in a mask of blood which the boy seemed not to have the strength to wipe away.

The security forces knew what had happened. Hiro Sasaki, well-known around here, had gotten his ass kicked along with his faithful companions. And who did it? Obviously, Osamu Saito and his minions who were all hanging around. So the fighters in their massive armor lined the supposed aggressors up against the wall and rewarded the so detained with a beating, even using their clubs. At the same time, taking advantage of the safe situation, the school doctors evacuated the victims to the hospital wing.

The staff of Gakko Academy had long been used to working in what amounted to a war zone, especially since a significant number of them actually were employees of the Ministry of Defense. Civilians, yes, but still part of the war department. So none of the security forces, nurses, or young doctors were shocked by the sight of the blood and injuries that the student wizards so commonly inflicted on each other. They all knew that the boys and girls could survive much worse.

And a medical brigade, called by the dispatcher, was already hurrying to the school from Yuki Ueno's clinic.

Chapter 8

Yoshiko Sakurawa

IN THE SCHOOL'S DOJO, which not all the teachers knew about and absolutely none of the students, a single fighter was training. His body was gracefully flowing from one stance to another, and his hands and legs were striking the air sharply, blocking, and stopping imagined holds and throws in their tracks. That kind of training would be enough in itself to impress anybody, but anyone watching closely would definitely be surprised by the hints of magical techniques scattered through this martial dance, which put Ketsu Aoki in the ranks of the strongest of all fighters.

Aoki had discovered this room in his first ever year working at Gakko Academy. At the time he was just sorting a bunch of junk in a huge basement. It turned out that part of it had been built according to the demands of war time and was intended to be a bomb shelter. It was a fairly big space that had electricity, water, and even its own heating system, so he had it cleaned, renovated, and turned into an exceptional dojo.

Makiwara, heavy punching bags, pull-up bars, dip bars, and some simply, dependable gymnastic equipment was all that punctuated the ascetic environment of the gym. But that modest set of equipment was not due to a lack of finances. The gifted didn't need any new-fangled electronics. They stopped functioning too often, being unable to handle the stresses that wizards put on them. The most durable object there was their own bodies and minds.

A young assistant, entering the gym, decided to not interrupt the head teacher's training right away. Ketsu Aoki himself, however, asked him to quickly inform him of what happened with some of the students of Gakko Academy. The legate gave his full attention only to a few of the adolescents. And today three of those had taken part in a bloody fight which left four wizards and one ungifted seriously injured.

"Mr. Aoki, another fight has taken place," the assistant said anyway.

"Tell me," snapped the head teacher, a little out of breath. Even for him those exercises were not especially easy.

"Persons from your special list engaged in

the fighting. Genji Tanaka fought against Hiro Sasaki, two members of his gang, and a second-year student. All of this was observed by Osamu Saito and some of the members of his gang," said the secretary, short and to the point.

"Recordings?"

"They have already been sent to your private mail, along with preliminary evidence from the participants," reported the young man, militaristically.

"What were their goals and the results, in short?" asked Aoki.

"Sasaki has severe trauma in the groin and several broken ribs. Two of his fighters have numerous injuries from a blunt metallic object, probably the metal ruler which was left in the collarbone of one of the attackers. The second-year Bo has a broken nose. Genji Tanaka has numerous injuries and broken bones. As for their goal, they planned to discredit the leader of the second-year D class with a defeat at the hands of the class outcast, the fat kid Bo.

"So I am to understand that the plan did not come to fruition. Who won?"

"In simple terms, two of the fourth-year D class fighters were left conscious, but if we take it in terms of relative strength and injuries, Tanaka was the most successful," the secretary said, permitting himself to make an independent observation.

"Well, that boy just gets more and more

surprising..."

*   *   *

Genji Tanaka's team had gathered together in the second-year D classroom. Takeshi and Ryuen Kato, the Wada twins and Ichiro Hattori had taken up a corner of the room with a few desks and were engaged in a whispered discussion. The rest of their classmates were pretending that they didn't notice the intrigue, but were in fact trying to hear every word. Yesterday some members of Hiro Sasaki's gang had tried to catch the leader of the class and beat him up, but instead the strongest fighters in the fourth-year D class had ended up in the hospital.

A real crisis was coming to a head at Gakko Academy. Akira Takada, the leader of a fourth-year gang, could now, during the war with the Mori clan, only take care of business on the phone, and her deputy, Butsu, was clearly not cutting it. The efforts of Genji Tanaka had now, for an uncertain amount of time, taken out Sasaki and two of his closest associates, cutting the head off of his forces entirely. As such, two of the three most important school gangs were left without a leader. This made a situation ripe for Osamu Saito to try to take control of the rebellious school.

But for the second-year D class those circumstances were just an idea. For now it was up to them to preserve their independence and

102

wait for the return of the boss. And, if possible, get revenge for Genji. Or should they just let Hiro's people burn with rage and a desire for revenge? There were rumors that the skeezy Sasaki had gotten a terrible injury and would be recovering for a long, long time. Moreover, he wouldn't be able to show any interest in women for at least a half a year!

"What are we going to do?" Takeshi Kato had taken on the role of leader in Genji's absence. He had so far actually been a perfect deputy, despite their previous differences.

"We should attack Sasaki's gang!" shouted Ryuen, a bit slow but fearless, but upon seeing the dubious faces of his classmates, he immediately shut up.

"They have the best fighters from two classes, each of which is older and more experienced than we are," objected Hattori quietly.

"They don't have a leader, though," continued the older Kato brother, weakly. Then he immediately contradicted himself, "Just like us."

"Maybe we could appeal to Akira's gang? Kiyoko is with us and knows about the situation," suggested Suzu Wada.

"Sister, then Genji will be in the hospital and we will immediately have ended up under the upperclassmen," objected her twin, Rika.

"I don't know why Genji doesn't want to join

up with Takada." Takeshi shook his head. "It's definitely the best choice. It all works out with Kiyoko, and Akira isn't going to make us suffer. Plus, she's leaving next year and then Genji will probably become the leader of the unified gang."

"Akira's gang has serious problems right now. I've heard that Osamu Saito has challenged Butsu to a duel, and his people are getting ready to attack the members of Takada's army in the schoolyard," Hattori, always well informed, stated. "Think about it, how bad it would be for us if we were with Akira!"

"Uh-huh, and we have to take into account that Osamu's third-years are a little weak against Takada's fighters, so they would be much happier to take us on," Rika Wada said, supporting him. "Plus the strong gangs are now fighting against each other, and maybe none of them will get around to us."

"I'm worried that Hiro Sasaki's people won't forget about us. If Takada's army gets into a fight with Saito, that's a problem for us." Suzu said, expressing a logical danger.

"Then, if it's not worth it for us to get protection from Akira, maybe, at least through Kiyoko or something, we could get Takada or Saito to destroy Hiro Sasaki's gang?" Takeshi Kato asked, almost rhetorically.

"That's an amazing idea," agreed Ichiro Hattori. "But how do we do that?"

"Tomorrow or the day after Genji will wake

up. Let's go visit him and get his advice on what to do," suggested Rika Wada.

"Yes, let's do that," Takeshi said, finishing the discussion. "And also, guys, when you're going through the school, make sure you do it in groups of two or three each. But it's better to not split up the class at all. Let everyone else know!"

* * *

I woke up, as usual, in the hospital, and as always, I was in a cast and a bunch of bandages, all smeared over with some foul-smelling ointment. I realized a long time ago that the locals believe that the worse something smells, the more effective it is. Jesus, these bandages really annoy me. Given my tattoo of regeneration, I would prefer to not have any ointment at all either. The only good thing was that all this fake medicine was hiding my real recovery from all the medical staff. But that would only last so long, so I had to get home as soon as possible.

Sheesh, with how often I end up in this hospital, I shouldn't have bought that office, but just built an administrative building right here. I think there's even a plot of land for expansion. Ah, but here I am, complaining. They're going to take me home soon anyway. You couldn't call my situation outstanding, but I don't think it's that bad. In any case, the rune of armor really reduced the damage. I mean, from the outside I like pretty banged up, but my internal organs were hardly injured at all, even in spite of the magical fists of those teenagers.

I was already thinking that I should do some tattooing, but which one, the second stage of the armor or the strength and speed? As usual, during these convalescences I spent my time with my Psy tattoos. Some time spent breaking them into their parts, and some time spent actually putting them on. But I knew from experience that I would not have enough Psy energy without some intense and pleasant sexual feelings. And where was I going to get that like this?

For the last couple days nobody but Yuki Ueno had bothered me. Only she had access to my body, for obvious reasons. Even the few procedures that were supposed to increase the speed of my recovery were done by her alone. And even though the head doctor acted very professionally and not unpleasantly to me, I couldn't get over the kidnapping and association with vivisectors enough to view her as a woman. Yech, it would be like having a snake in your bed.

On the third day I was able, just barely, to take a shower myself, or more accurately, to like in the bathtub and get wet. However, it was a pretty good jacuzzi for a hospital room. Or was that just something Yuki Ueno had done for the boss? Since I had come here last time, they had done some serious renovations, bringing in more furniture, probably for visitors. And I had managed to avoid any more of that greasy healing ointment, and only my bruises, swelling, cast, and bandages were left to remind me of the beating. Soon I would even be able to go home.

It was hot in the room and people rarely visited me. So I decided to dry off and lie down naked for a while. My skin was really itchy. I was getting new skin where the scabs had come off with the ointment, and it needed fresh air, not these crappy hospital gowns. Anybody who has ever spent more than a couple hours in bandages or a cast knows what I mean.

I had no time for that, since a sexy female figure appeared at my door silently and without knocking. The blinds were closed, so it was fairly dark in the room. I was supposed to be sleeping under a dose of tranquilizers that would down a horse, but my rune of regeneration had counteracted the effect. The girl took a few steps forward, apparently not noticing anything. It was clear that her eyes had not adapted to the semi-darkness of the room after the well-lit hallway.

And Yoshiko, which is who it was, had not yet figured out that the white spot on the bed was not a blanket, but my own body. I wasn't about to hide. I wasn't a young boy anymore, although in Genji's body you could dispute that... But, the former nurse, who was now the administrative director, had never once seen me naked, all this time, from the moment I ended up lying here in this world after the beating from fatass Bo, up until our time spent in the laboratory of psycho Professor Jackson.

Anyway, it was meaningful. I was once again in the hospital because of that chubster, and once again I was drooling over Yoshiko Sakurawa. The former nurse had found herself a medical uniform somewhere. The well-cut robe stretched over the ample form of the girl. Her buxom chest was popping out of her bra, and her wide hips and long legs very sexily defined an attractive triangle...

"Oh, Genji, excuse me! I thought you were sleeping." Yoshiko modestly covered her eyes with her palm, pretending she couldn't see me. Still, I could see exactly where her eyes were drifting to. "The doctors told me that you had been put to sleep. I just wanted to see how you were."

"The day we were kidnapped you also came to see me," I said, drinking in her figure with my eyes. She had definitely not been coming to inquire after my health then.

"Yes..."

Even in the semi-darkness I could see how Sakurawa was blushing. It was interesting that the sight of my naked body hadn't flustered her, but how she went red right when I mentioned that night. I was sure I wanted her, and now I was certain Yoshiko wanted the same thing.

"Come here," I said hoarsely.

The girl stepped forward as though hypnotized. I stood in front of her and eagerly embraced her right there. Our lips met in a kiss and our tongues intertwined. My hands slipped unimpeded under her robe. So nice, soft and yet firm, mmm...

She let out an involuntary moan of pleasure.

"Genji, we can't... ah... please. Ah... it's so good... we can go here..." Mumbling, almost incoherent, without resistance, Yoshiko babbled.

My intimate, dirty affections made her blush once again. But this time it wasn't shame, but arousal. With my free hand I pulled off her robe, literally tore off her bra, and pulled down her tiny lace panties. I pulled her towards me and felt her excitement across my whole body.

We went at it for quite a while. In a break in our affections the voice of reason compelled Yoshiko to lock the door, so we were no longer afraid of being barged in on.

"Oh, Genji!" Yoshiko smiled happily at me at last.

"That was amazing." I smiled back in response.

"Sorry, my throat is dry." She stepped away from the bed and grabbed a bottle of water from the nightstand. Her voice was actually hoarse. She had been groaning and holding back her cries so much that it seemed it had an effect on her vocal cords.

But I wasn't thinking about that. I had never seen Sakurawa like this before. Her slim waist led down to her wide, ample butt, her long legs... and between them... heaven... I don't know if it was because of her sex appeal or my rune of regeneration, but I was ready to go again, and I leapt up from the bed like a wild animal.

A little later I pulled away from my woman of the moment, completely drained, and we both dozed off for a bit. I woke up when Yoshiko, trembling, trying not to wake me, went to the bathroom. The sight of her naked body put me in the mood to go again.

I followed her into the bathroom. We began again, leaning on the tiles, then continued, sitting face to face under the warm streams of water in the shower, and finished with me holding her in the air. Drained, squeezed out like lemons, we returned to the bed. But Yoshiko, aware that the time for observation was coming, prudently put herself back together and opened the door. I threw on my pajamas and lay in bliss on the bed, covered by a sheet. If somewhere were to come in now, they would see a boy in his bed and his old acquaintance who had come to check up on him.

"Genji, I have to go now," Sakurawa said, a little shyly. These women... just a moment ago she was giving me everything, and now she was shy.

"Thank you, Yoshiko. That was the best time of my life."

Truth be told, I didn't know how to act in these situations, but I told the truth intuitively. Any insincerity would be clearly felt at a time like this.

"I should be thanking you, Genji. Don't worry. I also had a great time. If you think it's worthwhile, we can continue meeting in secret." To my relief, she suggested something that would work for both of us.

The only thing was her reaction to Fumiko... Jealousy could be a problem in the future. But we would cross that bridge when we got to it.

"You're the best, Yoshiko!" I thanked her honestly for my first and most amazing sex in this new world.

Chapter 9
Harbinger of War!

MY FIRST THOUGHT after my lover left was pretty dumb: *Ahhh, the rune of regeneration works better here than on Skayd! I could go ten times a night, for real!*

But maybe that was a cumulative effect from the hypersexuality of a teenager and the strange energy background here. Plus, the tattoo was just set better. I had done it slapdash and in a rush, but in this world tattoos on the astral body turned out clearer and less wasteful.

But I would be an idiot to think about that stuff and not seize the moment. I had certainly felt an influx of Psy during my time with Yoshiko. No, not an influx, but a whole geyser. And now that ocean of energy was swirling around inside my body, begging to be used. I had never heard of a mortal getting this much Psy. Now I knew why the ancients had so many tattoos.

For us, standing on the shoulders of giants, even thirty runes was too much. Why would you need that many if you could only use five or six at a time? And even then, the energy for that would not last long at all. But if the ancients could get this much energy, then the tattoos that seemed useless at first glance could be seen in a whole new light.

This way of getting energy, though, was a little embarrassing. No, I mean, it works for me and even more, I liked it a lot. It's just now... well, what, before any great feat I would have to seduce all the girls around me? Or, like the ancients, just get myself a harem? Hmm... well, at least now I knew why the great men of this world didn't stop at three or four wives, but also had a hundred or so concubines. That's a joke, of course. The local wizards don't their energy like that. But I do!

What to do with it? Okay, runes first.

I filled in the outlines of the strength and speed ones first. They weren't completely ready yet, not even a third of them, but everything I had spent a month working on was done in literally a minute. The excess of Psy filled up the gaps, made the marks, and connected everything. I wasn't able to do anything more though, to my own shame. But who knew what sort of luck I might have?

On the other hand, I didn't have a lot of juice left. Maybe I could put it in the rune of regeneration? Or shit, maybe I would, like some of those who drank one of the concoctions of the Ancients, regress to the age of three or four? Damn... well, it was just a little energy, and I wanted to try it out.

After a bit of thought, I dumped everything left right into the tattoo, to make sure it all ended up in one place, no doubt, and holy shit!

The effect wasn't too bad, but not at all like in the legends. My minor wounds, scrapes and scratches, healed up immediately, but the more serious ones stayed the same, at least as far as I could see. And then, as usual, I really need to eat, drink, and use the toilet. I don't know if these things are even related. But whatever, I spent the whole evening running from the table to the toilet. To hell with these kinds of experiments.

* * *

After my miraculous recovery, there was only one way to go. Home! To freak the doctors out, even in my own clinic, with my regenerative abilities that were no less than that of a gifted, well, not the best idea. So in the morning they took me back to the Tanaka home base. As per custom, I had to act like I was sick for a while longer, so I had some time for myself. One thing bothered me though. I couldn't get that much Psy at home. So, maybe I could drop into the office? The renovations were done, and Yoshiko was right next door...

Anyway, one of the features of the rune of regeneration was birth control. It seemed like the Ancients had had problems with too many children, so there shouldn't be any unwanted pregnancies in a situation like mine, no matter how likely it might be. A bit of Psy energy in the right place, and you get perfectly safe sex. So I got lucky here, and I might cause a lot of trouble with this uncontrollable desire... No, I wasn't going to be a predator, not at all!

Considering that I would never survive at Gakko Academy without some serious efforts, I had to get to work. My training continued at full swing. In addition to my general exercises, plus boxing and wrestling, I was also started on some other specific disciplines.

First of all, acrobatics with a focus on interior spaces, working on somersaults, leaps, and even how to fall.

Secondly, how to throw things. For that I was brought a real circus performer, a forty-year-old man with the talent of throwing anything. It seemed like putting a knife or an ax into the bullseye of a tiny target was child's play, and doing it with a fork or a spoon, that was the real trick!

Third, fighting underwater. The lessons were taught by a former naval instructor. It turned out that there were a lot of unique aspects to it and a lot of advantages for the ungifted.

In addition to the strictly military lessons, I started to be taught some practical things. Orienteering, flora and fauna, survival classes, woodworking and stone carving... It was very dry and condensed, but no less useful. All of this was done for the future, since sometimes academies trained their students in a year-long camp on tropical islands. Second-years rarely ended up there, but we couldn't rule out the possibility. However, those skills were not emphasized, completely voluntary, purely for my own edification.

But still, the most useful classes for me were the ones with Matvey Nikolaevich. He broke down each of my conflicts in detail, outlining plans for locations and probably trajectories of all the students and constantly made me think up non-standards ways to get out of situations. His own views were shocking for their simple but absolutely correct logic.

It was like a game of chess. The Yakut taught me to narrow down the possible moves of my opponent so I would be able to predict their next move. In addition, I had to leave avenues of escape open for myself. It turned out that I could, in some way or another, force my opponent to attack or defend himself in a way that worked for me. And that wasn't just theory, but I was constantly reminded of the effectiveness of its practicality and that kind of thinking improved my reflexes.

You might ask how Matvey Nikolaevich managed that. Very simply. Having heard from my father about my improved regeneration, he started not just sparring with me, but making his own students fight me. They could come at me in pairs, in trios, or even more. Although that clearly showed me that a real fighter, if he didn't fall, could only fight with at most two or three opponents at a time, otherwise the rest would just get in the way.

The training, working on my runes, and my own studies ate up all my time. Kiyoko or one of my guys called me every night to give me the news. A total war was raging at Gakko Academy. The absence of Akira Takada and Hiro Sasaki had thrown off the balance that had lasted for months. The fragile equilibrium had shattered and Gakko was overwhelmed with a new wave of duels and mass battles.

My guys treaded lightly, acting like guerillas behind enemy lines. They walked the halls in groups, rarely going to the cafeteria or the bathrooms, the most dangerous places in the building. I'm not even going to mention the schoolyard and the paths around the parking lot. Nearly all the students walked through there like it was a minefield scoped by snipers.

The powerful Osamu Saito was the worst offender. His captains committed atrocities on all the classes. The gangs would break into other classrooms and beat all the students up one by one. This should have forced the students to submit to Saito. However, it actually had the opposite effect, drawing out their resistance. Moreover, the armies of Takada and Sasaki would not let his outrages go unchecked. Even without their leaders, they were still powerful forces.

In short, the week passed like a single day. I couldn't manage to finish my Psy tattoos, even though I had been on the verge of it since laying the first part of the strength and speed ones. My arsenal of toys for the school had not been replaced, although there were plans. I was keeping them in reserve. But I had trained well and made a few preparations at home. I hoped that my tactics would surprise my opponents. Kiyoko was still at her estate, so we wouldn't see each other at school, and, to be frank, I was missing the girl a bit. Still, there was someone to comfort me there...

I was already in the habit of viewing going to school like going to war. In fact, it was a war. I had never been in the hospital as many times on Skayd as I have been here. Then again, there aren't really any hospitals there.

I put all my weapons under my clothes and in my bag, not forgetting my lead-weighted Gantan. Then I carefully checked my clothes and shoes, did my morning training, had breakfast, and headed to Gakko Academy.

This time I made it to the classroom without incident. Nobody was waiting for me by the lockers, and I didn't hear the click-clacking of Fumiko Ono's heels anywhere. English was not on the schedule today, and it seemed like my favorite teacher was working either in a neighboring school or at the university. Of course, I had to check. Fumiko had a flexible schedule, and maybe I was wrong, and she was sitting in her little office, waiting for her favorite student.

The class was on a razor's edge. Clearly the tensions of the last few days were taking their toll. It felt like a siege. The strongest fighters were sitting in the first desks and the row closest to the door, to the surprise of the teachers. Ryuen Kato had always taken the last rows, but now he was magnanimously enthroned as close as he could be to the teacher's desk, so distasteful to him. The strategy was clear. If our enemies attacked, they would come across the strongest fighters of the second-year D class, giving the others time to prepare a counterattack.

It turned out that the upperclassmen had already come through the younger ones. Osamu Saito had visited the second-year A class. In the end, Raiden Nakata, who was the leader of the class, and some of his friends had been sent to the hospital, although the A class had held out. Still, the large gang had literally terrorized the second-years. On one hand that was almost good news for me. On the other hand, Raiden Nakata was scary. From what I had heard, he lived up to his name, fast as lightning.

Matvey Nikolaevich had warned me to take wizards with that gift especially seriously. It was almost like a defect, since most of the ones who had it also were expected to have a weak gift. They were not strong, but to make up for it they were fast. They could cast a lot of mobile but weak spells and their reserves of energy filled back up especially fast. But all of that only applied to adult wizards.

But adolescents going down that path were very dangerous opponents for me. They trained in speed at the expense of strength. Even normal wizards are fast for me, and these ones would be just goddamn flashes. But, thank God, Raiden was in the hospital. Other news was that Takada's army, for God knows why, attacked the third-year B class. Possibly, Butsu had remembered that Akira wanted to subjugate some of the third-years, so he attacked a free class.

Makise Abe put up a worthy resistance to Butsu, or maybe Takada's deputy had underestimated the prodigy. The third-year B class had made itself into a killing machine by combining with two fourth-year classes, taking out a bunch of people, and now both sides were licking their wounds. And this played even more into Saito's hands. Sasaki had few people, and now many of Takada's were in the hospital. A great war was on the horizon!

I had only a small army at hand, and each of its warriors had just recently broken through. That made them weaker and less experienced than our main opponents. But it was not this sewer rat from Skayd's first rodeo. We had more than once defeated an opponent, not with strength, nor numbers, nor even skill. It was organization, cleverness, unity, and mobility. That would give us a chance.

Against us were normal adolescent gangs. The leaders found it difficult to hold power in their own gangs. Somebody was always challenging the strongest fighters in the hope of raising their position. How were you supposed to keep a dozen people in check if you weren't united by a common interest? The landscape at Gakko Academy was simple. The gangs basically hung out together, had the same meeting places, went to the same sport clubs...

My situation in that regard was a lot better. The Kato brothers, unwillingly, had made a great bridgehead. Them and their four vassals were the core of my fighting force. Add to them the Wada sisters, Rokero Abe, and Jiro Fukudu, and you got two captains with units of five fighters each. I had already set up that division and the twins were great companions to Takeshi and Ryuen, softening the idiocy of the later and the intensity of the latter

Ichiro Hattori would be the brains of our army. He was accompanied by a couple of the nerds in the class, who might still make passable fighters. But that wasn't the most important thing. Hattori had wide-ranging connections throughout the second-year through his club, which many disparagingly called the Nerd House. But it was an accurate name. The best and brightest from all the second-year classes and some upperclassmen too were in that group.

And I was not about to underestimate them. They would be wizards in a half a year, a year at most and would be able to get their own back on their former bullies. But even without that, the Smart Club was a great find. The kids were united by a common idea, not connected to any of the groups in their own classes, and for all that, it made for great reconnaissance. And so the first flashes of organization started to appear in my gang. We had two fighting units, along with reconnaissance and intelligence in the form of Hattori. And I was planning on expansion in the near future.

Dealing with Hiro Sasaki's gang now would be asking too much. The leader of the fourth-year D class had more than 20 fighters, powerful fourth and third-years. And the leader himself would soon be back at Gakko Academy. I didn't hurt him that much. The second-year D class was just objectively too weak to deal with an army like that. We would need new vassals and allies to face them on a level footing.

The first who came to mind was Hideo Takayama. His circumstances in his own class were fairly precarious, but he still was in charge of a third of the second-year C class. Thanks to Tomoko, Ichiro Hattori's childhood friend, and couple other members of the Smart Club, we were fairly well informed about the classmates of our own year. Even now there were five or six who might come over to my side. And if Hideo would join, that would double my army.

So, during the lunch break, instead of getting lunch, me and my fighters went to the C classroom. Intelligence told us that the majority of the class was eating lunch there. During these hard times, visiting the cafeteria was something only the dumbest students did, or the fourth-year armies. Still, eating surrounded by enemies and with your guard up could not be fun for a normal person. It seemed like they were going there simply to size each other up and rattle their sabers on occasion.

Takeshi and his guys went first. I came next along with Ryuen's group and some of Hattori's club members. It wasn't the best timing for going to that classroom. We would have to go to the neighboring wing, meaning we would have to come down from the third floor and then back up to the second. We knew where all the main gangs were according to the schedule and we tried to take the safest path. We also left a little later, hoping that those gangs would all be in the cafeteria already.

* * *

An armed neutrality was in place in the second-year C class. The two boys that Hideo had recently beaten up with Genji Tanaka's help in the cafeteria were the leaders of a rather loose group of five or six people. Takayama had three close followers among those who had been with him since the first year. The rest of the students had not yet decided which group to join, including Tomoko and the nerds from the Smart Club.

Some of them were scared of Hideo Takayama's fierce hotheadedness, and the others didn't want to join up with the former outcasts who now, after breaking through, believed themselves to be such great fighters. But all three sides were aware that a class divided would be easy pickings for the gangs. The first sign of that was when Hiro Sasaki attacked Genji Tanaka. Even though it was unsuccessful, the fourth-year D student's attempt opened the floodgates for hunting second-years.

Like a maniac unleashed, Osamu Saito had attacked the second-year A class, and Akira Takada's people had run ragged on the third-year B class. The only ones who had stayed out of the war so far were the second-year B and C classes, and you didn't have to be clairvoyant to predict who was getting attacked next. The upperclassmen only had two choices for three whole gangs.

Chapter 10

Allies

"GUYS, I THINK WE NEED to unite. Only together can we stand up to an attack by the upperclassmen." Hideo Takayama was talking to his own allies, but purposefully loud enough for the whole class to hear.

"You're one to talk about unification, Takayama!" screeched one of Hideo's victims. "All last year you beat us up and treated us like shit! How are you better than the fourth-years?"

"They beat you more, and there are more of them," Takayama said, logically and with a dash of humor.

The boy was tired of his prior ambitions. All last year he had tried to make a team out of his classmates using his fists and his feet and good old-fashioned profanity. But it turned out to be worse than if he had done nothing at all. Some of the frightened students held a grudge against him, and the others considered him to be short-sighted. Which, honestly, wasn't too far off. He wasn't fit to be a leader on his own. He loved to fight and could vigorously defend the weak, but he had not been able to achieve his goals carefully and cautiously or draw people to his side.

"It makes no difference, Hideo! Even if you united our forces, you wouldn't be able to take on the Gakko gangs!" shouted the prettiest girl in the class, Tomoko, as if she were striking with a whip.

Hideo wasn't crushing on her or anything like that, but he had tried to pick her up, although without any real success. But then that loser, Hattori, from Genji's class, had taken to visiting the girl. Maybe Hideo would try to eat with Kiyoko... and he probably wouldn't have any balls left... Takayama instinctively crossed his legs, covering his precious sack. Genji Tanaka had a dubious honor in the school, being the "Premier Ball Breaker". Hiro Sasaki was still in the hospital, even though nothing was threatening his life or his health. But they said his manhood was still in question.

Those sad thoughts were interrupted by the man himself. The leader of the second-year D class entered the classroom with an impressive contingent of his own thugs, threateningly many.

Out of a dozen fighters Hideo only recognized Tanaka's old friends, Rokero, Jiro, and the Wada twins, and he had heard about the Kato brothers. They were said to be heartless bastards. What were they doing, coming here to usurp power? What a turn of events!

"Greetings, Hideo," said Tanaka, meeting him like the leader of a neighboring state.

"And good tidings to you, Genji," Takayama said, not flustered, even though the brigade of fighters behind his conversation partner's back was clearly causing some tension, especially considering the rumors about the terrifying power of its senseless leader.

"Time is money, brother. I have come to discuss our problems in making a united front against the upperclassmen. Takada has attacked Makise Abe, Osamu Saito crushed Raiden from the second-year A class, and you have surely heard about my own fight with Hiro Sasaki?" Genji began his spiel. When did he become so eloquent? Last year he was stupid as hell.

"I heard, bro, and I was tickled by the results. You know the legend of the Great Ball Breaker is well-known in this school." Hideo couldn't help but tease him a little.

"Dammit, I knew that was gonna catch on," Genji complained and then continued, "Dude, I had no other choice. There were four of them and one of me, I had to make my last stand."

"Hahaha!" Hideo couldn't hold back his

laughter, imagining Genji literally standing on Sasaki's poor nuts. "Last for who, bro? Sasaki's descendants? Hahaha!"

* * *

"Hahaha!" Everyone around broke out into laughter. The story of how the leader of the fourth-year D class nearly lost his nuts had made the rounds, and many of the school's smartasses still doubted whether Hiro was even still a man. Like that wouldn't catch up to me eventually.

"Hideo, you know we didn't come here just to chat." I got down to more serious business.

"Ah, yeah, I guessed that, especially when I saw your douchebags filing into the classroom," Takayama said, once again unable to hold back and smiling wide.

"Hey, who are you calling a douchebag?" The Wada sisters acted offended. "Who are you to talk, Takayama, judging us? You douche around all year without a break."

"Hahaha!" Once again Hideo was tickled. Then, suddenly becoming serious, he said, "I hope that you, Genji, have not come here to get my class to submit by force."

"I wouldn't even think of it." I smiled widely, looking Takayama right in the eyes. "I have come to propose an alliance!"

"Hmm... and how would that be any different from you making us submit to you?"

asked Hideo.

"I would not beat you," and now it was time for me to make a joke, "across the balls, hahaha!"

"Poor Hiro... hehehe!" chuckled one of the girls.

"Darling, I'm ready to lose my virginity," said one of the Wadas, seductively.

"But I have nothing to help you with, hahaha!" said Hideo, playing along.

"Tanaka, are you proposing an alliance with just Hideo, or with all of the students in the second-year C class?" A girl, standing with two guys who Hattori informed me were members of the Smart Club, asked, butting in suddenly. God, they were real nerds... Maybe I was putting too much stock in my connection with Ichiro?

"Of course not, but I get that you are asking because there is no leader in your class, right? I am not opposed to any allies," I answered confidently, unintentionally brushing against the short skirt and tight top the girl was wearing. Damn, it should be a crime to walk around a school dressed like that.

"Okay. I, Tomoko Yasuda, and my friends are ready to join up with you," she said, decisively and also adorably. Ah, Jesus, this was the cause of all that strife between Ichiro and Hideo, and here I was, practically choking on my own drool. Get a hold of yourself, Tanaka. Women will lead you to nothing good!

"I am thrilled to accept your friends and you,

Tomoko Yasuda." I was trying not to let my "elevated" mood show, but the last words carried a bit of innuendo anyway.

Shit, I needed to go through the local myths and legends as soon as possible to find the source of this abnormal pull to the opposite sex. Something was wrong with me. Or maybe I should go to a fortune teller? I was ready right now to throw all my allies under the bus for one piece of ass... I mean, it was an amazing piece of ass, let me tell you! Why was she bowing like that? Was she trying to tempt me?

Hideo was looking at Tomoko jealously while she was making eyes at me. This girl was definitely manipulative, and Ichiro was right the first time, when he said she was using him to piss Takayama off. Now she was playing with his emotions, trying to get Hideo to fly off the handle and not solidify the alliance with me. I had to cut that off soon. I needed fierce hoodlums like that in my army, not a bunch of nerds and a sex-bomb. And she was a bomb, but in a gang war with the fourth-years that would do no good.

I didn't know what would have happened at the end of Tomoko's trick, but we were rudely interrupted. By that time me and my fighters had spread throughout the classroom. Ichiro and his nerds were discussing something to the side, the Wadas had joined some girls they knew, Jiro and Rokero were, like the used to do, sitting beside Hideo's headcrackers. This was perfect, clearly we were on the verge of a new alliance. Only those two dicks that had attacked Takayama in the cafeteria were staying apart. I mean, I had thrown soup bowls at them. You don't forget a heavy thing like that so soon. It goes deep. Not in the soul, but in the head.

And then Osamu Saito's fighters burst in the classroom. There were comparatively few of them, just ten guys. They come without their boss, just taking care of the situation in the second-year C class. This was definitely enough of an army to destroy Hideo and the other leaders of the class one by one.

I glanced over at the two outcasts who had gotten bowls on the heads. Hmm. They were clearly showing their emotions, not worried. It was obvious they had decided to take out Takayama like this and at the same time bought into the promises of Saito's group.

But Osamu's gang was not the best choice. And it was the rank and file that ruined their reputation, but the leader himself and his closest associates. The teenagers, or even already young men, had been corrupted by power and committed real atrocities. Abusing the weak, enforcing unquestioning obedience of the young to the old, inappropriate behavior with girls... Saito was gaining infamy, and that was only thing stopping the clever and domineering student from obtaining mastery over Gakko Academy.

"Hi everybody." A strong-looking boy greeted us.

To be honest, I could not for the life of me recall anyone from Saito's gang, and they had definitely sent the also-rans to Hideo, just three fourth-years and a few third-years. This was certainly not Osamu's elite fighters. And where was the man himself? I winked surreptitiously at Hattori. I hoped he would understand and try to find out where the leader of the gang was. His network of friends/informants was always in the chat, and maybe they knew what Saito was up to now.

"Hello," Hideo answered like he was the host.

But Takayama was looking at me. If we came to an agreement, I would stay there and fight with the C class. If not, then I would take Tomoko's people out of harm's way. I didn't think Saito's people would go crazy and fight both classes right away. Hideo didn't disappoint me. He nodded in agreement, letting me know that from now on his army would fight for our side.

"And a good day to you too." I redirected the attention of the captain of Osamu's gang onto myself.

"And who are you?" the fourth-year asked, rudely.

"Maybe you should come into the class politely and ask the names of those there before introducing yourself?" I purposefully spoke slowly and calmly, getting under the skin of our obviously hot-tempered opponent.

"Oh, is that any way to talk to your elders?" A third-year girl with a confident look impulsively interjected, trying to help her boss. No good.

"You decide who among you is the leader, and then come in again," I responded in the same calm tone. That just pushed the guy even further.

"Suki, don't interrupt!" shouted my opponent. "And you, son of a bitch, you're just asking for it, huh?"

"Me? Never! Put yourself in my shoes. I'm sitting here with my friends, looking out the window, listening to the birds singing, and here you come, shouting loudly, blaming me for something. You got it?" I said, sincerely and with a bit of a biting tone.

My opponent seemed to be confused. He clearly was a bit worried about getting into a conflict with so many second-years, and nobody seemed to acting rudely. And that fact, that nobody was afraid, or angry, or doing anything to deserve it, was flustering him.

"Hmm, okay, fine, forget it. I am the captain of Osamu Saito's army. My name is Manabu! My boss sent me here to the second-year C class to offer you the chance to join his forces!" The upperclassman's words were heavy and forceful. But in the light of my previous tricks his fervent speech seemed not threatening, just funny. Some of the second-years broke out in giggles. "Hey!

Are you making fun of me?"

"Manabu, they're just laughing. Is that not allowed in the presence of an upperclassman?" I said, breaking in quickly while my fighters pushed forward, spreading out in this place cramped with so many people.

"And who the hell are you, goddammit?" shouted Manabu intensely, baffled by my constant interruptions. I felt like he was already ready to beat the life out of me, but our superior numbers and my confidence were keeping the boy from taking any hasty actions.

"My name is Genji Tanaka, the leader of the second-year D class and the ally of the Tomoko Yasuda and Hideo Takayama, present here," I informed him, calmly throwing my Gantan back and forth between my hands. These simple movements seemed to somewhat hypnotize and even slightly take aback the rather confident Manabu.

"The Ball-Breaker... -Breaker... Sasaki...." All around the leader of the invaders, the upperclassman could be heard whispering. Dammit, the name had definitely stuck.

"Aaaaaa..." Manabu exhaled suddenly, clearly not wanting to risk his own balls. "How do you respond to Osamu Saito's offer?"

"We'll think about it," I answered for everyone, very skeptically, letting it be known that it wasn't going to fly here.

"Okay, don't take too long," Manabu said,

trying to be noble, which he would pay for. He shouldn't have let my reply go unchallenged.

"Are you giving us a time limit, Manabu? Maybe we owe you personally or your boss something?" I said, aggravating the situation, while loudly clacking the two balls together.

"Hey, I just wanted you to know that these kinds of offers don't happen every day!" the fourth-year said, trying to extricate himself from the situation.

"Oh yeah? Then this is some sort of honor for us?" I said, laying out another verbal trap.

"How not?" Manabu smirked, full of himself. "Saito's gang is the strongest in Gakko Academy, and there are a ton of people who want to stand with us!"

"Well, now then, why did you come with your fighters and request us to join your ranks? We would have to take that as you asking for us to become vassals, just like the rest of the school would, right? Manabu, I am not the best student at Gakko Academy, and also, as your associate rightly noted, I am younger than most. So then, it just be fair for us to wait our turn and let those who are older and better than us go first," I said, shocking Osamu Saito's envoys.

"I... what are you trying to say?" the confused captain scratched his head in bewilderment.

"We will join the glorious ranks of your army after the fourth and third-year classes have pledged their loyalty to you. It would be improper for the young to take precedence over their elders!" I had purposefully changed my tone from flippant to respectful, but those around me were not fooled by this false humility.

"Tanaka, that means you are refusing to join us..."

"Manabu, I said what I said. We will join with Osamu Saito when he has completely subjugated the third and fourth-year classes at Gakko Academy," I said, enunciating every word while clacking the Gantan together threateningly. "And remember, captain, you yourself said that there was no limit to the number of people who wanted to be under your banner. So where would the young ones be, if not in the very back?"

"I understand," Manabu said through clenched teeth.

The guy definitely wanted to tear me to pieces for that humiliation, but our numerical superiority and my terrifying reputation forced him to leave empty-handed.

When our enemies left we quickly agreed on the conditions for our alliance and cooperation between the groups. In general everything was clear, but we still had to discuss everything in more detail, dotting the i's and crossing the t's. I was a little embarrassed that Tomoko kept trying to get closer to me during the discussion. She would unintentionally brush me with her ample butt, then unwittingly put her hand on me...

What a bitch! These games were threatening to destroy the alliance I had just made with Hideo and might even put the loyalty of my intelligence officer, Hattori, into question. I, with great force of will, clamped down on my testicles, standing as far as could from my unreasonably sexy peer. If only you know much it took! But I managed it, and Yoshiko had at least alleviated some of this strain from my body. I would have to do it all again, just to make sure, otherwise I might once again end up in an awkward situation.

Happy with the results, and, most importantly, having avoided any unnecessary bloodshed with either our neighboring class or with Saito's envoys, my group and I headed back. We went the same way we came. Takeshi and his guys went in front as reconnaissance, while I was in the back with the main group. Considering that the upperclassmen didn't normally go around in big groups like this, it was a perfectly safe way to get around. The only exception would be if we ran into a unit going to a fight, like Manabu's fighters. But that was what Takeshi was for.

But the danger wasn't waiting for us where the Kato was going. It was behind us that we heard the bustling of a large force. Our new friend Manabu popped out from around the corner with the same army as before. We had just passed that corner where, except for one young guy, nobody was around. I was surprised, wondering what kind of brave person would be hanging around in the hallways alone while war was raging between the classes inside of Gakko Academy. My mistake. He was apparently a spy, waiting to bring out our enemy.

I only managed to nod to Hattori, a signal to warn Takeshi, when the powerful fighters of Osamu Saito arrayed themselves before us. We were about equal in number, but if we counted Takeshi's group, the we were a bit bigger. But Manabu was supported by battle-hardened veterans of Gakko Academy, while mine was just a damn dozen of newbroken, untested second-years.

The hallway was fairly wide. On my left flank I had Ryuen's five-man unit and a little behind them, panting, Takeshi's unit that had just hurried up was standing on my right flank, with Ichiro and his nerds behind me. Not the best defense, but the flank had already been entrusted to them. According to our plan, if anything happened, they would be supported on both sides by the Wada sisters, Rokero, and Jiro. But with such an inexperienced army all these tactical steps would not work out. That's why my Teacher always used to say, "War is nothing, it's all about the maneuvers."

Chapter 11

The Fight

MANABU STEPPED FORWARD a little, and I followed his lead. The two of us, as the commanders of our armies, met in the middle between them. He angrily sized me up. The aggressive expression on his face along with his determined pose told me that the decision had been made and the unlucky captain of Saito's gang had made up his mind to get revenge.

He definitely lost in the duel of words, and now he wanted to change it into a fight with fists and magic that would be a much better fit for him. But for some reason he either couldn't get right to it or he was taking his time. If that was it, then Saito's own gang was probably rushing here. Which would be really bad. But I was sure that my guys had called for Hideo's fighters and

Tomoko's nerds and they would be here shortly. So it was not in my interests to waste time. We had to fight.

"You really thought you could get away that easily?" Manabu began talking, but I had no time for pleasantries and threw my first Gantan.

Yeah, I was breaking the rules, in the grand tradition of a sewer rat. My weapon hit the impudent Suki, who definitely had some connection to Manabu, and who had just a bit ago interrupted our discussion. That wasn't some sort of revenge or a desire to hurt my opponent, just cold, cynical calculation. There were fourteen of us, including me, and ten of them. But each of the fourth-years counted for at least two of the lowerclassmen, meaning the advantage was clearly with Manabu.

And it was a big advantage that would only grow as the upperclassmen started taking out my fighters. So my goal was to reduce the number of our opponents as much as possible before the brawl started. Manabu, for sure, had already heard about my Gantan, he had even seen them in Hideo's classroom. That meant that the guy was ready to face them, given how confidently he was holding himself.

I never entertained the idea that the gifted had trained as boxers or whatever, but the still could dodge or block their top half fairly well. But everyone knew that they could hit you even on chest pretty well, although Manabu wasn't afraid.

Hmm... It was possible that the dude had put on some kind of armor or a bulletproof vest under his school uniform. If so, then my first hit wouldn't take him out, and I risked wasting the spheres for nothing.

That was why I targeted Suki. I hit her in the chest from a short distance so she couldn't block or dodge it. For that skinny girl a couple of broken ribs would be enough to take her out of the fight. One down. But I wasn't scheming to take out Manabu's girlfriend, no. It was him I was after. And the captain of Saito's gang didn't disappoint. The leader committed an unforgiveable error. Instead of coming swiftly to bear on me, he turned around upon hearing the pitiful cry of pain from the undeniably beautiful Suki.

I had just a few fractions of a second at my disposal. Manabu, as I thought, was covered in armor, and he may have even taken the time to put on a cup wherever he went off to. But because of Suki, the unprotected nape of his neck was exposed to me. Hmm... That was dangerous. I might kill him. But Matvey Nikolaevich had told me that wizards were pretty well protected in the weak points.

I took the shot. The boy was knocked right out, and my rune of concentration showed me that I hadn't overdone it. Two down now. But that was limit. Couldn't take it any farther.

Now there were only eight fighters in front of

us. The situation was already looking better for us. I popped my flail into my right hand and held my metal ruler in the left, pulling an angry face and taking a step toward the members of Osamu Saito's gang. Those guys were definitely afraid of my weapon's terrible reputation, and, stupidly forgetting any training they had, instantaneously covered their groins at the expense of their heads and bodies. Which is where I started swinging my measuring tool.

I was rewarded with shouts of pain. I did three or four hits in quick succession, like a sewing machine, swiftly blinding one of my opponents.

The seven remaining upperclassmen had not even started to react. It just so happened that Manabu was in front, with Suki and the guy who I had hit with the ruler right behind him. The rest of the fighters were respectfully standing a few feet behind their boss and were now staring in disbelief at the results of our short scuffle. Behind them the sounds of feet rushing our way could be heard.

Hideo and his thugs were dashing up to the battlefield along with Tomoko leading her nerds from Ichiro Hattori's club. That might not be the most threatening army, but now our enemies had nearly ten of our allies at their back, which was a whole new ball game. The upperclassmen, surrounded, demoralized by the loss of their leaders, were ready to give up, but this calculating sewer rat from Skayd was in way prepared to accept that.

I knew that even as a pair of C classes we were not up to tangling with Osamu Saito. Two third-year and one fourth-year classes? That was a fine enemy for Akira Takada, but not at all for a bunch of second-years. And there were definitely going to be major problems in store for us after today's small victory. But we could thin their ranks at least, if we sent some of Osamu's army to the hospital today.

Of course, the wounded would be back to get their revenge sooner of later, but time was the deciding factor now. Manabu was the leader of about a third of Saito's fighters, and once they were gone, he would be left with about the same force as Takada and Sasaki had. That meant that balance would be restored in the school, and none of the gangs would have enough of an advantage to subjugate the so-far independent second-years.

So, I carefully considered everything through the lens of my rune of concentration and shouted my command. "Fight!"

We swallowed up our opponents like two waves. Either in confusion or because the attack was from two sides, or maybe afraid of my reputation as the Ball Breaker — or possibly all of that together — Saito's fighters put up only token resistance. But the second-years fought like lions.

Book Two

Ryuen Kato knocked a fourth-year to the ground, and Hideo Takayama gleefully kicked the boy, splayed headlong on the floor, from the third-year A class. Takeshi and the Wada sisters ran a strong-looking boy into a corner and turned him into mincemeat. It was a short fight. Now those fighters from one of the most fearsome gangs at Gakko Academy were lying on the ground like broken dolls, while we, the second-years, breathing hard and wiping away blood, were taking stock.

"Did we win?" Hattori asked, smiling joyfully, if a bit uncertain. He had taken part in this kind of fight for the first time. And he had carried himself well, taking out one of the less weak fighters with the two other nerds.

"Aahahaxhah! Yeah!' Hideo Takayama shouted like a wild animal and took a step toward him. He was a bit scared at first, but then saw his outstretched hand shook it firmly. "You did well, Ichiro."

"Thank you, Hideo!" Hattori was genuinely happy to make up with his long-time malefactor. "And I want you to know that I am not trying to hook up with Tomoko."

"I have known that for a long time, Ichiro. I just thought you were a piece of shit. You weren't bad, but you never fought to the end, like today," Hideo said, explaining his sudden friendliness. "And I never fight about women!"

"Pfff." Tomoko Yasuda snorted upon hearing

that.

The sexy C class student had shown herself to be a fierce fighter, taking out a third-year nearly all on her own. Well, I had to admit that she had gotten a pretty weak opponent. But even the nerds from the Smart Club hadn't been useless. Maybe they weren't too bad after all.

"General," Takeshi addressed me for the first time with the title of the leader of the strongest gangs in Gakko Academy. "What should we do now?"

"Captain," I said, conferring upon him the title of my first officer, "we have to send this guys to the hospital, as I once did to you and your brother!"

"Why so vicious, Genji?" the Wada sisters asked. They, of course, knew what state the Kato Brothers were in when they were taken out of the showers.

"It's nothing personal, Wadas, not vicious at all. I do this to guarantee the safety of myself and my own as much as possible," I patiently explained, even though time was of the essence. The security forces, most likely, had already been sent to the scene of the fight. "If we put these guys in the hospital for a longer time, then Saito will have a third less of his fighters for a couple weeks. And that means they will hardly be able to stand against Takada and Sasaki's gangs."

"And he won't be able to get to us." The twins finished my thought in unison and enthusiastically set to crippling the unconscious bodies of our fallen opponents.

The cries of those unlucky ones whose arms and legs were being broken with magic seemed to reach the farthest corners of Gakko Academy.

What we were doing surpassed the pathology of students, but I had simply replaced murder with something that would allow us to avoid our enemies for some time. It was cruel, but pragmatic and I wasn't about to quibble about the methods of saving our skins. With the caveat, of course, that it didn't break the law. Then again, maybe I was opening Pandora's box and the level of cruelty at Gakko Academy would only increase from here on out...

While we were engaged in our dirty business I was once again surprised by the sluggish response of the local security forces. The school was not that small, but the security here had quite a few fighters, and their job was to predict and prevent conflicts. Those guys, if you believed the advertisements, were supposed to be always ready, well-equipped, and with a ton of helpful ways to suppress young wizards.

During the time we were fighting and then crippling our enemies, you could run around the school at least ten times, but Ketsu Aoki's men showed up only at the very end, as if they were purposefully giving us the time to finish. The administration was clearly up to something. I needed to look into this, which would give me a deeper understanding of what was happening at Gakko and how to survive here.

For the rest of the day, until the end of classes, we were on guard. Certainly, lady luck, smiling on us today, could always switch sides to Osamu Saito. At the same time, I was worried about the C class who had come into our alliance. They could end up unlucky too, which would, more likely than not, spell a sudden end for this new-found alliance of second-years.

But some good came from the fight. The untested wizards felt confidence in their strength and the support of their comrades. Fighting shoulder to shoulder together and getting their first victory over a powerful opponent had taken a flighty herd of students and made them more than a gang, but something like an organization. Now I had the task of forging a sort of squad out of these youngsters as soon as possible, one that would not go awry in the trash heaps of Skayd.

The most important thing now was not to lose our momentum and to anticipate the next few moves of our opponents. I hoped that our efforts to remove Manabu's unit from the board of Gakko Academy would pay off. Akira Takada would soon be returning to her own troops, something I knew because Kiyoko had recently let it slip that their war with the Mori clan would soon be ending. As such, Saito, having already attacked Butsu, would probably soon have to pay for his impetuousness.

Now Takada had two, maybe two and a half dozen fourth-years against the same number of Osamu's fighters. However, half of his army was third-years, which gave Akira a significant advantage. And if I help my girlfriend's sister... But I had to remember that I had unfinished business with Hiro Sasaki, who would definitely be looking for revenge when he recovered.

Hmm... an alliance of myself and Takada against Saito and Hiro... It might just work. Our enemies were head and shoulders above us, both in people and in the strength of their separate fighters. If we took the fourth-years, who were split down the middle, out of the equation then I could only field two classes of kids against three third-year classes.

I also had to consider who Makise Abe would end up joining. It made sense that we didn't have the best relationship. Considering how I had exposed his secret and the fights in the hospital and their consequences, it would be foolish to expect a warm reception from him. Moreover, Butsu had attacked the third-year B class on his own without Akira, so there was no hope of us both making an alliance with Makise. On the other hand, I did have his cousin Rokero on my side. Of course, that didn't really mean anything, but I could at least use it as a channel for opening peace talks.

I had two choices now.

The first was to get Saito, Sasaki, and

Takada to all fight with each other using tricks and alliances, while we keep our heads down for the time being and continue building up our army. I was already thinking about training together and introducing some new ideas. I needed to improve my soldiers so they would be ready to fight with the stronger and more experienced upperclassmen.

The second was to take control of all the other classes in our year, grow in strength, and wait for Osamu and Hiro to graduate. But then again, what was stopping me from doing both?

* * *

General Saito was on the verge of achieving his dream. Dominion over the rebellious Gakko Academy had tempted many brave leaders and would continue to tempt many more. But only Osamu had ever had a real chance to make it a reality. He only needed to get a couple of second-year classes and he would have enough fighters in his gang to destroy the proud Takada and the maniac Sasaki.

Having found himself so close to the peak, the gang leader was quite confident, but still careful. Osamu was not going to start his conquest of the second-years with the D class. And no matter what anybody said, Saito was not afraid of the impudent second-year, Tanaka. He was just aware that Hiro Sasaki, the psycho, would try again and again to get another D class on his side. And, considering Genji's fighting prowess, starting his search for allies with the D class was ill-advised.

That was why Saito had, after some consideration, send two of his captains to deal with the second-years, leaving Genji's class alone for the time being. Each of Osamu's officers had no less than ten soldiers at their command, around thirty percent of whom were in the fourth-year. It was an imposing force, and if you took into account that they just had to crush pitiful, newbroken second-years, there was no doubt they would win.

But the first roadblock came with the A class. Raiden Nakata had turned out to be a surprisingly strong fighter, and the unruly second-years under his command had nearly destroyed one of Osamu's units. Of course, the fools had, as predicted, been sent to the hospital, but you could not call it a clear victory. That meant they would have to visit the second-year A class once more, and get those stupid dumbasses in order, respecting the power of General Saito!

And now the biggest issue had come with the C class. Intelligence had uncovered an alliance between Genji Tanaka and Hideo Takayama there. In the end the group Captain Manabu commanded was laid out in the hospital, which, considering the damage done by Raiden's gang, had put Saito himself in a precarious position. Defeat at the hands of second-years and the destruction of nearly half of his fighters would be good news for nearly all the school's gangs.

A fragile equilibrium was maintained by Akira's absence from Gakko and the failure of her captain, Butsu, to take Makise Abe's class. And also, of course, Hiro Sasaki's extraordinary defeat in battle with Genji Tanaka. If not for that, one of those two gangs would be knocking on Saito's door. Those opportunists would definitely take advantage of his defeat in battle with the second-years.

The newbrokens were somehow very troublesome this year. A year ago, when Saito, a captain under his own boss, was suppressing the second-years of that time, there was a lot less opposition. No shortage of fights and battles, though. A single victory did not show your strength. Only resistance over the long time could show how strong these newbrokens were.

But Osamu knew from experience that crushing young wizards who had been heartened by victory would be much harder and take time. How unfortunate that it had started like this! There was a lot of work to do now. Only a series of defeats would make leaders like Genji and Raiden give up or join Osamu's gang at the rank of captain. He who was a general today would not be less tomorrow.

Now he should punish the D and C classes

for their resistance, but was it worth it to risk it now? Two of his three captains were in the hospital, and if fate smiled on Tanaka, the that could be the beginning of the end for Saito's gang. Leaders who couldn't win victories quickly lost those who joined their army out of fear.

Osamu looked at things carefully and realized that if they offered a third class support they would leave their leader.

Chapter 12

The Night Club

THIS TIME KETSU AOKI'S SECRETARY found him in his office. The head teacher had not been at the school all day, and the examination of the large battle that had led to ten students getting seriously injured had been put off to the next day. On top of that, the losing side was in a state where they could not give statements. However, a short report on such an important event still had to be given to the legate as soon as possible.

"Mr. Aoki, a large battle occurred today between two second-year classes on one side against a group of Manabu's students from the fourth-year C class." The secretary began his report.

"Who did Osamu Saito take over?" the head teacher asked calmly, as though it were an obvious question.

"Mr. Aoki, the captain of Saito's army did not win. The fighters of the second-year D and C class destroyed Manabu's forces almost without a fight," the secretary relayed the unexpected news.

Even before this the second-years were able to stand up against the gangs of the upperclassmen, a recent example being Raiden Nakata, but to win... That had never happened before at Gakko Academy.

"And, let me guess, the leader of the younger classes was, of course, Genji Tanaka?" Ketsu Aoki asked quietly.

"Yes, sir. Permission to speak?" The secretary was unfailingly respectful.

"Speak," answered the head teacher brusquely.

"Sir, why do you allow Genji Tanaka to use weapons?" The secretary asked a question that had been on his mind for a while.

"Officially, he does not use weapons," answered Aoki.

"But sir, his pens, Gantan, and of course, the flail... The security forces confiscate all such things from the students, because otherwise instead of training their magical abilities we would get teenagers fighting first with cold weapons, and then with firearms..."

"You are both right and not right. Genji is ungifted. He cannot gain ranks or train his spells. But once he decided to stay at Gakko Academy, then we had to find a way to level the playing field. We understand that, as does everyone else, so what our one ungifted at the school is allowed to do is not permitted for the rest."

"What if Tanaka goes too far and brings a—" the secretary tried to explain the problem, but was cut off by the head teacher.

"You know the rules. We follow the letter of the law. No lethal weapons are allowed with Gakko Academy!" Ketsu Aoki smiled slyly.

"But then he won't have too much..." The secretary was lost in thought, apparently going through the small arsenal of the hapless ungifted, thrown into the chaotic mess of these adolesecent wars, in his mind.

"Yes... As I already said, some people think that we are witnesses to the birth of a legend!" The legate voiced his thoughts out loud.

* * *

Nobody had bothered me or my allies by the end of the day. Either Osamu Saito was being too cautious, or Takada and Sasaki's gangs had taken swift advantage of his weakness. In any case, the rest of the day went by calmly. And in the evening we planned to celebrate our new alliance and first victory with the new members of our team.

It was a little too soon to have a party at the penthouse, since they were still finishing up some decorative work there. I decided it was time to fix the place up, change the design of the rooms, and add some more modern stuff in the interior. Now, in addition to the amazing sauna with swimming pool, the were putting in a bar, gambling tables, and some other stuff. And an arsenal...

Today we picked on of the popular establishments for young people. ABS night club was famous for its food, drinks, and peaceful atmosphere. Like Ginza, students from a few schools in the area liked to go there. But the club was not a place for couples. You went there to rest, dance, and drink.

Accordingly, the clan that controlled the building had made it clear that anyone who wanted to fight would have to do it at least one mile away from the club. Otherwise the powerful security forces would get involved decisively in the conflicts of the adolescents. A better place for second-years would be hard to find. Everything was exciting, safe, and delicious. The club had the reputation of being a kind of playground, since older students preferred other places.

All of the participants in the day's fight came to ABS, both those from the second-year D class and C class. It ended being a small group of about two dozen people. But there was plenty of space for everyone, since we took our seats at the tables on the upper floor balcony, where we could watch the dance floor and eat and drink in peace, when the need arose.

The Kato brothers, as was already their habit, paired up with the Wada sisters. Ichiro, to everyone's surprise, came with a girl from the A class. The rest all paired up as well. Except me, I stayed without a girl, like a good boy, as expected since Kiyoko wasn't there. I would deal with the girls I had, and not try to start any new romances.

But that was complicated right away. Tomoko, who was officially with the nerds, was constantly sending lustful glances my way. I was worried about my overdeveloped classmate. To tell the truth, she had a great body, and there was something in her face that was just... But this one more woman might be the straw that broke the camel's back.

I had my relationship with Kiyoko, Yoshiko's jealous, and the English teacher... Not to mention the deal with Hideo Takayama. Thank God that the thing with Ichiro worked out, but, in any case, to ruin everything with my friends over yet another lover would be the height of stupidity. But goddammit, I definitely was having a reaction to Tomoko! There were just too many girls in this world who were blowing my top.

I had done some digging about it. I had to dig through a ton of local myths and legends. I didn't find anything specific, just some rituals outside of classical magic. But they seemed to not be very effective or didn't promise any definite results. Maybe something like that had happened to Genji's body, but I couldn't rule out the concoction I had swallowed.

It seemed that the best thing to do would be to get some statistical information about all the girls I liked. But who was going to get me the medical records or family tree of someone like Kiyoko Takada? I could definitely get all the available information on Yoshiko, even though she herself probably didn't know anything about her ancestors. Common families didn't keep historical archives. There wasn't a lot of information, but my rune of concentration would do its job, and sooner or later I would get answers to all these questions.

But now it was time to relax. For the first time we had taken care of a serious opponent without losses, and my team was impressive, not the most imposing or numerous, but you had to take us seriously now. Takada and Sasaki had twenty fighters each under their command, while Saito had ten more. So my army was something. And if we could get the two remaining second-year classes to join up with us...

"Cheers to our boss!" Takeshi Kato raised his glass of beer.

"Cheers!" echoed his brother Ryuen immediately.

"Cheers! Cheers! Cheers!" The Wada twins, Ichiro, nearly all the guys immediately followed suit.

"Cheers!" Takayama joined in, even though he still wasn't quite ready to part with his dreams of independence.

"Cheers!" Tomoko Yasuda, having come unnoticed back from the dance floor, whispered almost directly in my ear. Her breath was hot on my skin, her firm breasts pressed against my back, and her thighs were wrapped around my leg. The girl was definitely playing with fire. "Shall we dance?"

"Of course." I didn't have the strength to refuse, and even a look from Takayama couldn't make me think twice.

Tomoko took me by the hand and literally dragged me to the dance floor. And then there began some crazy dance, with her tightly holding me to her luscious body. The beautiful girl clung to me, first dancing face to face and then turning around and grinding on me. Her ass was shamelessly up against my waist and her rhythmic movements were just like... well, you know what. This uncontrolled dance was already starting to attract the attention of those around us, but Tomoko kept going, utterly shameless.

The guys also joined us. We were trying to dance in a big circle. And the Wada twins were doing moves that were no different from Tomoko's, so maybe that was acceptable here? But I couldn't find anything like that in Genji's memory. Almost all of our guys danced, except Hideo. Even the shy Ichiro Hattori come out to the dance floor with his A class girl a couple times.

I was worried about my ally Takayama. I knew from experience that jealousy could drive a guy crazy, especially with teenage hormones and the youthful tendency to overreact. On the other hand, Tomoko had made it clear to Hideo that she wasn't interested in him. If Takayama was going to stupidly keep everyone away from Yasuda, well, that was his business.

Even so, I tried my best to stop her from her excessively obvious seductions. God knows, it was a herculean task. It would have been easier to fight with Hiro Sasaki again.

Even though I was on my guard, the problems came from where I least expected them. Hideo Takayama and Tomoko Yasuda, worrying my like a time bomb, didn't go off that day.

But the trigger was pulled by the up-and-coming brains of my outfit, Ichiro Hattori. The mild-mannered nerd, the smartest guy, a person who had managed to make good connections with many students at Gakko Academy, who I never expect to cause problems. And really, he didn't. He danced carefully, paying attention to his surroundings, sure of himself, but polite. I watched Hattori and I was happy for him.

No, the problem came from somewhere else. His girl, Amaya, who was also shy and smart, was the unintentional source of a conflict. Koji Kubo, one of the leaders of the B class, had come to club with his rival for power, Taro Kodama. They were there with some of their fighters, four with Kubo and three with Kodama.

It seemed like they had come to make peace, since nobody came to the club to fight. I missed them coming in. Maybe I was in the bathroom. In any case, they never came out on the dance floor. And we were relaxing, drinking beer, having fun, utterly sure that there wouldn't be any fighting at ABS.

* * *

Koji Kubo first ran into problems when he had superiority in force and superiority in numbers, but his enemy were still not submitting, still disobedient. Kubo, as soon as he came to Gakko Academy, had surrounded himself with friends and considered the B class to be his own right from the start. Naturally strong, of average height, but broad-shouldered and with a powerful body, he oppressed people with his unwavering confidence and physical prowess. The son of an Oyabun, raised in the violent traditions of the criminal clans, he knew how to settle disagreements both by force and with words.

And so it was even worse for him to have to go against the skinny, girlish Taro Kodama. And despite his seeming lack of physical strength, this upstart from an impoverished aristocratic family, even though he had lost, had put up so such a good fight that nobody would ever consider the young Kodama to be defeated. His stubbornness combined with his good nature drew allies to him, and now the second-year B class was split into two opposing camps.

Fights would happen in the classroom nearly every day, and when they broke through it had only intensified the conflict. The girls had joined with the opposing sides, and the war continued with renewed vigor. But now both Koji and Taro had recognized that their internal divisions were making them easy prey for the upperclassmen.

They could have joined up with different groups, but the experience of the last year had shown that the life with representatives of two different groups in one classroom was a constant torture. It was vitally important for them to find common ground and stop the fighting. Living always on edge, following each other's every move, was getting harder and harder.

"Taro, I propose that we make peace. We must decide together which of the upperclassmen to join with," Koji began this difficult discussion. He had started the conflict, and he intended to end it. And Kubo had come to completely respect his adversary.

"I am not against that," Kodama said in his usual curt manner. "But who to join? I will say this. I am in no way willing to join that asshole Osamu Saito!"

"I wanted to put forth the same condition," Kubo said in support of his former enemy. He refused with his whole heart to follow a leader without honor. Saito's reputation was too bad, a fact with many witnesses to support it.

"Good that we agree on that." Kodama sighed in relief, having been prepared for the worst if the stubborn Kubo had suddenly decided to join Osamu's gang.

"Hmm. Hiro Sasaki is also not a choice," said Koji.

The leader of the D's didn't take allies from other classes. The guy definitely was messed up in the head, and who wanted to follow a psycho?

"So that just leaves Akira Takada?" suggested Taro.

"Yes, but she's leaving in a year, and since they haven't been able to conquer even one class, we will just have the same problem next year." Kubo, without knowing it, had come to the exact same conclusion as Genji Tanaka and his gang.

"So what do we do?" Kodama was surprised by the fact that they couldn't make up their minds on who to join. The young aristocrat had come to ABS sure that the hardest problem to solve would be coming to terms with Kubo. And now it turned out that just making an alliance between the two opposing groups would not be enough to solve all their problems. To hell with the government with its system of training young wizards!

The talk between the leaders of B class was interrupted by a boy from Kodama's team who had been watching those coming into the hallway. In order to talk in a club with constantly pounding music, the boys had rented a special soundproof room. They could have spoken in a café and not gone through the trouble, but ABS was more useful than other places because of its policy of no fighting.

Here nobody fought in groups and even personal one-on-one conflicts were not allowed. Anyone who truly could not wait could take advantage of the dueling arenas, for a nominal fee. Everything happened in a civilized way there, under the watchful eye of a team of qualified judges and the necessary medical staff. So this was the perfect place for discussions.

The talks were going smoothly. But the boys nevertheless set up a look-out outside the door, since, no matter what, neither Kubo nor Kodama could truly relax after a year of endless fighting. And right then, while both leaders were stumped, scratching their heads, wondering which group to join, the look-out rushed into the room.

"Taro, Amaya is dancing here with some nerd from the second-year D class." Kubo looked at Kodama in confusion. It wasn't like Taro had been observed to be with any girl at all even once all last year.

"Okay, let's go take a look," suggested Taro, standing up. Koji recognized the look in his eyes, one he had come across numerous times right before another fight that more often than not sent both boys to the hospital.

Both leaders stepped out of the well-lit room into the darkness of the dancehall. They had a hard time getting their bearings at first in the flashing of the disco balls, light organs, and projectors, first illuminating the floor, then the hall. In any case, the loud music and roar of the crowd of teenagers would be enough to stun anyway who suddenly showed up in that environment of unrestrained merrymaking.

Finally they got used to it and could make out what was going on. Literally ten yards away from them a large group of students from Gakko Academy were enjoying themselves. It would be hard not to recognize the new celebrity, Genji Tanaka, one of the worst hooligans last year. But Koji and Taro had run across him them, and Hideo Takayama too.

Huh. It seemed like both D and C class students were here now.

But Taro had no time for that. He was at first surprised to see some girl he vaguely knew, one who certainly also studied at Gakko, lustfully contorting herself around Genji.

Jesus, her moves were way more than just suggestive, and anybody would want to be in the leader of the second-year D class's place right now.

But his army wasn't stepping away from their boss, and he could see, dancing near Genji, the twins that everyone in the school knew, and boys and girls from the classes in their same year. And one of the girls, shamelessly embracing some weakling, the young aristocrat was surprised to recognize as Amaya.

Chapter 13

The Duel

TARO WALKED ACROSS THE DANCE FLOOR like an icebreaker in the Arctic Circe, forcing dancers to step aside with his body, with a powerful wedge of friends and former adversaries behind him. Nearly a full ten boys and girls, hardened by a full year of ruthless fighting, they seemed sure of themselves and therefore imposing. A lot of people parted automatically before that dangerous force, vainly scanning the room for the bouncing. Everybody knew that group fights were strictly forbidden at ABS, but that's clearly where this was headed.

When they started coming after my intelligence officer, I was standing at the back of the whole scene. I was really trying not to cream my jeans at the intense seductions of Tomoko

Yasuda. But my infatuation with the female sex this time did me some good. The girl, performing her wild gyrations around me, suddenly froze and stared for a minute. Of course, I couldn't just ignore that behavior and not turn around and see what caused it. Just in time.

A couple assholes from the second-year B class, who were always fighting with each other, were making their way intently toward Ichiro Hattori, ignoring the rules of the club. The disturbers of the peace were supported by about ten fighters. But even on the dance floor there were significantly more of us, and our guys, who had been left at their tables with their drinks, were already coming up on the rear. My army may not have been entirely sober, but an advantage of twice their numbers meant they had no chance.

The matter never got to a brawl. The security at ABS demonstrated why their establishment was considered one of the safest in the prefecture. We were fairly softly dragged, literally, apart into different corners. So this was magic! As far as I could tell, the hemispheres of energy shields that separated the teenagers into two... no, three groups, were the work of two young people from out of the darkness.

The first one was coming down from an upper balcony, and the second one was coming from somewhere in the depths of the dance floor. Both of them were in severe black uniforms, self-possessed, cold, immaculate. And why not? The adult wizards had pushed the aristocrats' kids into the corners. One hemisphere held Hideo and his guys to the wall, another kept us and those dancing around us into the center of the dance floor, and the B kids were practically stuffed up against the room they had came from. A couple of them had even been thrown through the door.

Aha, this was my first encounter with real magic. Judging from the ease with which the two guys had separated three groups of teenagers, I would have a hard time of it in the future. Only if my runes could in any way effect something similar. And from what I understood, in addition to these defensive skills, the local sorcerers also had attacking spells. Thank God, only the most talented students could manage that much, and then only in the very last class, in a very limited way.

"Sirs, as you all know, fights at ABS Club are strictly prohibited," pronounced one of the wizards, his voice amplified by something. The music had already been turned off, the light show had been stopped, and the lights turned on on the ceiling, dispelling the darkness.

"We had no intention to," I said, raising my hands in surrender. Really, my team was just here to relax.

"Then what is your classmate doing, Genji!?" Taro Kodama shouted, beside himself with anger. My recipient knew him since last year. Actually, as my next step I was planning to get one of the two groups from the second-year B class. I had been leaning toward the weaker Taro. Koji, winning in the war, would never accept my help as a favor, but Kodama definitely might have.

"Hey, Taro, forgive me, maybe I'm not getting something here, but I didn't even know your class was in the club today." I was truly unaware of the reason for this conflict, but Kodama, as far as I could tell, was truly upset about something.

"That is just it! Your classmate is doing this behind my back! I'm sure that if he knew I was going to be here, he never would have dared." Kodama, furious, kept spewing accusations.

"Taro, would you just explain clearly?" Alcohol and the absurdity of the situation made me speak a little harsher than necessary.

"That guy over there," Kodama said, pointing his finger clearly at Ichiro and the girl clinging to him, "has offended my honor!"

"I told you to stay away from me!" Amaya said suddenly.

"Guys, can you please explain what is going on here?" I pleaded, annoyed.

But the resolution had to wait. The wizards needed to get the club going again. So me, as the obvious leader, Ichiro and Amaya, as the probably cause of the conflict, and Taro and Koji, as the initiators of it, were taken to a private room where we could talk in peace, under the supervision of one of the gifted. The rest of our people were taken back to their own places. My team went the tables on the balcony, while the B class locked themselves in their room.

"Young ones, can we consider this conflict resolved?" asked one of the wizards. "If not, we will have to kick both groups out of the club. In addition, if the instigators cannot justify their behavior, then they risk being permanently blacklisted from ABS Club."

"Good sirs," Taro said, calming himself down, "perhaps I react rashly, but I have a good reason for it. This girl, Amaya Kodama, is my sister, and her behavior is unacceptable! Amaya has recently become engaged to be wed, and her courting by this boy is something I take as an affront to the Kodama clan's honor!"

"That is not true, Taro! You sold me like a whore! Did anybody ask for my consent to marry that beast?" shouted Amaya, clearly continuing some familial fight.

"Shut up!" Taro reacted strongly. Then he blushed, because they were now airing their dirty laundry in public.

To be honest, I was somewhat surprised things had come to this. To me, the reasons for the fight were ridiculous. After all, Ichiro hadn't slept with Amaya, just danced. Okay, maybe a little too openly, but there were only a hundred or so people here. How had that riled up the normally calm and reserved Taro Kodama? Either this engagement was exceptionally important for the clan, or the Kodamas were a family of hypocrites. But the first one seemed more plausible.

"Taro, it seems to be that we have just been the victims of an inadvertent misunderstanding in your family affairs. Believe me, none of us meant to put your family in a bad light," I said, exercising my right as leader to speak on Ichiro's behalf.

"I didn't know anything about Amaya's engagement," Hattori said, backing me up. He clearly didn't want to cause any problems for his family from some innocent flirting. "I have been friends with her for a long time in the Smart Club."

"I know that," Kodama muttered bitterly. "But, guys, I have no other choice but to challenge you to a duel!"

"Are you nuts, Taro?" I was upset. The guy knew that there had been no ill intent, but he was insisting on escalating the situation. "And why BOTH of us?"

"Genji, don't be offended. This is nothing personal. I am just afraid that the family Amaya is betrothed to will take advantage of today's conflict. But we have our plans... Anyway, I have to keep the clan safe. The best way is a duel, or a public apology from Ichiro and yourself, as his general." Kodama give his fairly long speech.

His motives might have been a little clearer now, but they didn't seem any more logical to me.

"Taro, what is making you put these clan problems of yours on me and Ichiro? Hattori was just dancing with your sister, and I wasn't involved at all. Are you not worried that, by giving in to one side, you won't offend another? I won't just leave it at this!" I pushed it a little, feeling completely within my rights. Whatever relationship the Kodama clan had with Amaya's future clan, it could not be worth it to drag in third parties.

"I understand that, Genji. But still, Ichiro danced with her, and you did nothing to sto—"

"And I didn't intend to," I cut Taro off sharply. "What reason do I have to forbid my people from dancing with girls who come to our party of their own accord?"

"Young men," the wizard watching our argument, silent until now, suddenly broke in, "if I understand correctly, the representative of the Kodama clan will not leave without a duel, and the opposing party considers his reasons negligible?"

"Yes, exactly," I said, immediately.

"That is so," Kodama conceded to the words of the security forces worker of the club.

"Let me suggest something that will be amenable to both parties."

After waiting for us to nod in agreement, the wizard continued:

"Kodama requires a public resolution of today's conflict. We need not quibble about the reasons for that desire, although I believe they are substantial. On the other hand, the indignation of the young man, madam Amaya, and even more so Genji, since they did nothing untoward. But perhaps Kodama or his friend Kubo could suggest something to the opposing side that would justify a conflict. Or might Genji Tanaka himself see a way out?

"Hmm, then everyone would believe we were fighting about Amaya, restoring the honor of the Kodama clan, but for ourselves it would be a different conflict, something so that neither Genji nor Ichiro would bear a grudge," Taro said, thinking out loud, then asked suddenly, "Tanaka, am I right to believe that you decided to take over all the second-year classes?"

"Yes," I said, not hiding anything.

"If you win in this duel, I and my people will pledge our allegiance to you as general of Gakko Academy," Taro offered, unexpectedly.

"Hey, we didn't agree to that!" Koji Kubo, up until now silent and calm, suddenly got upset. "Don't forget that we made an alliance today!"

"Hey, Kubo, this is clan business!" Taro had definitely got himself in a bind. He was dealing with family interests, trying to finish things amicably with my gang, and now he also had to worry about his classmate. I did not envy him.

At that time I starting sending energy through my rune of concentration and modeling possible outcomes. The duel itself was unavoidable. But the fight could turn out many different ways. Taro would attack Ichiro first, most likely, winning due to his experience, and then he would attack me. If Hattori didn't fall right away, then I might have a chance... but Kubo interference introduced a completely unknown variable to this already fairly complex equation.

"Then can we duel two on two?" Koji brought up an interesting idea.

"We are not equipped for team battles, only one-on-one duels," the ABS Club employee answered immediately.

"What about a system of individual fights? Two duels and then a third one between the winners, if they are from different teams?" Koji said excitedly, obviously a big fan of fighting.

"So, let's draw lots and fight. If Genji's team wins, then the whole B class will become Tanaka's vassals. What do you think?" Taro asked, happy to have found a solution.

"It doesn't seem too bad," I said after weighing the pros and cons. Then I asked, "But what do you get if you win? I mean, besides Kodama solving his clan problem."

"Yeah, whatever," said Koji Kubo accommodatingly, quite generous it seemed. "If fate smiles upon me and Taro, we will take an invitation to your penthouse, since everyone is talking about how cool it is."

"Agreed," I said, decisively.

I think the guys were intending to join me anyway. Today we would have an outcome that worked for everyone no matter what. We would fight, and if I won they would swear fealty to me according to the gentlemen's agreement. And if I lost, then we would make an alliance of gangs on equal footing, which was not bad either. Formally that was our relationship with Takayama and Tomoko too, even though their hostility to each other meant that the C class was still on top.

And Taro would also have a good outcome for his clan's plans. Although, because of them, we decided not to draw lots. Kodama had to guarantee that he would fight Hattori, and if he drew the lot with Kubo, then Taro's chances of dueling him were halved. Plus, there was a non-zero chance that the young aristocrat would lose to me, which would make it quite unlikely that he would face Ichiro. So Taro and Ichiro would fight the first duel, and Koji and I the second. If the winners of the first two rounds turned out to be from different groups, then there would be a third, final match to decide the winner.

The managers of ABS turned out to be crafty businessmen. By forbidding group fights they increased profits right away. First of all, the safe environment attracted quite a lot of clients. As my Teacher used to say, "He who doesn't fight lives to see another day." And a lot of different people came here. Lowerclassmen, single people, and other guys from different schools. Secondly, there was the advantage of not have expensive property destroyed. If there were no fights, there were no broken glasses, busted chairs, or money wasted on cleaning.

But most of all ABS made money by setting up duels. The fights went from uncivilized, murderous acts to fascinating spectacles. What's more, the customers themselves entertained the crowd for free, and, it must be said, fairly regularly. It seemed the duelists themselves had to put up the costs of renting arenas and the on-staff team of highly qualified medical professionals. So you had yourself a super profitable business.

A modern arena materialized, for lack of a better word, in the middle of the dance floor. It seemed that some of the equipment had been hidden beneath the floor, rising up automatically, while the rest was brought and set up by the efficient workers. Everything had been made to the highest standards of technology and in the fashion of the battles between wizards that were popular in the country.

Naturally, group battles were more popular, but here there was only an arena for duels. Which made sense. Group arenas were more complicated and cumbersome technical matters. A normal club couldn't manage that. But the arena for two gifted was exemplary. The view was good, with cameras all around to show it on-screen, with a protective octagon and mats that were hard but would not cause injury.

Taro Kodama and Ichiro Hattori came to the arena first. Both of the fighters were given athletic uniforms, like the smooth ones that cyclists wore. Ah, yeah, that would make judo holds pretty hard. No helmets, no gloves, no cladding on the legs either, goddamn full-contact. And I was to understand that you couldn't bring weapons either.

But it was coming to it. The time had long passed for me to try dueling with the gifted without an ace up my sleeve. Starting with the experienced upperclassman had been dangerous, and this was only a slightly easier version. I didn't have any real conflict with these guys, so it would be like sparring in close to real conditions. Just so. My armor would protect me, and I knew well how useful my tricks were in duels with wizards. And I already had a good estimate of when I would be able to finish my runes of speed and strength.

By this time Ichiro and Taro were both squaring up in their corners of the arena. Taro was not that tall and had what looked to me to be a fragile frame. The perfect picture of a pampered aristocrat. But, judging by the last year and his fame as a fighter, the heir of the Kodama clan was not that weak. His duels with the stout and short Koji Kubo had already begun to take on the air of legend.

And here is where my fighter failed. His

fragile, sunken chest, which had never once known a bench press, his lanky arms, his chicken legs. The ridiculousness of the entirely unathletic Hattori was even more emphasized by his athletic uniform. The super-modern fabric was not just supposed to not block heat exchange and mop up sweat from unwanted areas, it also highlighted the athletic muscles of the fighters, if they had them, of course. But in Ichiro's case it just brought out his physical failings.

However, Hattori did have one clear advantage over his opponent. He was tall, in comparison with Taro. So the brains of my army should be able to stand against an active opponent, with the right tactics, keeping him at a distance with his long arms and legs. He just needed to precisely counter him and seize the right moment. I shared those thoughts with Ichiro, giving him a few tips in case Taro might close the distance.

Chapter 14

The Outcome of the Duel

GONG!

Ichiro clumsily took the center of the ring. His physicality was not at the level where he could move around actively, so from the center he could dominate and make use of his advantages in the length of his arms and his mass to full effect. Taro was as swift as expected. The young wizard was working hard, not preserving his strength, circling Hattori like a pack of wolves chasing a deer. Just a pack, it seemed, the boy was everywhere, trying to attack first from one side, then the front, even occasionally trying to run around behind.

But my intelligence officer was holding is

own, not least of all due to his well-chosen position and economical movements. Kodama was trying to break through Ichiro's defense with his speed and by applying pressure, but getting past those extremely long arms was no easy feat. He was running the risk of getting hit by a lucky hit, but it would be no less dangerous for it. And these were two gifted fighting, so any attack could be the end of the battle.

Taro lived up to his reputation as an exceptional fighter. All of his bobbing and weaving around Hattori was like a wave of water, drawing attention. The aristocrat carefully picked out the weak spots in his opponent's defines and without a second thought, threw himself into a dedicated attack, diving under those long arms and landing a short, powerful punch to his liver. Ichiro was definitively staggered.

But Kodama, not satisfied with that, tried to add two more to his head, finishing what he had started. It was a logical move. Ichiro, having taken one to the liver, threw his arms up, trying to defined his vital organs, although all he had to do was work his elbows and move his arms. But my "genius" just didn't have enough experience.

And Taro's pair of hits nearly went off. The first hit was a tester across Hattori's jaw, while the second should have knocked him on his unprotected chin. But! Alright! I could that Ichiro had a trap in store. Our nerd wasn't so simple after all. He waited for the hit, blocking it a bit clumsily, then planted a ringer on Kodama's head when he fumbled the attack.

The B class student was staggered, taking a fair hit. But now you could see Hattori's inexperience. He should have developed his advantage and taken out his opponent, but he never expected to be so successful, so, missing his chance for a counterattack, once again went on the defensive, giving Taro time to collect himself. After that sobering hit, Kodama would not make a similar mistake again. He was taking his opponent seriously now, and for the rest of the fight he pummeled Ichiro's defense with a flurry of jabs.

In the end Hattori let a few powerful hooks and jabs through, the round ending in a knockout for my intelligence officer. But everyone around us, including the B class team, recognize Ichiro as a decent opponent, which was no small thing for the former nerd and outsider. His reward for the fight was sharp gasps and sympathetic glances from Amaya Kodama, who had been left under strict supervision by her brother. She couldn't come near us, but it was clear where her sympathies lay, despite the foreboding look in Taro's eyes.

However, for me, the best thing that Ichiro did was to thoroughly exhaust the aristocrat. If I could deal with Koji, then at least I wouldn't have to face another fresh fighter full of strength. Yes, he would have time to rest while I faced my opponent, and if I won I would have to do basically two fights in a row. But I wasn't going to think about that now, first I had to take care of Kubo.

The arena was well lit, with the light of the projectors making almost a separate space, leaving me alone with my opponent. In the background I heard the murmur of the crowd and saw the washed-out faces of the spectators. We were surrounded by empty space, with a spotlight on me and my opponent. He was calm, collected, ready for victory. Kubo knew that all of my surprises had been taken from me and I had nothing to hit him with. So he was powering up his fights with energy, ready to crush the fragile body of an ungifted.

We were nearly the same weight, but I was taller with longer limbs. That was one advantage, and, taking my runes of armor and regeneration into account, I was probably about as well-defended as a wizard, having the ability to restore myself right in the battle, a significant bonus to my constitution. As for minuses, the stout Kubo was not the best opponent to have in a fight, being strong, heavy, and yet nimble as a fox. And, of course, any of his hits, powered-up with magical energy, could be a knockout for me. But whatever, before I managed to get this armor even a glancing blow could have done that to me.

I stood to the right of Kubo. In this position there was only one possible attack, a side-kick with my right leg. To do a punch or a grab I would have to open up my body, which would cost precious seconds. And I could only defend myself with the same stupid sort of direct kick, or by running, which was not ideal.

But actually that was just a crude set-up for me. What was my opponent thinking? The start of a duel, and he's trying to test me out, this guy who only has one direct hit with one leg available? Is the trick too obvious? Those were the thoughts I could read on the puzzled face of Koji, carefully keeping his distance.

I'm not going to even say that I went for it, just kicking forward. It wasn't useful for its strength or speed, but the effect of the push. I wasn't afraid of failing, so I hammered at Kubo's defenses. He had, with reason, thought he could catch me in a side-kick. But the force of my hit made the broad man fall back, and I repeated it immediately.

Koji was forced to step back, and I flipped onto my hands and spun into his head with my left leg. The wizard managed to block, protecting his face, but I just ramped up the attack with my whole body. I wasn't doing any real damage with my attacks, but I was still maintaining the law of conservation of energy, powerfully pushing my opponent, throwing him off balance.

I learned my lessons from Matvey Nikolaevich well. The gifted might have impregnable defenses, and they might not feel hits, but they are still physical objects with a certain mass. And, by applying the right amount of effort to the right point, I levered the stone named Koji Kubo. I did another roundhouse kick, hitting him in the same place.

But the B class student quickly recovered, and my hits weren't powered-up anyway, so they couldn't do any real damage to my opponent. The wizard started acting like a real boxer. He covered his body with his elbows and his head with his fists. From time to time he would come out from behind his defenses and throw some magically-powered jabs and crosses my way. That was dangerous, since, sooner or later, he would get me into the corner and beat me up with no skill involved.

But I had a better idea. I waited for the right moment, then did a nice, fairly pointless roundhouse kick. I hit my opponent, but just for show, a glancing blow. However, each time before this I had done two kicks in a row, charging up my legs by going on my hands in the finest Brazilian style. So now, Kubo was automatically waiting for the second kick, stepping forward a little and getting ready to grab my leg and throw me to the ground.

I did not disappoint him, spinning, but instead of hitting him on the head, I did a powerful attack on his leg. Something clearly cracked, since I smacked it with circular force, from above. I felt like Koji would definitely have some loss of mobility until the end of the fight. Oh! It was even better than I expected, since he was definitely limping, though he was trying to hide it.

I had to take advantage of this temporary leg up, since who knew how good his regeneration was? I put on more pressure, cranking the pace of the fight up as much as it would go. I was now using my hands, even though that was dangerous. But I had to take him out as soon as possible. Otherwise the risk of getting got by my opponent would just go up, and I would get tired, not good considering if I won I would still have to take on Taro.

Being in a rush would cost me. Koji had given up the initiative at some point, retreating into simple defense, so I was not worried at all. By that time I had hit him a few good ones and was pretty sure in my reasoning that he was on the path to defeat. But what do you know? Kubo unexpectedly tore out, doing literally three or four series of violent attacks. I managed to meekly run away from most of them, but a couple of follow-up hits nearly knocked me to the tatami.

Shit! They hit so goddamn hard, the fucking mages! I was nearly done for, with just my armor keeping me from failing completely. It was now my turn to simply defend myself. I slithered around like a snake, hopped like a gazelle, and ran like an injured hippo. Just ten heartbeats and my rune of regeneration would clear the fuzziness out of my mind. But I wasn't in a hurry to show that I was on the up-and-up.

Kubo continued to press his advantage. In the heat of battle the boy had completely forgotten I could grapple. He fought like a kickboxer who had come from regular boxing, always using his arms, rarely, almost never, his feet. And so he believed wholeheartedly that nobody would get him in the legs or do a throw. And once he completely relaxed, having almost hit me in the liver, I skillfully came up from below and did a classic takedown.

After that, while Koji, shaken and disoriented from the fall, had not yet managed to get up, I grabbed his foot and, yanking it around, applied some classic pressure. I turned it with my whole body, so that Kubo, unlike what he would normally do, tapped the mat almost immediately. It was clear that I had nearly spun his foot clear off.

There was a short break where I got congratulations from my team. Hmm... from some of them very warm congratulations. I was pumped up by the fight, sweaty, and in way fit for hugging. But now Tomoko kissed me in a way that, I swear to God, made me want to go fornicate immediately. The girl had clearly learned the seductive arts somewhere, in just that short moment of contact her charms managed to literally rub across all the important parts, and her hands flowed over my whole body.

Yeah, those kisses aroused me. It was frightening to think what would happen if we were left alone...

Right now, after the fight, riding a wave of adrenaline, I was especially receptive to her and her almost feral lust. My nostrils flared like a bull's, drawing in the sweet aroma of her body, with the taste of her lingering on my lips, ahhhhhhh... Okay, I need to get myself back to normal. And this escapade with Tomoko was pretty effective at calming down my hyped-up body. That was exceptionally hard to do. Usually adrenaline didn't let you leave the battle state, so a fighter might burn out before the second duel. But now I did it once, and boom, shut off!

After a short time I fell into a meditative state. On Skayd we just did this to collect Psy, but here I was apportioning it out. I pushed an ocean of energy through my rune of regeneration, soothing my sore muscles, saturating my blood with oxygen, healing micro-tears, and closing up small bruises. Small things, but all together they would have slowed me down.

Besides that, I poured energy into my rune of concentration. Now, more than ever, I needed a clear and sober view of things. Taro Kodama was not the most physically developed teenager, meaning that before he became a wizard, he won using his brain, speed, and technique. But then he got these devastating attacks and improved defense. That kind of enemy was one of the worst and most dangerous for me. I wondered if he was stronger than me physically? Fragile, significantly shorter and skinnier... Maybe I would walk away with an easy victory?

Gong! I hadn't decided which tactics to use, but the fight will show me what to do. My trick with the side-kick would not work a second time, though. Kodama was smart and undoubtedly learned a lesson from Kubo's sad experience. He moved cautiously, testing my defense with precise pokes from a decent distance. It was hard for him. I could easily keep the young aristocrat at a distance due to my height and long arms. But he had clearly been taught how to deal with opponents like me, and he managed to use his speed and well-trained dives to get away from the last flurry of hits.

I was also carefully, dodging at the foot and a half range, where I would have him within arm's length. Underestimating Taro would be stupid, but drawing things out was not in my interests. The statistics were in his favor, since any good hit could knock me off my feet, and the longer the duel, the more likely it was for me to take that hit.

It looked like the phase of trying each other out was over and the time had come for a concerted attack. Was it risky? Yeah. But losing the initiative was even riskier, so onward!

I came right out the gate with a barrage of Taekwondo attacks. Straight to the body, side-on to the head, sharp down, feigning a sweep, roll, low kick. The last one was key, the first three were whatever, but I didn't care about them at all. He put some distance between us, stopping for a moment, and then I put the pressure on again. Only now I could see from Taro's squinted eyes that he was ready and planning a counterattack.

Well, that was just what I was waiting for. I began the same way, straight-on, then side-on, and then I sharply pulled back. Kodama, a little late, tried to close the distance, or, more precisely, he was doing everything on time, but I had predicted everything in advance and avoided his attacks just a bit earlier than he expected. Taro was losing it, and I, breaking all my patterns, came in with both of my fists on his head. Considering how I been avoiding using my arms at all, this came as a great surprise.

The aristocrat, taking a left hook and then a right hook, was thrown off, and then I threw him over myself. What I was supposed to do then was guarantee my victory by pinning my opponent to the mat. He was on the ground, and I was over him, so I could do a joint lock, but the trick wouldn't work with the gifted. So, after a very short consideration, I started to just pound Kodama's head into the mat. I slammed it without hesitation, quick and sharp, so that the wizard could not come to.

The boy had an unbelievably strong shield,

so my heavy hits hammering down from above were not having the desired effect. The aristocrat, rather than losing consciousness, was actually trying to avoid them, actively moving his body and legs in an effect to get away. I was really hoping that the referee would stop this beating, but no such luck. Before it was too late, I jumped to my feet and, in defiance of all rules, drove my knee into Taro's head as he stood up after me. Luckily for me, magical duels don't have any rules. You can even knock someone in the crotch, if you really have to.

My opponent went down again, and I again started beating on him. This time, though, I used my legs to add weight to my hits and work more meaningfully through the wizard's protection. But Taro was still fighting and suddenly grabbed me by the leg. Jesus, it was like being caught in a vise, then an unbelievable force overturning me onto the tatami, with my leg, caught in this bear-trap, nearly cracking in the iron fist of the gifted one. He had definitely put all the reserves of his strength into this one, since my rune of armor had all but turned itself inside out.

I quickly kicked out a leg and, turning on my back, started kicking the wizard wherever I could. I was only using my good leg, which seemed to be doing okay. I myself was just barely avoiding losing consciousness from the pain. Kodama definitely broke something in my leg. As I said earlier, his grip strength was so much that the boy had literally crushed my muscles and skin with his iron fingers. The referee stopped the fight. To be honest, I could no longer see my opponent, and I was just throwing at random, but considering that I was still conscious, it was called a victory for me.

Shit! If would have better if I had taken down two Kubos. This was a Pyrrhic victory. The B students, at best, had got me only twice, but twice was enough! I wasn't even going to consider the bruises. But Kubo, as far as I could tell, had broken a bone in my face with just a flick of his left hand, which is not even to mention the leg that Taro had been able to grab and squeeze practically to death.

Oh yeah, I got it now. I was no match for wizards in holds, joint locks, and stuff like that. The gifted couldn't always pull something off with their strength pumped up, but when they did, it was like a ton of bricks! It was a good thing he hadn't got me by the neck, or I'd be speaking in a falsetto for the rest of my life. Ha, if I survived. Oh, I might pass out and hurt later. No, I have to hold on now. There can't be any doubt of who won.

I started to get up, first on all fours, shamefully, then I managed to get on one knee, and then I was surrounded by strong but soft arms. The devil take her, Tomoko Yasuda!

I was weak and couldn't even make it to the changing rooms on my own. I could have done with some help from my closest companions, but those assholes, happily winking at me, weren't even helping Tomoko. Sons of bitches, how was this delicate girl going to drag the wounded hero to that faraway room? And why the hell would you leave me with this nympho? I thought my friends would save me from trouble, but they were just paving the way for it.

My only hope was Hideo Takayama's jealousy, but no luck. He had backed off, the bastard, creeping on some big-titted beauty, not even throwing a glance at Tomoko. He just congratulated me on my victory and, like the others, left me to my suffering. The girl was panting, constantly dragging me toward the changing room, and there was nothing to save me. I would give up, just so I wouldn't break, all I could do! How was an injured man to resist this much pressure? If Kiyoko yelled at me, I would say that I had resisted tooth and nail, but my wounds were clear, what could a man on the verge of passing out really have done?

But when the moment of truth was right around the corner, the club's medical personal stopped us. The politely, but firmly, separated me from Tomoko. They put me on a stretcher and took me to the medical area, where they clean my scrapes and bruises, and most importantly, put a tight bandage on the leg that Taro had crushed. Of course, they also smeared everything with that foul-smelling ointment, but whatever, I would wipe it all off at home. The local doctors had no idea that my rune of regeneration would work without that disgusting goop.

This time I didn't go to Yuki Ueno's clinic. I was in pretty good shape. My wounds looked bad, but there were no obvious dangers, even by the standards of local medicine. So all that was waiting for me was home, and, most probably, another marathon training session with Matvey Nikolaevich. He tripled his efforts every time I ended up in the hospital. It seemed like the martial Yakut took every hit I let through as his own personal failing. But I was not against all that work, as long as it brought me good results.

Chapter 15

Old Secrets

IN AN OLD BUT FAIRLY LARGE home in the center of the city, the small family Kodama gathered together. The place where their home base was located was quite meaningful. The once powerful clan had been able to afford the most expensive land in the city. But those days were long gone, and the only thing remaining from their former glory and wealth was this estate. It was, you could say, the most valuable property remaining to the Kodama name.

But you would be wrong. The family had managed to retain something even more important. Knowledge. Ancient scrolls, records, and secrets transmitted by word of mouth. Magic is the growth of power. If you have it, then you can change reality around you. While you are weak, your own body is the limit, but the stronger you get, the more you are able to the change the world. You won't find many secrets here, other than methods of teaching. But everyone says that the modern schools are the best you can do.

It was said that wizards used to be stronger, but at the expense of many lives, when only one out of ten would survive, at best. It wouldn't be okay to even imagine using those methods today. But there were many families who retained some of it. In addition to personal power, there were also a few dozen rituals known throughout the world. It was fundamentally a different kind of magic, more like shamanism. At least the inner energy of the gifted was used as little as possible in them.

It was not known who brought these secrets to the world and when. Legends called them gods, while the chronicles named them something else, a forgotten race. But the fact remained, if you followed the instructions precisely, you would get the desired effect.

There were no apocalyptic rituals, or castings, as they were also called, among them. That was probably what had saved the world. If there had been something outrageous in there, then people would long since had killed each other off, either seeking to acquire the rituals or with their help.

Nevertheless, the rituals did provide some

useful things, and the results of some of them could be considered miracles of nature. However there were not very many known castings, and nobody had managed to make changes to any of them. So the results depended entirely on the precision with which the instructions were followed. Sometimes even a speck of dust, falling into the performed magic, could drastically alter the effect.

At the height of their power, the Kodama family had three rituals. The knowledge and records of two of them had been lost more than a thousand years ago. At that time a miracle had preserved only one heir of the of ancient name. The last and most valuable ritual had vanished without a trace along with the head of the clan more than five hundred years ago. Since that time, the Kodama clan had grown weaker and weaker, sliding inevitably toward their current condition.

The only thing that the ancient family had left was information about what effect the ritual had and approximate knowledge of how and with what you would perform it. The Kodamas would occasionally find traces of their castings being used. It must be said that just because one family lost a specific ritual, that did not mean it was gone forever. Many clans had had knowledge about castings, they bought them, traded them, seized them by force... Or lost them, like the Kodamas.

Book Two

All of the members of the family were in the room. The younger Kodama was telling his father what had happened.

"Father, today I was at a meeting with Koji Kubo at ABS night club. We agreed to make a truce, but that is school business..." he said, stopping suddenly, knowing that his father had no interest in those adolescent problems. "My people noticed Amaya on the floor, dancing with Ichiro Hattori, a student from another class."

"Go on." His father suddenly perked up, shooting a strict look at his daughter.

"Recalling her engagement, I was forced to challenge Hattori and Tanaka to a duel," Taro said, speaking more confidently, seeing his father's interest.

"Why was Tanaka involved?" asked the head of the clan succinctly and then answered himself, "Hattori is part of his gang, is he not?"

"Yes, dad," the younger Kodama confirmed his father's guess. "But Kubo was also part of it, so we set up two duels with a third deciding one."

"I get it." The head of the clan cut off his son's explanation.

That kind of duel had been popular among wizards for hundreds of years. It was entertaining and the results didn't allow for any doubt, plus there was more room for tactics and strategy. A newbie could be paired with a powerful veteran or the favorite could be pushed to a decisive duel, anyway, there were a bunch of combinations.

Aristocrats especially liked them.

"I beat Hattori and Genji Tanaka won against Kubo. In the deciding match, Tanaka knocked me out," Taro said drily, setting forth the facts without unnecessary details.

"Hmm... Son, the result is not important. What is important is that you fought for the Amaya's honor and left no doubt that the intentions of the Kodama family are serious," the head of the clan praised Taro, uncharacteristically serious for his age, and then addressed Amaya, "And you, my daughter, will be punished for your carelessness!"

"Dad, was not finished," interrupted Taro.

"Speak," said the elder Kodama, shocked.

"At the end of the duel with Genji Tanaka, I grabbed him in a "bear trap" using all of my energy. But he was able to break free, and, without losing consciousness from the pain, beat me down, literally tearing victory out of my hands!" The normally calm boy was suddenly very expressive.

"Perhaps I am not understanding what is so interesting about that?" His father crooked his eyebrow in confusion.

"Oh!" Amaya covered her mouth with her hand and spouted, "Dad, Genji is ungifted!"

"What?!" The head of the clan, always so strict and reserved, leapt out of his chair and began pacing nervously. "Are you sure?"

"Yes, dad. I told you about Genji Tanaka. He

terrorized the first class all last year. But everyone knows that's a bad strategy. If your recent victim suddenly breaks through to a powerful gift, then you can't avoid your fate. But it was even worse for Genji. He never broke through at all. I've heard that his mother is ungifted," Taro said, coming to his own conclusions.

"Wait, wait, is that the boy that Bo put in the hospital?" recalled their father.

"Yes, dad," confirmed Amaya. "But then Genji got even with the fatty. The slimeball tried to catch him in a trap, selling him out to some fourth-years."

"Amaya!" said the head of the clan, admonishingly.

"Dad, there is no doubt that Genji is not a wizard. Or better, no doubt that he was not a wizard!" said Taro, enigmatically, but all the Kodama family members understood what he meant.

"Why are you so sure of that? You think he has been hiding his gift?" the elder Kodama asked doubtfully.

"In the last year Genji has taken part in numerous fights and each time he has ended up in the hospital with unbelievable injuries. Besides fatass Bo, he fought with the Kato brothers, with Hiro Sasaki, with Makise Abe, and with a bunch more people. As such, the whole school is talking about how Tanaka took out the strongest fighters without magic. There are rumors that he took out two champions from Okubo Academy on his own." Taro set forth his detailed evidence.

"Hmm... that seems true. The clinics can confirm it, most likely. But to hide your gift, suffering that much..." The head of the clan had begun thinking out loud.

"That's what I mean, dad," Taro said, enthusiastically supporting his father's thoughts.

"Okay. Then let's look into it. Did he use energy while dueling with you?" The elder Kodama picked up the scent, and, like a bloodhound, fixed on it with all his might. The old fighter knew clearly that you couldn't lie in a duel. The duelist could sense each other clearly, meaning that Taro should have been able to learn a lot about his opponent.

"No, dad, he fought without magic. 100 percent. It's just..." the boy started haltingly.

"What? Taro, right now you can and should tell me any ridiculous suggestion you have!"

"My hits... You know, I can throw a good punch, if I power up my fists with magic... And I managed to land a few good ones on him. But he withstood them. Ungifted! You remember when you took me to a gym group with ungifted, so I could feel the difference? Genji is not a wizard, but he is no ordinary boy. He is somewhere in the middle. And then, the "bear trap"...

"Tell me a little more, how did you do the hold?" His father was trying to find some discrepancies, since it was too unbelievable to think that the long search of the entire clan would finally find victory due to a simple school fight.

"He tricked me, got two hits on my head, and got me in a throw. Then he started beating me, first with his fists, then, realizing that he couldn't beat me that way, with his feet. I caught him and squeezed him, putting all the rest of my energy into it, like you taught me."

"Were you groggy, maybe you imagined it?" asked his father, doubtful.

"No! I squeezed his tissues and muscles, there was blood spurting through my hands!" Taro replied, animatedly defending his position.

"It's true, dad. I saw it too. The wound was disgusting," Amaya said, supporting her brother.

"The "bear trap" on an ungifted... That should have either broken his leg or ripped it clean off!" His father was still doubtful. But he was himself wondering why that hadn't happened. "Unless they did the ritual on him! But what about girls? Amaya?"

"No, dad, I didn't feel anything." She blushed. It was always embarrassing for her to talk about that, especially with her father. But when the topic of the Kodama clan's ritual came up, it was always that that was one of the most important things.

"Dad, Tomoko Yasuda was hovering around him. And she was acting extremely forward. And they also say that Genji unexpectedly won the heart of the only heir to the Takada clan," Taro added.

"Hmm... It's very close..." muttered the elder Kodama.

The family had come across traces of the lost ritual hundreds of times before and always come up empty-handed, or, just a stone's throw away from their goal, lost men, money, and power. The ritual had become almost a curse for the clan, dashing their hopes.

"Kids, we have to follow up on everything. Everything must be done as carefully as possible, and we might have a chance!"

"Dad, if everything goes well, will you cancel my engagement?" Amaya asked desperately.

"My daughter!" the head of the clan began strictly, then cut himself off when the voice of a loving father started to talk. "Yes, if it turns out right, we will cancel the engagement."

"And it is true, dad, that Bo the fatass turned out to be a completely useless person. They say that he had a crush on Kiyoko Takada, but a lot of people think that his family just wants to marry into the Takadas," Taro said, supporting his sister.

"Okay kids. But until we decide what to do, do not make any plans. Right now we risk losing what little we have left!" their father said, ending the discussion.

Book Two

* * *

Genji's parents rarely had the chance to be alone. The life of an Oyabun forced Goro to always be with his brothers in arms. The clan's territory had expanded broadly, and their ten captains put the Tanakas practically on the same level with the strongest criminal clans in the city. Real estate, the port, trade, all of that took his time. In addition, he had to fight with his rivals, the forces of the law, and the industrialists who had lately been gathering sizeable armies. There was a lot to do.

"Goro, what do you think about the ritual?" asked Hena, when she finally managed to find some time to be alone with her husband. Lately, in part due to Genji, the Tanakas' affairs had been going quite well, and the clan had made money to hire enough fighters and wizards that nobody around would dare to start a war with them.

"Hena, all the signs described in the instructions have come to pass. Except one! But he is definitely stronger. They said that he would not take hits. And his regeneration... All of that points to success, but just..." Goro inhaled sharply, impatiently waiting for the ancient miracle to finally take effect.

"Maybe we don't have all the instructions and we did something wrong? This attraction...

the sexual one... maybe the strength is connected to it somehow?" suggested Hena.

"Hmm...maybe. Our experts noted a significant increase in Genji's abilities on the day that he met with Yoshiko Sakurawa. Until then there were no sudden bursts like that. Either we did something wrong or we didn't interpret the instructions correctly. I mean, anything is possible, considering how I got my hands on the documents. You know that the smallest mistake could mean that we get a completely different result."

"Maybe we should then set up the conditions for Genji to... meet girls?" Hena suggested, somewhat embarrassed.

"Why do you think I allowed him to get an office with an apartment like that?" Goro asked, grinning.

"But our son might do something stupid with his classmates. Wouldn't it be better to just bring Eika back?" Mrs. Tanaka said, doubtfully.

"Ha, as if our warrior woman wouldn't do something stupid herself. In that case I would prefer that Genji do something stupid with the Takada heir. Then again, maybe the ancients had a reason for giving so many to their wizards. Maybe that is because of people like our son?" Goro said, jokingly, but at the same time aware that his words had a kernel of truth in them.

It was always like that with the rituals. Seeming trivialities played a major role, while the important things, or what were presumed to be, didn't matter at all.

"So what should we do?" Hena didn't want to the leave the problem unresolved. "Is it okay for Eika to come back to our estate?"

"She might be over it, who knows? On the other hand, our son is home so often from his injuries that we might not even have to wait for the processes caused by the ritual to start. Then we would be wasting our time. So, something might have to happen to him at home," Goro said, coming to a conclusion.

"Yes, but you will just have to be here less often," Hena smiled slyly.

"And why is that?" The imposing Oyabun frowned in spite of himself.

"The servants have taken your prohibitions to heart, so if you hang around the estate our son will never have a chance," explained Hena, chuckling.

"So it is decided? We bring back Eika, but under strict psychological supervision. If she starts losing it, then we have to send her away for good. And I think we should keep her out of the estate's security forces. The girl will be in an unstable emotional state, so it would do no good to depend on her in a fight," Goro said, settling the matter.

"I agree. It is better to consider that she is not even here than to depend on her and be disappointed when we need here," Hena said, supporting her husband wholeheartedly.

As if anticipating the end of the conversation, an assistant brought the news that the heir had returned home. Not on his own two feet, but with the help of medical workers. The incorrigible boy had once again gotten himself into a fight! The only good time was that since they were bringing him home his injuries couldn't be too bad. If the ritual didn't work, then they would have to remove him from any educational institution for wizards, but Hena and Goro still had a faint hope in their hearts that it would work out. And that meant that Genji would have to continue to maintain his position within Gakko Academy!

Chapter 16

Eika

I CAME HOME LATE in the evening. All the time they were treating and transporting me, I was completely engaged in regeneration. The smell of the local ointment was nearly insufferable, and the sooner I could heal up my wounds, the better. I would wipe it all right the hell off, since it could only be like a millionth of a percent effective. They might smear it all over my skin, but whatever, to hell with, just don't let that smell get in there, please God...

My mom sighed a little, but not as much as before. It seemed like she had gotten used to it. She even seemed to be kind of happy that, instead of the usually path of school, hospital, recovery at home, I had managed to skip a step and come straight home. On the whole I was not suffering nearly as much in comparison to the last times.

The bruises and small cuts, they didn't matter, even for a regular mortal without enhanced regeneration they would only take about a week to heal. You wouldn't even have to go to the hospital. No need for any special treatment, just antiseptic and better food. As for my leg, it was not so positive. Taro Kodama could easily go to a factory and work as a metal press.

Goddamn! How do you squeeze skin like that with your bare hands? What kind of effort did that take? If I recalled correctly, my armor should be able to deflect the energy pulses of direct attacks, like from the local firearms. Then again, that was when it was fully done, and now I had just a fifth of it. And I suspected that the first stage of the rune was more like a base for the next ones, so its effectiveness in defense was not a straight twenty percent, but less than half that.

But even so... I could see the places where his hands had come in contact with the dynamic defense of the frame, which had withstood that vicious pressure and redistributed it across the tattoo. It just hadn't been enough, and all the skin, meat, blood vessels, and blood looked like they had gone through a food processor. The boy might have weak magical potential, but his grip was fantastic.

But on the whole I had gotten lucky. We went to the bar to celebrate a union of two classes and without too much fighting ended up with a third ally. The only one remaining in the plan was Raiden Nakata, although, to be honest, I was apprehensive about him. Maybe just forget about him, the monster? It seemed like even Osamu Saito was giving him a wide berth, so it was no shame for me to feel afraid of him.

Right now Makise Abe was looking like the better choice, although I had beaten him up once. But it would be humiliating for a third-year class to submit to a second-year class, so if the foolish idea to subjugate the only still independent third-year class even crossed my mind, I would have to reserve my bed in Yuki Ueno's clinic in advance. There would be a lot of fallout!

And now I was bored, lying down, recuperating. They knew my habits at home, so there was a ton of food in my room, and I was chowing down on poultry, fish, meat, vegetables, and fruit. I always had seeds, nuts, and berries at hand. That was how I replenished my vitamins and nutrients. The rebuilding of my body was going well. Even though I had taken care of the B class, I still had to keep strengthening my body. The runes of strength and speed were not far off now.

Anyway, about them. As usual, I was spending all my free time on them. Using my concentration, I was able to work quickly, and I had already done a bunch. At this rate I would be able to put them both on quite soon. That was essential right now. Each of them should, on their own, give me a substantial bonus, but my experience on Skayd had shown me that they went well together, multiplying the effect. From what I could tell, when the tattoos of strength and speed worked together, they multiplied the effect by twenty percent, maybe even thirty.

I only had a little Psy right now. But there was no way to just get free energy at the estate. I would have to overcome it slowly, step by step. Kiyoko had not called. She either thought that I was sleeping, knocked out by anesthetic, or somebody, definitely one of the Wada sisters, had already told her about Tomoko Yasuda. And even though I had resisted heroically, I just knew that a fight was waiting for me. Given Takada's preparation time, she was going to wring me out for sure. What kind of life was this? All roads lead me to the hospital, hahaha.

Ah, but if Kiyoko visited me, what a load of spirit and vigor I could get from her. Well, yeah, but, there was no way, aristocrats, clans, and all that stuff... I needed to go to the penthouse more. I felt good there and Yoshiko was right next door. But that was a pipe dream, and the simple reality of it was that I was going to sadly fall asleep while tattooing these runes. But where was I going? I had to do something! My opponents were getting stronger, not by the day, but by the hour, training their magic, sharpening their claws. I had to get one over on them somehow.

I woke up in the morning in no particular mood. I had a fair amount of success and my injuries were not so bad, but still, I was bored. Not by life, but by these constant fights. It wasn't really that different from Skayd, but I was hoping to relax here, enjoy my life...

To get rid of my ennui, I had a hearty breakfast of an enormous six-egg omelet, a pair of tomatoes, an onion, a generous helping of sausage, and a whole mountain of fried bacon. I polished it off with a whole liter of fresh-pressed orange juice and a couple of muffins with nuts and dried fruit. All in all, it was a real mouthgasm. The food in this world continued to be one my greatest pleasures!

After that satisfying breakfast I moved onto my aquatic procedures. I threw away all my bandages. Thankfully my tattoo regeneration had, overnight, closed up my open wounds and I had absolutely no more need of bindings and ointments. I drew a bath at a comfortable temperature. There were bath salts and body butter in bowls on the shelf. I tossed a couple into the water, not even looking at them, then jumped in up to my head. Ah, what a great thing the ofuro was! It was no steam bath, but it was too soon for me to be going to the sauna right now.

In the tub I had special handrails with moveable shelves, so I didn't have to just stand

and splash around, I could lie down and think in comfort. The Tanakas were no strangers to modern accessories. It seemed like it was a classic from the past, wooden tub, but in fact it had a powerful motor inside, so while lying down I could also turn on a gentle jet massage. I wasn't up to anything stronger right now. My wounds would hurt, but these fine but powerful streams of water were just what the doctor ordered.

I relaxed and, calmed by the water, with a full stomach and pleasing thoughts, seemed to even doze off a little. And that is when I had a strange dream.

At first everything seemed to be perfectly logical. I was dreaming of naked ladies, but at my age and with my particular condition in this world, that was totally normal. But the last times in my dreams I had been visited by Yoshiko or Kiyoko. I might even expect Tomoko Yasuda, since she had left a real impression on me.

But now, out of the blue, I started dreaming of Eika. With my life going so fast, I basically had already come to consider her a ghost of the past. I hadn't seen her for a month, and for the current me that may as well have been ancient history. For the first few days I was still remembering our adventures, but then everything was swept away by all the hectic events in my teenage life. But now I was dreaming about her. Maybe the ofuro tub reminded me of her. She did once give me a nice rubdown in here, mmmm....

Book Two

Goddammit, it was just a dream!

I opened my eyes wide and saw the charming serving girl in front of me. Eika, completely naked, was standing up to her neck in the water. Her face was turned coyly to the side, and her hands were working completely underwater. In my surprise at what was happening I came with a loud moan. What the hell was going on here?

"Psst… Genji, your parents are not home, and I thought since we had some time… but still, you can't be so loud." Eika placed a finger on her lips adorably and gave me a coquettish glance. All the while her other hand never stopped.

"You… you're… you're back?" I couldn't articulate clearly. You try talking when your downstairs is being manipulated so professionally, God…

"Yes, they took me back. I have left the military wing of the clan and will no longer be a soldier in the Tanaka army. Now I am a serving girl again, and it looks like they have assigned me to you," she explained briefly, and then with a lusty smile said, "The time has come for the heir of the clan to has his own personal serving girl."

The meaning of the term "personal serving girl" took a few minutes to get through to me. Eika stealthily pressed a few buttons and the board I was lying on automatically lifted my body above the water. Her head bent down and I could no longer see her beautiful eyes. But all my thoughts flew right out of my head.

Her intimate maneuvers were driving me wild. It seemed like this heavenly pleasure would last forever. She could take me right to the point of climax and then stop, taking time to breathe, and then continue her sweet torture. Jesus, it seemed like Eika had not gone off to take her exams in the magical ranks but rather... Well, some other skills. If there were a ranking system for these abilities, my serving girl would be no less than the level of a Shihan.

She took me to heaven once more, and now I wanted to give her some pleasure. No good turn, haha... I slid off the board to the bottom of the tub and stood up. I wrapped my arms around the girl and we melded into a passionate kiss. At the same time I lifted up her light body. In the water the athletically dainty Eika seemed like a doll. I put her on the board and...

"Sir, no, you don't have to... ahhhh, ah! Yes, yes, yes! Oh my God..."

I didn't take her very long to reach climax. Either she hadn't been with a man for a long time, or it was due to my strange influence. But there was no time for considering any of that. We were both through the roof with desire. A few minutes ago Eika was trying to stay quiet, not letting out even the tiniest squeak. But now she couldn't hold back her moans. She was even biting her lips so hard it drew blood.

Then she retreated into herself for a while,

literally hanging off of my neck. The girl was still crying, coming down from the powerful emotions and reactions of her body, but I, like a heartless bastard, went from calming strokes along her back to her thighs. But what else could I do?

I couldn't help but react to her hot, enticing body. I carefully lifted Eika and lowered her down onto myself. The serving girl gasped and tearing herself away from my neck, gazed at me with half-closed eyes. But as soon as I started moving, her surprised turned into waves of pleasure. The girl moved back and expressed her approval of what was happening with a load moan.

"Ah, God... Genji, yes, yes, keep going darling!"

Eika was driving me crazy with her groans and dirty talk.

In the end we nearly fell into the water when, exhausted and satisfied, we separated from one another. We lay on the board, catching our breaths. Eika, from time to time, would kiss me and lazily run her fingers through my hair. We were silent, since we didn't even have the energy for conversation. Then we decided to get out. Normally I would just confidently jump over the edge to get out of the ofuro, but now I had to use the wooden steps.

Eika went first, with me supporting her. That was a big mistake. As soon as her butt appeared out of the water, I couldn't hold myself back. Like a sea serpent I jumped out the water and onto the first step. I placed my hands over the powerful but tiny hands of the serving girl, pressing my body against her well-built figure.

The second time was even better than the first. This time we were in now hurry, going a long time, drawing out each other's pleasure. Then we took a shower, but neither I nor she had the strength to go on. Naked, we moved into the bedroom and spoke to each other for the first time since it started.

"Genji, I want to be with you, but it can't be like it was today! Dear, I just lost control completely. Imagine what would have happened if someone came in?" Eika was really worried about what had happened. A high-ranking wizard, having trained for years in self-control and discipline, she had all of sudden lost herself entirely. And not for just a moment, but for a whole hour!

"I don't even know what happened myself. I was completely asleep, and you started first," I said, putting the blame back on her. And nobody was going to bother us, I was taking a bath, after all.

"I was so happy that they let me come back, and your parents were both away..." Eika began sweetly excusing herself, embarrassed, but I couldn't hold back again and literally forced her to stop talking, closing her mouth in a passionate kiss.

She could only protest with her eyes. She

gazed askance at the clock, pointing out that we didn't have any more time for loving. Then she put her fists against my chest. But we both knew that was just a game. A wizard of her rank could, if she wanted, toss me right up to the ceiling. But her playful resistance turned us both on and she gave in again.

We tried to keep the miraculous dance of our two bodies going as long as possible. There is only a kaleidoscope of scenes in my mind, and I could not recall later how long our lovemaking lasted. I was no longer there. I only came to my senses when Eika, taking her leave, kissed me on the cheek. My arms instinctively wrapped around the serving girl, already clad in her uniform.

"Genji, shh..." She pressed a finger against my lips. "Dear, your parents are already home. I have to run."

"Okay, then I will wait..."

I fell asleep again. That was in fact a perfectly normal reaction for a boy of my age. But it was not normal for a Psy master with two-fifths of a rune of regeneration. Considering my hearty breakfast and the ocean of Psy I got after sex, I should have been running around like crazy. But I slept like a baby. Something was definitely going on with my body.

I woke up after thirty minutes or an hour of healthy, tranquil sleep. I looked at myself and freaked out. Jesus! There were no traces of bruises, injuries, or any other problems on my body. So what, if I was in a fight between rounds of sex I could tangle with any of the local monsters? I checked my astral body and my reserves. My energy was significantly more than it had been after I had been with Yoshiko. Perhaps it was because Eika was a wizard?

Part of the energy, apparently, had gone to each of my runes of its own accord. The concentration, regeneration, and armor ones were working for no reason, but at full power. The tattoos of strength and speed had once again expanded out into the contours I had already placed. I just had to apply my full strength, and would have a whole ocean of it at my disposal immediately.

And I did! What was I worried about? I had checked the patterns ten times over, part of the runes was already going, and when would I have so much energy again?

A hot wave rose up from me, washing over my astral body, seeping into all the cracks. The energy was lashing against the edges, and then, stabilizing into the prepared Psy channels, began to light up a miraculous tattoo.

Shit! That was definitely not me! My delicate constructions were but scribbles compared to what was now showing up on my astral body. These were finished tattoos, the work of Psy masters at level five hundred. I had gotten more than I bargained for, it seemed.

I could feel it burning even in my physical

body. A little sharp, but still, not a bad feeling. It was like my astral muscles were charged with the work, starting to grow, adding new strength and energy to my body.

Hmm... I would have to rethink my whole training regimen.

Chapter 17

"Shadow"

AFTER DINNER I WAS COMPLETELY READY for training. Matvey Nikolaevich and his team were supposed to come only after three days. They had been told that I was injured again and couldn't work. But then this thing with Eika happened and I was miraculously healed. It also seemed that my parents were used to my abilities, or they just weren't paying attention to them. So I went out after my hearty lunch directly to the running track. I know, I know, you're not supposed to. But those rules are not for people who have five full Psy tattoos.

I started light, speeding up after five go-rounds, and only the tenth I put my whole heart into it. Goddamn! Of course, these weren't the same limits I had on Skayd, but the results were exceeding all my expectations. This speed was insane! I didn't know what was going on in the Nakata family, but I felt like I now had a chance against Raiden, no matter how lightning fast he might be.

I was working with the shadow under my feet.

Well, of course, the final answer would come from Matvey Nikolaevich, but everything was still too bad. I would have to train up my motor skills up from literally nothing. I was not equally fast everywhere. On the whole, all my muscle groups were working faster now, but my arms, to exaggerate a little, were twice as fast, while my legs were one and a half times as fast. Everything was a little more difficult, with my biceps, my triceps, all of my muscles out of balance.

Obviously, they were connected to each other, with one moving the other, but since I was out of balance I couldn't feel my body. It was as if a nimble acrobat had been crammed into the body of a boxer. It was like I could walk, I could run, but if you made me do a backflip I would break my neck on flat ground. I knew that the speed of each individual muscle or group of muscles was perfect, set by the creator of the rune. But my body was far from perfection. I would have to put it in order with a lot of training.

The problem was that in these conditions all my work came to naught. One-two punches, throws, kicks, everything needed precision, and right now I didn't have it, at least not until I could get these new feelings into my nervous system. I knew, now, that all of my training would have to be done using my rune of concentration, which I knew from experience. It would help me take charge of my body faster. Here was another reason to get my two runes done quickly, otherwise the process of mastering these new possibilities might take months.

I tested my strength. In the same way, it was better than I though. Bench press, weight training, dip bars, planks... I would have to change up my whole workout. My body exercises were now only important for improving my coordination. As such, my weight had practically stopped being a burden on my body. Maybe Matvey Nikolaevich had something like the stick push-ups in his bag of tricks? I would have to seriously rethink everything. Some of my trainers were now just useless. I would tear off all the bandages, ignoring most of the weights. Ohhh, now it was finally time for the tractor tire! If I pulled it off then Matvey would have to find something heavier.

Hmm... What else could I test? I went to work with the equipment. The inflatable punching bag went about as bad as I expected, since I just didn't have the accuracy. I was just happy to hit the thing. Of course, at the last hits the bag tore open at the seams and fell apart.

Whatever, I would just buy a more durable one. My elbows and knees did even worse. My coordination was abysmal. I mean, these strong hits were only worthwhile if you didn't have to hit a precise target. The punching bag was big, so it was hard to get a glancing blow.

So I had to work, work, and work some more. Shit, I had five more unbalancings ahead of me. Maybe I should have just sucked it up and done them all at once? No, the full runes of strength and speed would have taken years. It was worth it to strengthen my skeleton and my tissues. And I had others I needed to do. Otherwise my own physical abilities would have done me more damage than good. I would do everything the right way. Maybe it would be easier next time. Besides, I had already gotten my body in the right condition for the first one, now I would just have to train my abilities.

So I could stop training for that. But I still needed to swim a little. That would charge me up a little and give me some coordination, and it didn't depend on strength or speed. That was the easiest way to give my muscles and my spine a little break.

Then I sweated in the sauna a little and went to my room.

I didn't expect Eika in the evening. My parents were home, and it seemed like she hadn't yet decided on another meeting. Still, something was telling me that without my father's approval, and more importantly, my mother's, these little dalliances could never have happened at home...

On the other hand, it would be too presumptuous to continue our rendezvous while my parents were at home, so I acted in the understanding that she would not come. And on top of that, I needed a little break from my rune of regeneration after that. Not physically, but morally.

Around evening I did a lot of reading, busying myself with my studies. Then I called some of my guys.

Hattori had kept his ears to the ground and let me know what was going on at Gakko. The upper-class gangs were, to put it lightly, dismayed by how quickly our class had taken over the second-years. As a matter of fact, there were no more divisions to be made at the school. Raiden and Makise were too tough of nuts to crack, and our three classes were seen as very dangerous. Any gang might now end up with nothing at all if they attack the younger ones. Unless Takada, Saito, and Sasaki could somehow come to an agreement amongst themselves.

Takeshi was occupied with building up the military wing of our gang. You could make a serious force from the three classes. The Kato brothers had ten fighters behind them, the same as Koji Kubo and Taro Kodama, basically. Hideo Takayama's class, though, was not so lucky. There was dissension, there were the nerds under

Tomoko Yasuda, and so a full-fledged military group had not been able to be made yet. But it was just a matter of time. The boys that Takayama had beaten up would join the majority sooner or later, and the members of the Smart Club would turn out okay. Magic had a way of doing that.

Kiyoko called me a little later.

"Hey, how are you?" A sweet voice came over the phone.

"Everything is okay. I got messed up a little again, but less than usual." Honestly, I was happy to get a call from the Takada heiress.

"The war with the Mori clan is winding down. Soon I'll be back at school, and you're not even there. I miss you." She spoke openly.

"I miss you too! Don't worry, I won't be at home long. Everything is okay, actually, I just have to heal up a little and I'll be back at Gakko," I said, fibbing a little.

"No, Genji! Don't hurry on my account. Gakko Academy is not the kind of place where you should be when you're wounded, especially in your condition."

Damn, how well finished these clan girls were! They put men's interests above their own feelings and desires. Kiyoko was just a perfect candidate for a life partner.

"Well, we have a lot of guys in our gang now. I think they can watch out for me at first." I said, casually bringing up my new army.

"Genji, you literally took over two classes in a couple of days. They will not leave you in peace now. The upper-class leaders will be trying to knock you off your high horse, and it will be much more useful for them to set up one-on-one duels than full battles. So you won't be able to avoid the challenges. Trust me, I remember how much Akira fought when she was starting on the road to supremacy at Gakko. And the whole time she was being watched out for by the older classmen," Kiyoko said, sharing valuable information.

"I got it. Okay, I will come back to school when I completely ready," I said, decisively, calming down the girl who was actually completely worked up. An absolutely exceptional military partner, and she could help in business, and as for the rest, well, judging from what I already knew, you couldn't scoff at that either.

"Yes, Genji. Right now you should be thinking not just about yourself, but about the people who believe in you. A general of Gakko Academy is more a politician than a fighter!" she said, clearly quoting something, and then laughed like a delicate little bell.

"That was great, hahaha!" I laughed at her joke in support.

"I heard that from one of Akira's guys on her birthday. After which she shattered his nose and broke his arm. The dumbass was trying to hit on her," said Kiyoko.

Book Two

"I see that Akira is very strict with the theorists of school wars." I was teasing Kiyoko.

"Ahhh, my sister hates guys who can't support her and women." My girlfriend was telling her sister's secrets. "What do you think of the games, by the way?"

"Games?" I was a little shocked. I was definitely up to my ears in problems, and now there were games. "Jeeez, to be honest, I think you're a bit cuckoo."

"Hey, not cool, General Genji!" Kiyoko reminded me of my responsibilities. "A self-respecting gang should put forth a team in the games, at least if we want to retain our independent status. But right now even our strongest fighters could hardly hold out against the fourth-years."

"Hmm... Is it really that important?" To be honest, I had never made the connection between these school conflicts and an athletic discipline.

"Genji, it's like you're from outer space," Takada said, surprised. "Winning a championship in the games would be a million points plus to our reputation, and anyway, we are going to have to deal with fighters from other schools sooner or later. And they size each other up first off by their ratings in the games. If we stay at the bottom of the school's ranking, then a lot of generals will not take your status seriously, and we won't be able to avoid fighting constantly."

"Uh, yeah..." I hadn't considered that.

Jesus Christ, what kind of planet was this. Shit! They made all these dumb customs for themselves, and now I had to deal with it. I would have to quickly look over the stupid rules for the local tactical games and figure out what they were and how to do it. I think I need to find literally any way to get out of these societal obligations. We were already up to our eyeballs in school fights anyway.

"Just talk to Hattori. He's probably already thought about all of this anyway. At least you won't have to plan our strategy from the ground up," Kiyoko said, giving me another piece of exceptional advice.

Yeah, I was definitely going to marry her. If she was even half as good in bed as she was at giving advice, I would never be able to find a better woman. Hmm... And you could have a few wives here. With permission, of course.

"Thank you darling," I said, sincerely. "I will definitely think about that. Especially since I have quite a bit of time on my hands now."

We chatted for a good hour, discussing school matters and our plans for the future. We went over the people in our three classes, discussing the leaders of the other gangs and their strategies. Kiyoko was extremely well informed about everything that had happened in her absence, the fight with Manabu's army, the duel with Kubo and Kodama... Somebody was definitely keeping the younger Takada in the loop. I was sure that wouldn't have happened unless the Wada sisters were involved, which meant that the matter of Tomoko was sure to come up. So I could not relax, preparing myself for the difficult topic. But Kiyoko tactfully avoided the topic, and was ready to sigh in relief when I received a hit below the belt, after we had already said our goodbyes.

"Tanaka, I get it, and I'm not against you having other women along with me, but if you and Yasuda hook up behind my back, then I will tear your balls off and rip all of that little skank's hair out!" She said, finally, and hung up.

What the hell was that? Shit, how was I supposed to take that? It was like I was allowed to do it with other people, but also like I was gonna be castrated by hand? But I had heard about the alternative logic of the local women. It had to exist, for sure, but I couldn't find it, even with my rune of concentration. So there was only one thing to do. Tread lightly, with small steps, like a sapper in a minefield. But there was another, more cowardly, thing to do. Put everything in the girls' hands. They would take care of each other, and I would have my pick at the end, ha.

So, broadly speaking, I was in an ambivalent situation. I had gotten stronger and faster, which was good. But now I had new problems in the form of the upcoming tactical games tournament and fear for my secret, which Kiyoko was somehow unknowingly threatening. To hell with her, with Tomoko, that was far away, but how would she feel about Yoshiko, Eika, or even possibly Fumiko Ono? I had already really messed up there. Would she punish me for it? Like grinding my balls beneath her heel...

There was only one thing to do. I had to train. I seemed to have squeezed everything I could out of my runes. Now I just had to use them right. Wait! Dammit, I was the idiot, this was what my one-track thinking meant! Yes, yes, yes, let's go through the runes again. I couldn't remember much, and besides, some of the Psy tattoos were considered completely useless, childish. They were taught so young adepts could learn Psy, since they were simple, but they had no use at all.

But here one was, in all its glory. "Shadow". A completely useless ability on Skayd. A Psy master with that tattoo could disappear for a short time, literally just one or two seconds. It was a kind of trick, not visual, but like suggestion. Considering that ninety-nine percent of the inhabitants of Skayd used neural networks built into their bodies, and the weirdos who didn't have them wore tactical glasses and external comms, the shadow trick didn't work at all on our world.

Nobody cared about it, and most people thought it was straight bullshit. Only old descriptions and the fact that it worked on young children proved that it had some trifling effect. But here, on Genji's world, two seconds, or even just one second of invisibility could give me a great advantage. Besides, the tattoo was actually really simple. Of course, if I had armor. It completely copied the contour of the body and lay right over the skin of an individual.

Without even moving from where I was, I began to reconstruct the tattoo using my tattoo of concentration. There were not too many elements. I thought it would take me only three or four days to do the whole thing. So I would have to reevaluate all the runes I knew about in light of this new reality. I had already done that a couple of times, I thought, but somehow I had overlooked the shadow. Who knew that the most useless rune would have its time to shine in a different world?

Anyway, rest was now just a dream. Instead of getting a good night's sleep, I set about going through my slender deck of runes and trying to put them to good use in my current reality. Nothing helpful except the shadow one, there was nothing else. Or, more precisely, all of the Psy tattoos were useful, but my schedule for doing them hadn't changed. The only thing was that I could push it back four days and work on the rune of shadow out of order.

I woke up in the morning with high hopes. Damn, a little selfish, sure, but I needed just a little bit of Psy for the rune of shadow, and I didn't think Eika was against it. But I was wrong. My mom and dad were at home and I was expected for a family breakfast. On the other hand, I did need to speak with my parents about my new abilities. I needed to know if I could trust Matvey Nikolaevich's team with those kinds of secrets. Anyway, I, to put it mildly, had broken out of the usual norms of development. I was not a wizard, but the changes were surprising. It would be okay if it were just a growth spurt, but these massive leaps...

We at breakfast, as usual, the three of us. The table was covered in meat, fish, and eggs. It was interesting how I saw Goro in this body as a world-wise, elderly man. But in fact, Genji's father was still young. He worked out constantly, and the rank he had achieved spoke to his outstanding abilities. To become a Shihan at that age you either had to have a whole clan school of aristocrats at your back, or an inhuman sense of purpose, iron discipline, and an indomitable will in addition to exceptional talent. Goro worked on himself twenty-four hours a day. There was no other way that a former orphan could have become the leader of an independent and successful clan.

At first all three of us were quiet, just eating our food. Jesus, just one morsel of this food would make it worth the transfer from my world! And bless the fights at Gakko just as long as we have these fruits. And the fish, and the meat, all worth it. People have been killed for less on Skayd.

I worked hard all night with my Psy, and before that I trained diligently all day. On top of that, the runes of strength and speed were transforming my body to the perfect kind for one of them. So I wanted to eat like a whole pack of wolves.

Mmm, fish with marinated radishes and hot peppers and flavorful spices. The spiciness was brilliantly offset by the wild fried rice and the mango juice, masterfully made in our own kitchen. It wasn't too thick, as it often was with this fruit, nor was it too watered-down. No, no such blasphemy was allowing in our home kitchen. The thick pulp was carefully kept in check, and the sweet, fragrant ambrosia was carefully poured into a carafe. I enjoyed every bite and every sip, mmm...

But now it was time to get down to brass tacks.

Chapter 18

Listen to Your Gut

"DAD, I NEED TO DISCUSS an issue with my trainers," I began, tearing off a massive piece of tender, melt-in-your-mouth stewed meat with berry sauce. Before that I had scarfed down nearly half a leg of mutton under the astonished gaze of my parents, like I considered it just a prelude to the fish, rice, and tons of veggies.

"How so? Do you want to add something?" My father with a difficulty I understood well tore himself away from his omelet, stuffed full of streaky bacon, springs onions, and chopped tomatoes.

"No, dad, something has changed in my abilities."

Upon hearing that my father exchanged a knowing look with my mother. What was going on. I was trying with all my might to explain my antimagical abilities, and now they had their own secrets. And my announcement hadn't occasioned even a bit of surprise, no, it was more like they were expecting it. No, even more like the had been wanting it to happen. Well, what was I supposed to feel now?

"Hmm... Explain that in more detail. Is it about your physical abilities or something supernatural?" asked my father with barely-concealed expectation. Seriously, what was going on?

"Uh... I'm just talking about my physical abilities," I clarified. Although my tattoos of armor and shadow would be incomprehensible for local science, they were still not magic, and not an achievement by local thinkers. And the rune of concentration was completely fantastical.

"I understand," said my father, a little disappointed, but he perked up immediately and inquired, "So what has changed, son?"

"Um... I have become faster and stronger," I was haltingly trying to express how the new runes worked, deliberating how to explain my new abilities. Just like the regeneration, I didn't know how to justify it. Okay, before I was recovering a little faster than a mere mortal, but now I was reviving like a damn phoenix.

"All within possible norms," muttered my father, once again sharing a glance with my mother. They definitely knew something. I need to try to get some information out of them. In any case, it would make it easier to hide my Psy tattoos.

"Mom, dad, do you know what is happening to me?" I decided to ask point-blank, feigning ignorance. If my abilities somehow correlated with the local magic, that would be an undeniably good cover. It would be like hiding your drugs in a cache of illegal weapons. My parents would be hiding their own secret, and right under their noses I would keep the secret of my transfer from Skayd hidden.

"Never you mind son. It's possible that you are breaking through somewhat late. So it's a little strange, with invulnerability like wizards have, and then strength and speed... It's very similar, just not all at once, somehow one at a time. But perhaps its best to keep it a secret. I think that if you don't exceed the limits of a normal person to intensely, it won't give rise to any questions. And those who encounter it and know what is happening..." explain my father, losing himself in thought.

Hmm... My father was hiding something. He definitely knew more than he was letting on. But no matter, I was sure he was acting in Genji's best interests, which were also my own.

"Son, we can't tell you everything now, but trust me, the changes in your body are only for the better. However, not everybody is going to look at those changes in a good light, so the longer we keep them a secret, the better," added my mother, but she also left all my questions unanswered.

Ah, to hell with it, I was just happy that my parents' secrets and my own lined up so well. It seemed like there was an absolutely solid legend about me for the locals. As far as I could tell, my parents, after my recipient was put in a coma by fatass Bo, carried out some kind of magical ritual. It didn't matter which one, but maybe that's why I ended up transferring into Genji's body.

They acted, doubting, obviously, whether they were right or what the results would be, but now they thought they were getting confirmation that everything turned out right. But there were certain people who wouldn't like that. Or, maybe, some people were looking for the ritual, or even for the people who had gained superpowers from it. So Goro and Hena would do their utmost to keep my secret, which worked out great for me.

"Mom, dad, I understand completely, and I also think that these changes should be kept secret. That's why I brought this up," I said, returning to the topic at hand. "My trainers will definitely know that my abilities have increased significantly. Matvey Nikolaevich constantly pays attention to my physical parameters, and now I have added a lot to them. At the same time, I have lost some of my abilities, showing that my increase in strength didn't happen naturally, but by using magic…”

“Don't worry, son. We have an agreement with your trainer's team. From now on you can consider him and some of his specialists to be a part of the Tanaka clan. They will be working not only with you, but also with our military teams. Their methods have proven to be fairly effective against gifted of the first ranks, which may give us an appreciable advantage over our competitors,” said my father, dispelling all my doubts.

“But anyway, darling, Matvey Nikolaevich does bring a lot of extra trainers to Genji. Maybe we should warn him about it,” my mom said, worried.

“Absolutely. I will talk with him. And the specialists that were in close contact with Genji will be replaced with equivalent clan trainers,” responded my father immediately.

So, by the end of breakfast, all my issues with the training team were resolved. Now I could consult with the specialists about how to quickly and effectively get my body working right again, without worrying. Ah, it was like a weight off my shoulders. I had taken a liking to the martial Yakut, and his team of daredevils had helped me a lot. Without those obsessed madmen I would long ago have been eaten alive by the students at Gakko Academy. So it would have been a sad day to have to part with such exceptional teachers.

After breakfast I devoted some time to

training by myself. I tried various exercises, jump rope, somersaults, parallel bars, the obstacle course. My muscles would definitely balance out sooner or later, but time was of the essence. The sooner the better. Then I went for a swim and took a sweat bath. It was too bad Eika wasn't there, but she was trying not to be around me while my parents were home. But I had all but confirmed that our little secret was at least sanctioned, if not completely approved by either Goro or Hena.

After my training I set about working on the rune of shadow. On the whole my day had passed quietly and as planned. For everyone else I was still in the hospital, or at least recovering at my family's estate, so nobody was bothering me. I had accomplished quite a lot and was just getting ready to turn in when I heard a light knock on my door. Eika slid into my room. She had found a moment to slip into my part of the house. She put a finger to my lips and without a word set about her task of corrupting a minor.

At that time, just in my skivvies, I was already ready for bed. But as soon as I saw her familiar figure, I jumped up and pressed her hot body to my own.

Everything was amazing, but as soon as I finished, the lovely nymph moved away, jumping out of the bed and, without even showering, ran off. To tell the truth, I had no idea what happened, since she had done everything so fervently. So now there was a pressing question. Who was taking advantage of who? As far as I could tell, Eika had satisfied her carnal requirements and dashed off back to her work. That was that! Hmm... Well, I wasn't against it at all. Much less since everything was so pleasing to me, and on top of that I got Psy energy into the bargain.

This free Psy was just amazing for the contours of the tattoos I had already prepared. I finished the shadow one in record time. This planet was a real paradise for Psy masters. Now I had to think about my strategy for using this ability. Also, in addition to disappearing, I could do it selectively, either for everyone around, or just for certain people. It was like I was just dug out of people's brains. Which meant, if I didn't abuse it too much, the ability could be a secret for a long time.

Each individual opponent would just think that they had lost me from view for a second. And if I follow that up with some kind of hit, they would just think it was a trick of the eyes. Nobody around would notice me blinking out, since I would be completely visible for everyone else. Damn, most teenagers would be too embarrassed to even admit that I had disappeared for a second. And the cameras would help me, since they would clearly be in my favor. Did I disappear? No! Stop telling tall tales.

Hmm... Should I trust my parents or my

trainers with this secret? Probably not a great idea. No good would come of it, and it would only lead to unnecessary doubts and questions. What would Matvey Nikolaevich say, especially if he had never come across anything like that before? Of course, all of my trainers together might be able to think up something useful, but it wasn't worth the risk. I would figure out myself, with the help of my tattoo of concentration.

And my own personal hell started in the morning. Matvey Nikolaevich, inspired by my father, it seemed, as a personal thank you to him, rushed to the estate at the head of his own gang of loyal experts. Up until then I was had considered myself, with reason, to be a responsible person, striving for self-improvement, but that pack of wolves in the form of the martial Yakut and his minions showed me beyond doubt that I was a slob, an idiot, a lazy piece of shit. I had had a good thing going, and now I couldn't even lie down happily.

All of my protestations that I was working, that I was trying to get the most possible good out of what had happened, were smashed against a wall of contemptuous apathy. It was doubly bad for me since it had been so difficult to get these tattoos. I'm not even going to mention Skayd, but even there I would have accomplished something. If not for the unexpected bonus I got from sex, I would still have many months of tough work ahead, like a miner in the asteroid belt.

Gakko Academy

But all my spiritual agonies didn't even so much as give Matvey Nikolaevich pause, and I spent the whole day as a lab rat. Huh. Skayd hadn't left me, even here. I don't know what the hell was going on in the perverted minds of my trainers, but all day long they kept coming up with the most unbelievable tests for my body. Sometimes all together, like colleagues, and sometimes separately. So I started to get the impression that these, pardon me, motherfuckers were competing to see who could think up the worst task for me. And just a little bit again I was sad that I might have to part with them. Dumbass!

First I had to jump into the sky. Yeah, you heard that right. I wasn't supposed to reach a specific height, oh no! They were demanding that I at least take off from the ground, if not reach escape velocity. My teachers, it seemed, had decided that along with strength and speed I had acquired the ability to levitate, or at least had gotten rockets installed in my ass.

Those thoughts were obviously their problem, and it wasn't my job to fix the sick heads of these deluded fools. But those pricks supported their vague tasks with clear punishments. What was the goddamn use of trying to get ready for my fights at Gakko when my own trainers hit me harder than they did at school? They beat me so mercilessly that I would have preferred to just get into it with Akira, Saito, and Hiro right now, no training.

After jumping into the sky, I was lifting things, at first large ones, and then massive ones. Of course I realized that Matvey Nikolaevich was trying to get a clear understanding of what I had attained, that is to say, he was trying to find the limits of my abilities. But could he not do it in a more humane way? And, to be frank, the Yakut was finding the limits not just in training, but for me myself. How the hell was I supposed to know how many pounds I could lift?

Well, on Skayd I could take three or four times the normal weight for an unmodified recruit, and that was good enough. But here they were trying to find the limit down to the pound. I felt that, despite everything, they were now planning to increase it. And how would they do that? These sadists only had one trick: give me harder tasks and beat me worse for not completing them.

Jumping rope, lifting weights, running, acrobatics, push-ups, parallel bars... And on top of all that, they tested me in what seemed like every known form of combat. Anyway, by the time evening was upon us, I was thinking that they wanted to punt me into the unknown cosmos, so that I could subjugate the galactic sectors inhabited by aggressive wise guys with my bare hands.

They didn't let me go for lunch, and I threw up my breakfast by the first half-hour of training.

They only let me drink, and not nearly enough. At the same time, those dicks treated themselves to delicacies from our kitchen and slurped down all kinds of juice. Ahhh, I hate them!

And when I had finally finished all my exercises just good enough, my bewildered trainers gathered in a huddle and whispered amongst each other for a long time.

Jesus, I needed to deal with this, take some time to do the tattoo improving my senses of sight, smell, hearing, taste, and touch. They weren't the top priority, but it would be amazing if I could listen in to what those people, in their unjustified belief that they were real teachers, were whispering about. But those runes would take a lot of time and effort. They were very fine, delicate handiwork. It wasn't about improving the sense organs, but more about building up a system to be able to turn the abilities off and on and make them work in a more directed way. Otherwise you would get a whole bunch of problems instead of any benefit. Imagine it. You're hearing every sound amplified ten times over. It would drive you nuts. I mean, it had happened before.

After all that whispering, Matvey Nikolaevich went off to the main house for some reason. Had he just decided to go bug Goro Tanaka? As if all this hoo-ha had ended for me with one more sad experience with its own different consequences...

I saw it clearly. In just a few minutes the

head of the clan would come rushing out of the house. Around him there would be a crowd of security forces, gesticulating wildly, joined by other members of the criminal syndicate. Some new hell was on the horizon! And there was nothing I could do. I couldn't go against my own parent.

At a sign from my father, some sort of movement began deep underground. Grinding, groaning, tooth-shaking sounds of metal machinery moving. Given how surprised my trainers started chattering, I realized that Goro Tanaka could astonish even that pack of fighters with something unique. Within the span of literally just half an hour a whole complex of intricate exercise machines and mechanisms had appeared over a fairly wide area.

Something was stirring vaguely in the depths of my recipient's memories. I stepped up my rune of concentration and immediately knew what was in store for me. Oh, the devil take them all! These old miscreants, with my father in charge, had decided to test my rank. But what was good for wizards was death for normal people. Genji had dreamed of taking this death course, invented thousands of years ago, but I had no such ambitions. Son of a bitch, I, of all people, knew for damn sure that my abilities were in no way magical.

The processes in motion were now nearing completion, and my asshole was clenching with trepidation. I was used to that feeling from Skayd, and here at Gakko Academy, damn it to every fucking hell, it had developed into an incredible sign of trouble.

My rune of concentration was at full bore. Its only task was to find a way to get out of this upcoming torture. But the excited look of my father and the enthusiastic shouts of Matvey Nikolaevich and his gang left me with no hope. Fuck! Now I wish I was just getting a beating again. And I was despairing that I was going to be taken away in a stretcher again. Oh, what use was it? My gut had learned its lesson, and now there could be no mistaking the outcome!

Chapter 19

The Test

TESTING GROUNDS FOR CHECKING THE RANKS of the gifted were, in general, controlled by the government. There were well-regulated standards on the difficulty of the obstacles, and the all-important matter of balance between the strength of the trainers and the danger for the person being tested. The empire could not afford to lose wizards while testing their ranks! But, at the same time, the obstacles should be difficult enough to make the rank of the gifted clear.

But some clans, especially criminal ones, did their own ranking, without official documentation and all that nonsense. It made sense. They could keep their true strength a secret, avoiding the threat of having their fighters drafted into the imperial guard, and there were other benefits too.

Even the aristocrat clans tried not to let the true ranks of their wizards become public knowledge. So this stuff was widespread, even though it was expensive and not always safe.

Something told me that my heroic father's last concern would the safety of the one being tested. I was sure that we had the harshest homemade stuff that could be gotten, if not in the whole capital, at least in our area. There wasn't anything too complicated in it. Our ancestors had made it thousands of years ago, so copying the ancient models with modern technology was no problem. Of course, not every clan could afford arenas like this, and a functional polygon was not cheap. You had to get some gifted, and the higher the rank of the person being tested, the better the testers had to be.

Given all this work that had been done, they were just going to send me, right in my workout clothes, without letting me put on a helmet or even body armor (and I saw there was some available), through the test for wizards. Those goddamn idiots, I was not a wizard! The only thing they put on my body were some sensors. These people here had some scientific experience, hadn't they ever applied it to people? And what about international conventions? But these criminals didn't give a shit about that, and who was I going to appeal to, if my own dad was the one putting me through the wringer?

The idea of these tests was simple. They put

the beginner wizard into the center of the polygon, which meant taking me through an underground passage and using an elevator to take me straight into the box that I had thought was the goal. But no, I was mistaken, that was just the starting point. The goal was to break out of the maze at any cost, which was, in itself, a training ground for developing the strength of the wizard. It was clear that they wouldn't just let me out.

And here I was inside of a rising elevator, which, instead of a marker of which floor you were on, had a countdown showing when the doors would open. Three... two... one... Motherfucker! All four walls of the elevator crashed down around me. Here I thought that one door would open and I would have some time, sitting in my box, to look around. But I didn't even have a single second to get my bearings, incomprehensible objects were flying at me from all sides, obviously some magical stuff.

Now I understood what had pushed that crazy Yakut to test me in this thing. Now I had to jump, and I had spent half a day breaking world records in jumping!

Not wanting to rush in blindly, I tried to look around my starting area and find out where the least dangerous path to the edge was. How could I look around, though? I was jumping and flipping around in place, and these vile magical attacks were only growing in intensity.

Ah, even my rune of concentration wasn't helping. It was just a damn maze all around. I had to depend on my intuition. But what intuition? The attacks were coming from all sides, and I had to get to where there was the least amount of them. The magical ones were different only in scale so far. More small ones, less big ones. I felt like the damage would depend on the size, so it would be better to avoid the big ones. I had already let a couple small ones through, which felt like being punched by a charged-up wizard. So what would happen if a big one got me?

I ran. It couldn't be that hard. No matter how big the polygon was, it was still smaller than the estate, which meant that the distance from the center to the edge was not too much. I could make it out. Oh goddammit, don't jynx it! It looked like the goddamn hallway was moving. Part of it shifted sharply to the right, and then began moving up and down. The system was redesigning the maze, and the magical attacks continued their assault. I had let quite a few through, mostly on my body, but a few times they had whizzed by alarmingly close to my head.

What now? They couldn't disorient me, of course, even though that was clearly their intention. But those who ran from the space hermits onto an unknown multilevel space station would end up in lost in a labyrinth of your own making. But here we had gravity, and that was a connection to some kind of guidepoint. Then again, the hermits couldn't shoot you from all sides, dammit. But everything was too much like being hunted, stunned by the stoppers, and then on a skewer, food for those piece of shit cannibals...

For now I was just running, but I didn't like that I didn't have the initiative. I was clearly being directed by this thing, led to where the collective twisted mind of my team of trainers, under the command of my father, intended me to go. And that was no good. I didn't like it when somebody decided for me where I was going to go and how many hits I would take. I needed to break the mold as soon as possible, otherwise I wouldn't get through this at all. I was not a wizard, so moving like them was no good.

I tried to suddenly change directions. Ah, they suddenly changed the maze as well. If I did that two or three times, then my puppetmasters would start to wildly mess up the changing corridors. What was the point of all that fuckery? They were trying to wear down the wizard's reserves, which I didn't have. My speed was falling though. The things were hitting me more and more often, which was doing no wonders for my mobility. They had hit my extremities not just once or twice. My legs were done for, like I had taken a good low kick. I won't even mention my arms. I had to defend myself with my shoulders and elbows a few times, when I couldn't dodge. I really doubted that I could even use my upper limbs, even if I had to.

While trying to make things easier on myself, disappointed in my effort to find a good strategy, I suddenly stumbled across a dead zone. At first I didn't believe it, but in the next hallway it happened again. The maze was made from standard moving pieces, which meant that in every one a dead zone should be found. So what was it? Another trick? A mistake by the builders? Or maybe there just weren't enough wizards?

But I didn't have the luxury of choosing, so I just dove into the safe space. If I didn't catch my breath now, then the magical objects would beat me down without any tricks anyway. The dead zone was not big. I could barely squeeze myself in. But at least I could breathe and think a moment. I had been jumping around like a frightened deer, not knowing where I was going, without even a second to look around, so this moment of rest was a gift.

I filled my tattoo of regeneration with Psy. I needed to get rid of this swelling as soon as possible so I could prepare myself for what was next. Knowing Matvey Nikolaevich, I could easily predict the way it would go. He wouldn't give his opponent even a second of time, just pressure, attack, pressure, attack...

Book Two

*   *   *

All the walls in the observation room were equipped with monitors. Every participant within the polygon was observed by several hidden cameras. Moreover, the whole scene was taken from multiple angles, allowing the mainframe computer to make a life-size, 3-d image of what was happening. The audience also had motion detectors, mass detectors, and more. And the one being tested was also outfitted with a whole suit of tools, giving precise information about his physical state and location.

At first Genji was just wandering aimlessly through the maze, same as any other testing their rank. But all of that chaos going on within the polygon at the first stage of testing was there for a reason. It weakened you, disoriented you, made you anxious. Only when the candidate was on the ropes would they unlock their full potential. Otherwise it would never appear, staying hidden inside. That was why these psychological preparations were necessary.

But the one being tested had found an unexpected way out. The was a flaw in the finished design of the maze, one that its designers had either never considered or just considered insignificant. Most likely the latter. To figure out that there was a dead zone for magical attacks, you would have to watch it for a while in peace, and the boy definitely wasn't supposed to be able to do that. Plus the size of it was so very small, how would he ever notice it?

But fact remained that the Tanaka heir had leisurely sat down within the whirlwind of magical attacks was either calmly resting or just meditating. The absurdity of what was going on had thrown the experienced examiners completely off-kilter. The newbie, who should have been dashing around the halls like a monkey, desperately trying to save his skin, was sitting calmly, practically sleeping, eyes closed, paying no attention to the concerted efforts of a whole team of wizards.

"What's happening?" asked the Taekwondo trainer, perplexed.

"I don't understand it myself," answered the technician in charge of working the polygon. For the last few minutes he had been frantically flipping switches, reconfiguring the machine, but to no avail. He just couldn't get to Genji like that.

"He found a dead zone," said Matvey Nikolaevich, calmly, having been carefully observing how the situation played out, first on this monitor, then on that one.

"There's no way!" answered the technician, even more upset, still frantically pulling at things on his control panel.

"And yet it is true." The aged Yakut spoke with the calm of a god, and there was no arguing with him. The fact was staring them in the face.

Genji had found a spot to rest and relax in peace. The first stage of the test was threatening to end in a fiasco. Not for the teenager, but for the examiners themselves.

"Matvey Nikolaevich, is this in some way connected to the supernatural abilities of my son?" asked Goro Tanaka.

"That depends what you mean. If it is magic, then no. But that does not mean that your son does not have a superpower. Genji is incredibly intelligent and crafty. In times of stress he thinks much faster than his peers, and, if I can be honest, faster than most people with much more experience in battle. That is your son's most valuable and unique ability." The normally laconic trainer gave a whole speech.

"Hmm... What do we do now?" The technician asked out loud, puzzled. "He's broken the whole test, just resting. We won't be able to get a real result. How are we going to get him out at all?"

"Try a new configuration of paths. Maybe he'll fall for it?" one of the clan's officers suggested.

For a good ten minutes they built up various hallways and paths in front of Genji, trying to lure him out of the dead zone, but all their attempts failed miserably. The boy was completely apathetic to what was happening, and as far as most of the observers could tell, even fell asleep for a bit while the adults did their utmost to get the testing procedure, which they had thought was perfect done to the finest detail, back on track.

"Turn the hallway he is sitting in," said Goro Tanaka all of a sudden.

"Sir, that command is strictly forbidden. The test subject could fall into the gears and die!" protested the technicians, whose hairs were standing on end at that suggestion. The father of a child was suggesting that expose his own heir to a possibly fatal risk for no good reason!

"It will be on my head!" roared the head of the clan, and all questions or objections withered on the vine.

The part of the hallway that Genji was sitting in started to turn in random directions. But it still wasn't that fast. If the young man just stayed where he was, then his life shouldn't be in any danger. The centrifugal force was so small that there wouldn't be enough to move a human body, and that didn't even take into account that the technician, along with the turn, was also changing the angle of tilt, imitating a docking with other sections of a massive labyrinth.

However, the test subject suddenly showed an interest. While in motion the magical attacks stopped and the curious boy headed right for the edge. The examiners decided he was just watching the machinery, until someone suggested that he might risk jumping over to another section. But it would be totally insane to do that while it was in motion. But the truth was beyond anything they could imagine.

* * *

I sat calmly in the dead zone and meditated. I sent all my built-up Psy haphazardly through my runes of concentration and regeneration. My body was back in fairly good shape, and my mind was still looking for a way out. I could run through the corridors and sit for a while in the dead zones. But what would that get me? All the segments were as alike as identical twins, and, given that they were constantly moving, I would never make the slightest bit of progress towards my goal.

Even if I could move in the right direction, the operators would just flip a switch and send me right back to the center. That had already happened. More than once, under attack by these magical strikes, I made it nearly two-thirds of the distance from the center to the edge, but that was only if I could trust my sense of direction and my internal meter of speed and time. However, whenever the goal was near, they would just turn me around back toward the center. And no matter how hard I tried to turn back in the right direction, I endlessly strayed from the right path.

That meant that was completely at the operators' mercy, and as soon as I flagged at all, I would take a ton of damage from the magical attacks. And then they would take me to the next test. And what would that be? Maybe a duel with a real live person or some weird mannequin with attack and defense functions. But whatever it might be, by that time I would be weak and exhausted. My internal clock told me I had been there for at least a couple hours already. I hadn't eaten, I hadn't drunk anything, and all the while I was actively moving and getting hurt. All of that meant I would soon be totally worn out, feeling apathy, losing my will to win.

Perhaps the locals were used to this kind of exam, but the sewer rat inside me was in full revolt. Freedom. That was the only thing that you fought to the death for on Skayd. It was only the possibility of making your own decisions and acting in accordance with your own desires that inured the humble sewer rats to their miserable existence. But now I felt like a caged animal, being led to the slaughter, hogtied around the neck and the legs, and I absolutely could not bear it.

And then, all of a sudden, fate handed me an opportunity. The barrage of magical attack suddenly stopped. But I knew enough to realize that I shouldn't be expecting present from the examiners. That meant another trick. And it happened almost immediately. The whole part of the corridor that I found myself in suddenly started to turn. In short, I felt like nothing good would come of this.

Before that I had seen a few gaps in the distance, the kind that were made in mazes fairly often, but this was the first time they were in the part that I was in. At first I tried keep myself steady, but the speed and incline of the hallway were not too bad, and I could just keep my balance without too much trouble. Since the onslaught had stopped, it made sense to look around, so I carefully approached the edge.

It was worth it to be careful. I could expect anything from my father and Matvey Nikolaevich. They might up the speed and tip me right over. Oh, unlikely! Inside the polygon there were dozens of moving mechanisms, turning and working. All sorts of gears led from gigantic electric motors to cogs and wheels that were responsible for the turning of the segments around their axis and the change in their inclination. All of that was connected to a massive complex that enabled the masterfully redesigning of the labyrinth on the fly.

I watched the moving parts as if in a trance. Those who have taken apart a watch and seen how the dozens of cogs work in tandem, silently, will understand what I mean. I turned on my tattoo of concentration and there it seemed like I found my way out. Maybe not the best one, but I had a chance to escape from the trap that my trainers had set for me.

Chapter 20
Unintended Result

ALL HELL BROKE LOOSE in the control room. The Tanaka heir had suddenly made a move, flattening his body across the floor of the moving hallway. His pose, his tense muscles, his gaze fixed ahead of him. He looked like a leopard about to pounce on a deer at the watering hole. What was Genji even looking at? He was definitely getting ready to jump!

"Stop the machine!" shouted Matvey Nikolaevich.

But it was too late. The boy shot up like an arrow and made a strange dive into the jumble mess of the massive polygon's moving parts. A shocked silence hung over the room. All of the engineers, having already given their warning, were thinking only one thing. Falling in there was certain death!

"Stop the machine!" an engineer shouted into the radio, and the machine department of the polygon, located somewhere deep inside the building, began systematically stopping the always-turning corridors.

Everyone there was afraid to even look at the head of the clan. Goro's face had frozen into an inhuman grimace. He stared into the monitors, running his eyes over each one, hoping to find even a trace of his only child, but in vain. Only one person was still calm in the room. The old Yakut had immediately seen with his experienced eyes that Genji had jumped to a specific point.

He hadn't even intended to jump from one part of the corridor to another, no. The boy was playing a trick. And given Genji's careful, meticulous nature, he would be prepared to guess that the boy had found some clever escape, and that the chance that he had survived was much higher than most people thought. Genji Tanaka might be considered rash, too willing to take risks, but his trainer know for sure that behind that mask was hiding a careful, deliberate fighter, who only took risks when the chance of winning was not just high, but absolute! It was a different matter entirely that he was ready to sacrifice things that would be unacceptable for a normal person for the sake of victory.

He could have said all of that, but the Yakut wanted the surprise that his student was obviously planning to come off as he wanted. It would be a lesson for Goro Tanaka. He had chosen to risk his son's life just like he risked those of his men. But when it is your own flesh and blood, there is a big difference. Was it worth all this? All of the adults here, including the head trainer, had gone too far. The voice of ambition and hope for new discoveries had pushed them to expose the young man to an unjustified risk.

After a short pause the whole crowd, both the technicians and the fighters, all rushed off in search of the young master. Goro Tanaka personally led one of the teams. They had a long way through the whole of the machine ahead of them. On top of that they would have to search every nook and cranny and all the maintenance holes. Only one person remained in the control center. Matvey Nikolaevich decided that he would learn about everything right here, not leaving his spot. And in just a short time the Yakut began to chuckle, hiding his smile behind his hands.

* * *

I was searching for something like the eye of a hurricane within the chaos of all the moving parts, a place where I could once again sit and chill. But right next to me there weren't any. Clearly, to turn something as big as part of a hallway, you needed a whole bunch of moving parts, and considering the speed and angle of inclination, their connections to each other had to be densely packed all around. The whirring movement along the vertical and horizontal axes completely ruled out the possibility of any person being there without putting their life in danger.

Any parts like that elsewhere would only be because the turning was not so intense there. In any case, you could only stand underneath there when that miraculous machine had come to a complete stop. Which was too bad. Until the operators came to their sense there was nothing stopping me from going back to my starting point. Which was only threatened by the unplanned movement of these massive metal parts and also the possible damage to my long-suffering body.

But when I had almost given up hope, I suddenly spotted a transport brace on the neighboring ledge. It seemed like the individual segments were connected by it to supports and moved. It was obvious that none of its connection would go right by the corridor itself, otherwise there would be too much risk of a breakdown or the machine might just break through the floor or the wall of a segment. Which meant, if I held on to the brace, I would be in a relatively safe place!

But there was only one brace here, and that meant I would have to hold myself parallel to the lower segment. So I would be looking like a kind of flag. If I sagged at any point then I would find myself suddenly within the meat grinder between some massive toothed cogs. How long would it take them to stop the machine?

Okay, let's think about this. I am sure they are watching my moves on the monitor. I jump, and everyone is in shock. Let's give them about fifteen seconds for that. They're not girls there, but real men. Okay, fine, half a minute. They are serious men, maybe it will take them a while to get there, like for my dad. Then the command, stop the machine! Another half a minute. Then the question of getting the automatic systems to work. Everything is electric these days, but the inertia of a heavy machine, powered by electronic motors cannot be undone by anyone. Okay, creaking and winding down, another minute. That meant I would have to hold myself on the brace for two minutes, but I would give myself at least more, just in case.

I had held myself like a flag on the parallel bars before, but there the angle was different, and the grip was comfortable. But right now I had three runes in my favor, strength, speed, and regeneration. Plus my armor rune, in the worst case, would come in handy. It was decided. Let's go! I waited for the right moment. I had to jump in the right way, so no part of my body or my clothes fell into those deadly grindstones. If they pulled me in it was all over.

I took off my tracking sensors in advance, throwing them onto the ledge. Let the examiners worry. It would at least throw them off my trail. I only left my "pass" with me. It was a little button with batteries. Before the test they told me that as soon as I passed through the doors I was looking for, they would notice it and open the way. Yeah, I hadn't yet come across any doors, but I kept it just in case.

I jumped. Throwing myself forward, I canceled my momentum with a dive and slipped under the neighboring segment like a fish. During this process I used a moving shaft to fine-tune the direction of my flight. This was no circus trick, but an extraordinarily dangerous and extremely complex feat. If not for a detailed plan, created using the rune of concentration and running an ocean of Psy through my tattoos of strength and speed, I would never have been able to pull it off.

I grabbed the brace, but my legs were dangerously close to the gears. It would have been even worse later. The machine moved in a circle and was coming closer to me. I chose an opportune moment and stretched my body out parallel to the base of the segment. Alright, now to let time pass.

The first minute. I held on, clenching my teeth. The position was not comfortable. I had to tense up all of my muscles to remain horizontal. After thirty seconds one of the shafts would move away a little and I could allow myself a little bit of leeway in the angle of my body.

I changed it, but that was a mistake. Now it was even harder, and I no longer had the strength to get back to my initial position. I put all my Psy into the rune of strength. Even the concentration rune, which I kept constantly fed, was on the strictest of rations.

The second minute had passed. According to my optimistic prediction this execution, falsely labelled an examination, would soon be over. I put a bit of energy into regeneration. I had to pep up my overtensed muscles.

Damn! The third minute had passed. The machine was beginning to stop everywhere, but there was a lot of inertia, and close to the center, where I was, all the fearsome cogs were still in motion. It was clear that the automatic shut-off worked from the edges to the center, so as not to damage any connecting parts. That would be at least one more minute, and I was at the least of my strength.

I toughed it out, although in the last seconds my legs were leaning against the shafts as they stopped moving. It wasn't dangerous, but it let my legs and the muscles in my body relax. Now I had two choices. I could go through the maintenance pipes, or I could go back up and leave like a free man. Both choices had the same amount of risk, so I chose the cleaner and more comfortable path. Having to crawl through any more machine oil, nah, screw that.

Book Two

* * *

To get through the tangled mess of maintenance routes, you had to walk through machine oil up to your ankles. Our day clothes and workout uniforms were mercilessly splattered with oils of all types and colors. People were picking through the cogs with difficulty due to the darkness, and in some places they ran into a rain of drizzling oils, wherever the moving parts required that sort of constant upkeep.

After a couple minutes, the whole group of regular guys looked more like a maintenance crew that had just finished a week's worth of work cleaning the engines of at least a battleship. People's exposed body parts and clothes glistened with oil. Shirts and kimonos that had been all white just moments before were now nothing but dirty, greasy rags.

But they continued trudging forward, trying to get to the scene of the tragedy as soon as possible. It was possible the heir was lying there, waiting for help. And his sensors clearly showed where he was. The only question was, was Genji alive or dead?

And then, like a bolt from the blue, a mechanical voice rang out from the intercom over the polygon:

"Candidate Genji Tanaka has passed the test for the rank of Kohai. A new record for the

Tanaka clan has been set, with the test taking zero point one minutes!"

The system carried the news to all the speakers in the estate, even those in the parks and squares. The announcement system was intended for wars or emergencies, but the polygon also had access to it.

The people rushing through those tons of metal and machine oil stopped and stared at each other in disbelief. There wasn't even anyone to explain what was going on. All the operators were here too, searching for the young heir. Then they started to worry that someone might have turned the polygon back on. Right now you smash them all up into a fine paste. No, the mechanisms were stopped at the lowest level, that was clear. Then what the hell was happening?

"Candidate Genji Tanaka has passed the test for the rank of Sempai. A new record for the Tanaka clan has been set, with the test taking zero point one minutes!" said the mechanical, synthesized voice, coldly.

And almost immediately:

"Candidate Genji Tanaka has passed the test for the rank of Sensei. A new record for the Tanaka clan has been set, with the test taking zero point one minutes!"

"Dammit! He's walking through the halls, opening up the doors with test bracelet!" The head technician finally caught on.

"Shouldn't there be gifted examiners of the higher rank there?" came a confused voice.

"They are all here," remarked another, gloomily.

"But... is that allowed? The technician asked himself.

"Genji Tanaka has actually passed the test. The rules say by any means possible. If the candidate passes through the door for a Sensei, then he is a Sensei," someone quoted from the imperial laws.

"Well, it's a good thing thus isn't an official polygon," sighed one of the members of the examination committee.

"Ahhhh, huh..." hemmed the head technician, forcing a cough.

"What's wrong?" asked Goro Tanaka, immediately suspicious.

"Sir, as per your orders, our polygon has gone through all the necessary steps with the government commission, meaning the results of the tests are all recorded by a program with the head of gifted affairs in the Ministry of Defense."

"Oh you... what...!" The head of the clan was swearing internally, but he immediately set to contacting his lawyers.

They would have to get the test results cancelled as soon as possible. What a mess! An ungifted had achieved the rank of Sensei at the age of eighteen. They couldn't let that information get out, or there would be no way to avoid a scandal. It was good that it would be considered utterly impossible, meaning that almost nobody would doubt that some sort of ridiculous accident had happened.

I was in no hurry, practically sauntering from the center of the polygon to its edge. Nobody was moving the corridors, nobody was throwing magic spells at me, and didn't have a care in the world. Hmm, it was pretty fancy, as if it was something elite. All over were bas-reliefs, paintings, and other sculptures about the great deeds of wizards.

On the other side of the door was a plain dueling area, an arena for magic battles, basically the same as the one I tested out at ABS Club. Nothing special, some signs of techniques that had been used, wear and tear, and the same style as an ancient dojo with the requisite bas-reliefs. I opened the door with bracelet, and feeling like I should hurry for some reason, went through the next one. And now there came an automatic victory voice...

Oho, I passed the Kohai exam. This was going to be fun, ha!

I passed through two more rooms. That made total sense. The highest ranked person in the clan was my father, who was a Shihan, I had heard, meaning we couldn't confer any ranks higher than Sensei.

Having finished the test, I headed outside and ended up at the backdoor of the estate. Of course, no one was there to meet me. They were probably looking for my remains, chewed up by a machine. But I was here, whole and unharmed.

What to do now, I asked myself, shrugging. I had done quite a lot today, even before the polygon with my exertions at the hands of those damned trainers. I wanted to eat and drink. And I wanted Eika too, ha. But that woman was definitely not going to show up around me. No, I was sure my dad was going to be rushing here in no time. But honestly, I didn't feel guilty at all. Those adults had set up a tricky test, and I passed it. And if I broke some rules, well, that wasn't mu fault. Nobody had explained anything to me, they just threw me into the polygon and started pummeling me. I was well within my rights.

On the way to my part of the house, I requested that food, juice, water, everything that was in the kitchen and more, be brought to my room. There were already snacks, dried fruits, nuts, some cookies, and jerky in my room. I put all of that on a tray and, cramming a handful of it into my mouth, headed into the bathroom. I made no distinctions, chewing everything indiscriminately, stopping only to drink water. I had burned an exorbitant amount of calories today, not even taking into account that goddamn test.

As far as I could tell, my runes of strength and speed took my successes as some sort of effort to activate my tattoos. That was why they were working so hard to get my body in the right shape. I had already seen a layer of fat literally disappear before my eyes, while some places my muscles were swelling up. But all of this was at the expense of a huge amount of calories and building blocks in the form of proteins, fats, and carbohydrates. So I was trying to replace them at the same rate.

Right as my tub was reaching enough water, I heard a careful knock at the door. That would probably be my food. But my heart was beating in anticipation, since I knew that knock very well. Only one person's delicate but powerful fingers announced their presence like that.

I was not disappointed when Eika came into the room, pushing a little table in front of her, laid out with all sorts of plates, bowls, pitchers, and even a small pot, heated right on the tray by a miniature range.

In spite of the delightful aromas wafting from those delicacies, I paid no attention to the food. My hungry gaze drank up the familiar figure. Eika was in her usual uniform, but I knew what charms were hidden by the serving girl's plain outfit. Her thick, powerful thighs, her perky breasts, her flat stomach, and her sweet lower parts...

"Genji, no!" Eika had guessed my intentions and quickly started explaining, worried, with good reason, that I would quickly go from looks to action. "Mr. Goro Tanaka and Mrs. Hena are not far away at all. I have heard that they are coming to see you."

"Eika, they will take at least twenty minutes to discuss what happened," I said, trying to turn my desires into reality. "I want you so much. We can do it!"

"Genji, I am also impatiently waiting for our next meeting, but control yourself now. We risk losing everything we have for one indulgence," the serving girl responded, entirely reasonably. But, seeing my despondent gaze, she added, "I will come here tonight!"

"Okay." I just barely could overcome my instincts to tear off the clothes of that female, the ones hiding her treasures from me, and take her roughly, right on the floor.

The spicy, high-calorie food heated up my throat with an invigorating stream that poured on to the fire of hunger that was raging in my belly. Along with the celebration of my stomach I climbed into the tub full of warm water and lay back across the board. Now I could sate my hunger, calmly, reasonably, with what god had sent me in the form of my parents and the sexy Eika. Damn, we definitely could have done it.

Chapter 21
Not Enough?

IN THE HALL shared by every wing of the main Tanaka house, the lady of the house was angrily chewing out her husband. The serious man, head of a criminal clan, a person who had taken his wrath out on more than a hundred powerful competitors and ruined businessmen, stood in front of her, his head hanging pitifully. If he could have, he would have hidden it under his armpit, but his bull neck didn't allow him that sort of flexibility. There was only one person on Earth who was allowed to speak to Goro in that tone. And Hena had been doing it long before they had united their destinies together.

At that time he had been kind of shy in front of the lanky girl, skinny from malnourishment, who was always striving for justice everywhere, not even giving up in the presence of dangerous hooligans like Goro Tanaka, who even at that time already had the entire orphanage cowering in fear. Despite his physical strength and decent talent in magic, the general of the teenage gang had bowed his head before Hena's beauty, and since that time what he feared most was disappointing his one and only woman.

"Goro, what the hell, did you leave your mind at the office or forget it at the supermarket? How could you expose the boy to such a risk? He is not a wizard! Who even considers throwing an ungifted boy into the testing arena? He could have been killed in the first five minutes there! Just one hit by a big sphere, and then a couple more small ones would be enough!" Hena always tried to keep herself in check, speaking in an almost exaggeratedly polite manner, but only when it wasn't about her only son.

"Hena, don't get too worked up, please, I can explain everything," Goro shrank away from fear of what was coming. "Genji displayed outstanding results during training, so Matvey Nikolaevich and I decided that it looked like a delayed break through... I mean, first there was the regeneration, and then the strength..."

"And you, the two old idiots you are, based on your own presumptions, threw him into your damned contraption on the very first day! Dumbasses!" shouted the lady of the house, furious, and all the servants hurried to get at least two rooms away from the hall. Falling into her hands now would be tantamount to suicide.

"Dear, we have gotten the testing polygon fully certified. It matches up to all the government's standards, including for safety," Goro said, hurrying to voice his protests.

"What?" Hena said, shocked, remembering clearly that the polygon had been purposefully kept off the government registry so as not to give away the forces of the clan. "Why the hell did you need to do that?"

"We needed to prove the presence of gifted fighters for the security agency that we were making for Genji. To get a license there we had to fulfill some requirements. I was afraid of sending my people to other centers or, God forbid, the imperial ones, so I was forced to register ours. And for the clan's needs we will build another one on the base in the nearby district. Our organization is growing and using the polygon at our own estate is not that convenient," said the head of the clan, laying out his motives point by point.

"Get out of here! You freaking idiot, you put our son through a polygon certified by the Ministry of Defense? You have lost your goddamn mind! You either drank it away or give it to one of your massage girls! You dumbass!" shouted Hena furiously, taking the conversation further than it had ever gone before. But it wasn't like you could have called it casual before.

"I already told you, the polygon has been tested for safety! What's the problem?" Goro asked, desperately trying to argue.

"Idiot! Your goddamn polygon is safe for WIZARDS! Try to get a certification like that for ungifted, and you'll realize what the problem is!" Hena hit her husband with an ironclad argument.

"Darling, I was completely wrong. Forgive me. It will never happen again!" Goro, guilty of all charges, began backpedaling.

"How are you going to get the test results cancelled?" asked Hena, reassuring her fool

"The lawyers are working on it. Everything is cut and dry. Genji is obviously not a wizard, and no way could an eighteen-year-old boy pass the test with a rank of Sensei," reasoned the head of the clan.

"That is good, then. Goro, are you sure he wasn't hurt?" asked Hena once more, furrowing her brow. That was the first thing she had asked and only calmed down when Eika confirmed that the young man was in one piece, without even a scratch on him. Considering that the serving girl was the only person who had been able to carefully examine Genji after he came back from the test, her claims were believable. But it was worth it to get one more dig in on his irresponsible father.

"I am one hundred percent sure, darling, that our son was not hurt," answered Goro quickly.

"Just know, if he ends up crippled again, it will be all your fault!" threatened Hena, at which the Oyabun closed his eyes in fright. His wife knew how to get revenge, and her creativity had been infamous even back when they were in the orphanage.

"Henaaaa..." His pleading thundered through the whole district, completely sincere, fully understanding and full of fear.

* * *

The echoes of my parents' argument could be heard even in my bathroom. That was even in spite of the fairly good soundproofing and the not insignificant distance from my bathing area to the main hall. I felt bad for my father, yeah, but it was also for the best. My mother might not be able to smarten up the reckless Oyabun, but at least my dad would stop carrying out experiments that were so risky to my life and health.

And maybe even my team of overly demanding trainers might be reined in a little? But there I was probably mistaken. The trainers had proven the usefulness of their training with results, so they weren't going to just let me be. And I still needed them. Despite all my progress, I was still weak against the monsters at Gakko Academy. There were beasts there that could, in the right circumstances, squash me like a fly and never even notice. I was exaggerating a little, scaring myself once again, but better not to ride this new victory too high.

While my parents fought I casually finished off the pot of miso soup, then I moved onto a dish with crab meat and snacked on all the fresh-caught tuna sashimi. Having sated my first hunger, I pushed the tray with food away for a while and enjoyed diving under the warm water. It was so nice to wash off all the dirt and sweat, especially with this real water, and not some disinfectant solution. I wasn't even going to mention the tendency of the locals to add butter, salts, and other luxuries to their baths.

Only one thing was bugging me. Eika and I definitely could have done it! The shape of her athletic figure was exciting my imagination. On the other hand, there was only a little bit of time left until night. Calming myself with that thought, I celebrated a well-deserved avoidance of another set of health problems. After washing all the grime off, I decided not to deny myself anything and started filling up the water again. Although I did wash off the ofuro using a special nozzle on the faucet.

While the water was filling up, I indulged in my gluttony once more. I was actually trying to draw out my time a little, knowing that neither my mother or my father would bother me in the bath. I had no desire to see the guilty face of my mother or the even more guilty face of my father right now. I was sure that my parents knew that I was totally all right. Eika must have, at the very least, told them how I was. It was not for nothing that she had inspected my body so diligently. Clearly it wasn't to satisfy her own lust, but rather as preparation for a report to the head of the clan, or rather his wife.

So I had a good reason to hope that my parents would get tired of waiting and hold off on their apologetic conversation until tomorrow, and then everything would just work out. And bathing was really very nice. The second time I washed myself without moving too much, which is to say that I got wet and then lazily grabbed pieces of meat, and then fish from the plate. Did I have to right to relax? I sure did!

Tap, tap, tap! Tap, tap, tap!

Dammit, could my parents really not wait? I looked at the door in trepidation, then with excitement as Eika came daintily slipping in the bathroom. The girl, not saying a word, started slowly undressing, trying to tease me. The jacket of her uniform fell to the floor, then her white blouse, and almost at the same time her severe gray skirt. She was left in only her underwear. The serving girl looked at me slyly, then did a few shameless dance moves.

Jesus! I almost jumped out of the water like a dolphin, but was stopped by a commanding gesture, after which the impromptu striptease continued.

One! I was blinded by the hemispheres of her perfect, perky chest. The girl moved toward me like a nimble kitten. Two! Her tiny string bikini dripped downward, leaving nothing to the imagination. Ahhh! This tub had become some kind of vicious cycle for us, since all of my greatest sexual encounters with Eika started here.

"How did you manage to come so early?" I asked after we satisfied our first craving.

I could go for many times and for a long time. That was why men had devised the tattoo of regeneration, otherwise why would there be so many patterns on the crotch?

"Your parents argued about something for a long time, then they made up and went to a restaurant. So I..." explained Eika, but I pulled her close to me. "Genji, what, again? Give me time to breathe!"

"No way. We don't have a lot of time, and I intend to use it as much as possible!" I said, almost growling.

I got a whole ocean of Psy today...

* * *

The time allotted for my imaginary recovery passed by in a flash. Matvey Nikolaevich crammed in so much training that I could barely drag my feet. If not for my runes, then I would have to face no improvement in my abilities, and at least exhaustion, if not, more likely, just getting killed by all the stuff the Yakut and his evil team had me do.

And they all set about tasking me after the had their "slightly" messy adventure in the machine oil, while I was strolling through the clean corridors of the polygon. But formally, that was not my fault, and actually the unlucky exam was publicly, at the insistence of my mother, no less, recognized as a mistake. But I suspected that they held a grudge for the trick with leading them the wrong way and throwing away my sensors. Otherwise how could you explain the fervor of those sadists?

Squeezed out like a lemon, I recovered only thanks to my Psy, and in the evening I set out for a nightly sex-marathon with Eika, who was as insatiable as I was. Sometimes I even started to doubt my own abilities. That sort of the thing was even beyond the rune's capabilities. But my reward was a girl leaving towards the morning on shaking legs.

But I myself was extremely tired after the marathon. I was almost not sleeping at all, especially since after Eika left I was trying to master all the Psy I just got. It was actually starting to less and less each time. I had to either take a break or, possibly, try with a different girl. Hmm. I had some strange abilities. I was holding on only because of the runes, but it was clear they had their own limits. Anyway, this time I went to Gakko Academy with hardly any rest at all. But there would be a place to catch up on sleep.

Kiyoko was already waiting for me in the classroom. The Takada clan had finished their war with the Mori clan and my girlfriend, along with her older sister, had been back at school for a few days. I knew all the subjects very well, so I could take the last desk in the lessons and try to get some rest. The teachers at Gakko paid very little attention to their students, since the goal of institutions for wizards was something else entirely. So I had ample opportunities to catch some rest.

And around the corner I would have the opportunity to test my theory about needing to change girls to increase the flow of Psy. I had at least two possible candidates for that experiment at school, Kiyoko and Fumiko, the English teacher. That was if you didn't consider Tomoko Yasuda's crude efforts. And after classes, as the boss, I had every excuse to attentively check the work of our general director, Yoshiko Sakurawa. The future was looking bright.

Remembering that experience was born from painful mistakes, I tried to much sure I was as well-equipped for school as possible. Who knew what was waiting for me within one of the most dangerous educational institutions in the city? My flail, my ruler, my tactical pens, the Gantan, steel-toed boots... Just everything that my trainers could work up for the self-defense of an ungifted in a school for wizards. This little ritual with my kit had already somehow become familiar, even calming.

Like a warrior, sharpening his sword before battle, I inspected my ruler, putting its edge in the rays of the sun streaming in. Checking their balance carefully. I arrayed my metal pens into different pockets. I made sure that my flail would quickly and easily fly out of my sleeve and roll the heavy Gantan balls around over my palm. Now we could even change the lead for a heavier metal, since my runes of strength and speed would turn the dangerous weapon into one that was entirely fatal.

As usual, I was a little late arriving to school. I approached the lockers in hope that I would hear the familiar click-clack of heels behind me, but no such luck. Considering that we didn't have English class today, the chances of meeting with Fumiko without Kiyoko around were close to zero. Too bad, but what could you do? I headed off to class with a heavy heart.

But I didn't manage to make it there without a new adventure. Some poser threw a big coin at me. I walked through the school with my Psy tattoos cranked up to the max, so I automatically caught the little round thing flying towards my head and just as automatically threw it back at the clown sitting on the windowsill.

Book Two

The boy definitely wasn't expecting me to respond so quickly and took the coin square in the nose. Humiliating. To tell the truth, I wasn't really aiming at all when I sent the metal circle back at its owner, I just had a guffawing mug in front of me and decided to wipe the smug smile right off it without even thinking about it.

The hooligan clammed up after getting conked on the snout by the piece of metal. He clearly had some comment ready, hoping that the coin would smash into my nose and not his. But all his faux-politeness dissipated when his own weapon came across the bridge of his nose. You couldn't argue that he didn't get hit across the face by the same thing he was hoping to get me with.

"Hey, what's wrong with you?" asked my aggressor, absurdly.

"Me? Nothing. What's wrong with you?" My tone was deliberately causal, while my eyes scanned the hallway and its several doorways for friends of the kid. If this was a trap, then he definitely wasn't alone. They might attack in a group, so I had to ensure that my back was safe in advance.

"You threw a coin at my face!" The idiot was still trying to blame me for it. What was even going on here? But there was no one around, which meant that if there was a fight, it would be one on one.

"Oh yeah? It seems to me like I was just

giving back what you threw at me," I said, smiling wide. Before a fight you had to undercut your opponent's vigilance, which would give plus twenty points to your attacks, ha.

"You're a confident guy!" The hooligan walked toward me, having hopped down from the windowsill. "It seems I was wrong. This is my coin, and your response was the right one."

The boy seemed stringy, dry, average height, and with a vague, almost gray appearance. But his eyes... His eyes gave away the predatory animal that was hiding in the shape of a nerd. The unknown guy stood firmly, and his deceptively light figure covered sinews, muscles, and tendons that were hard as steel. One more dangerous opponent. I wondered where he was from. All the while the teenage boy was approaching me, then offered his hand for a handshake.

"My name is Raiden Nakata, and I am the leader of the second-year A class," the leader of the gang, smiling in his superiority at once having managed to destroyed the pretensions of Osamu Saito.

"Mine's Genji Tanaka." I smiled and shook his hand back.

The body suddenly became serious. That means he also hadn't recognized me on sight, but had definitely heard about my previous deeds. It was not surprising. Nakata, as far as I knew, had come to Gakko around the end of last school year, becoming famous as a fighter shortly after he broke through, and was now testing his mettle in the school war.

"So you are the one who took over all the second-year classes except mine?" Raiden asked, making sure. I mean, who knows, maybe I just had the same name and surname as the leader of the second-year D class.

"Yes, but if you're wondering, I didn't force anybody. We are allies now, not vassals and lords," I said, trying to dispel all the rumors and insinuations going around about me in the school as soon as possible.

"I understand. Then we should discuss what to do next," suggested Nakata.

"I am ready at any time, but it would be better if the guys from the second-year B and C classes joined us," I responded immediately, not putting off the task.

"Agreed. Let's get together today after the lessons and have lunch together."

"Definitely. We have a lot to talk about," I responded in agreement.

Chapter 22
An Intense Lunch Break

IN THE CLASS I WAS MEET with the excited and hopeful gaze of Kiyoko, cheerful greetings from the warriors of my army, and a downtrodden, fearful fatass Bo. That last one I made sure to not pay any attention to. Gakko Academy itself would punish him for his betrayal and cowardice. Pussies didn't last long in this school. Maybe that was the reason for the government's policies? We, the teenagers, lived like we were in a state of war, and all of our behaviors and character traits were under a magnifying glass here.

It was hard to wear a mask every day for four years, and even harder if you spent all four of those years in constant battles. You couldn't make fake friends here, because the time might come when you would have to take a beating for them. You couldn't throw out false accusations, because you will have to pay for every careless word. If you fell in love, that would be your weak point, and they would try to get to you through that attachment, but a girl could also be a source of strength.

And it would be the same in your adult life. Graduates of the school knew how to choose the right kind of military girlfriend, one they could protect who would not end up being a victim. Here the leaders of the gangs learned to take responsibility for their subordinates, and their vassals mastered the difficult science of raising up their boss with their own strength and honor, thereby raising up themselves as well. Gakko was a real school for life. I could not imagine a more effective way to teach the fickle youths.

With their almost unlimited power, money, and strength, unimaginable for normal people, the members of the powerful families were a hearty mess of arrogance, contempt, and personal license. Why should they strive to climb the wizard ranks? That was definitely difficult and painful, more so when you already had absolutely everything. Why would you try to learn anything when thousands of people were already working for you? Why try to control yourself when you were stronger than a thousand normal people of your own age?

But nobody asked those kinds of questions at Gakko Academy. Here the ranks were a way to survive. Your intellect would help, sure, if you hadn't been gifted with enough strength. But pissing off your peers was basically a death sentence. Everyone here was gifted, all from rich families. Perhaps the government was not wrong to bring us all together here. They just worried a little about giving rise to excessive cruelty. The students were actually right on the edge, and at any time it could break out into all-out war.

The classes went by quickly. I mean, how else, given that I, as planned, was sleeping every available moment. I had the last desk, with the broad back of Ryuen Kato blocking me. I got in some good sleep.

During the break I touched base with Hideo Takayama, Koji Kubo, and Taro Kodama. I told them about the upcoming meeting with Raiden Nakata. Tomoko Yasuda was also essentially a leader of one the teams in our alliance, and it would be a good idea to let her know too. But I was too scared to, with Kiyoko right next to me and her threat vivid in my mind. I give that dangerous task to Hideo, plus he had a crush on her anyway.

Usually the guys ate lunch in the classroom, since the school was still basically at war. Also, all the leaders were back. Everyone was waiting for Akira Takada to send her fighters against Makise Abe or to personally challenge the flippant third-year to a duel. Otherwise the reputation of the strongest gang in the school would be open to doubt.

For the same reason, a punitive raid by Osamu Saito's army on the second-year A class was also expected; these upstart nobodies had to be punished. In principle Osamu should also do the same to me, but thirty fighters, even if they were second-years, would not be that easy to defeat, and he could lose up to half of his army. That was a serious risk.

On top of that, Hiro Sasaki also owed me a beating, since I was sure he had not forgotten the whole thing with his nuts. But here we could keep everything at the level of a personal conflict, since my army had basically nothing to do with Sasaki, and his issue was only with me. Moreover, the upperclassmen had attacked some punk in a group of three and still, by all counts, had messed up. Getting revenge for that would be indecorous, to put it mildly, and if Sasaki brought it to open conflict he would be shunned by the whole school.

And that was not a figure of speech. There were a lot of so-called neutrals and loners at Gakko. Nearly a third of each class didn't belong to any gangs. Some of them simply by force of their character, while others were just seen as weaklings, and it didn't matter if it was a because of a lack of spirit or of body. But there were some that choose to be alone on principle. They could go against the gangs, acting outside of the unwritten rules. That was how they survived. If

Gakko Academy

Hiro, theoretically, decided to recruit loners into his gang by force, then they would unite and resist. That was how they dealt with those who acted badly.

And Saito was not far from that. He was skirting the edges. Hiro Sasaki was a decent guy on the whole, bunch when it came to the letter D, he was an utter maniac. I was worried that he wouldn't see the limits of decency and try to take revenge anyway. But I was not alone now, and we could definitely stand up against our enemies.

In order to make it count, we decided to eat our lunch in the cafeteria today. A deadly locale, given the situation in the school. But if we continued to sit in our classrooms, then we would just remain the downtrodden second-years for the upperclassmen. I could not allow them to think that, otherwise there would come a time when the leaders of the gangs would start splitting my army into pieces.

*   *   *

Gakko Academy's cafeteria today was like a battlefield where three hostile armies had all of a sudden run into each other. Nobody knew what to do in that situation. If you got in a fight with one of them, the third one would happily sit back and watch, reaping the rewards afterward. What about a war between everybody? What for? That would only make the second-years happy.

Book Two

Each gang took a different corner. Boys and girls deliberately spoke loudly, forcing out laughter. They all wanted to show the other sides that they were not afraid in the least. Tensions were rising in the room. Now Captain Manabu isn't happy with the aggressive behavior of one of Hiro's foot soldiers, now Butsu is exchanging looks with someone in Saito Osamu's circle...

At the same time, the leaders of the school gangs were sitting respectfully at a table in the middle of the room. The talks hadn't started in earnest yet, and they were all pretending to be really involved in their food. Still, young mages did need quite a lot of calories, and nobody here was suffering from a loss of appetite. Even the skinny little Akira ate more than a regular special forces fighter could get through in a whole day.

The Gakko Academy cafeteria was pretty nice. You wouldn't get any delicacies there, of course, but there were fresh meat, fish, in-season fruit, and vegetables always in abundance. Nobody was complaining.

Saito preferred the classics, fish, rice, and a bunch of vegetables. He was himself like an eel lurking in murky waters. Cold, dangerous, with a terrifying, serpentine gaze...

Hiro Sasaki went in for European cuisine. They said that his family had lived among the Gaijin for a long time, and maybe that's why he was so weird? He looked like a normal guy, hardly different from any of his peers. It was just his eyes, those of a straight psychopath and his touch of insanity and that frightened all of his potential opponents. What could you expect from a man who had gone nuts? He could fly off the handle in the blink of an eye. He had no reason for his insane fury. His own nature was reason enough.

The only more or less normal person in that trio seemed to be Akira Takada. An attractive girl with a lovely, athletic body, highlighted by her short skirt and the uniform jacket hugging her torso. But your first impression was misleading, since Tanaka could never have become a general at Gakko Academy if she hadn't had an explosive character and carefully hidden aggression. There was a warrior hiding inside the girl, one that was constantly blood-thirsty, and once she let it out, neither Hiro nor Osamu would be able to stand against her primordial rage. Symbolically, today Akira had chosen blood sausage with vegetable garnish.

Gathered at that table were real monsters who could, with a single sidelong glance, scare the majority of the students at the school into hiccups. Even alone they were worth a whole army, but with their fighters behind them they were ready to tear up the whole district.

"Okay boys, have you eaten? Is it time to get down to business?" Akira started the dialogue first.

The girl was the champion of the school,

after all. Hiro had taken his lumps from Takada about four times. It seemed like the poor sucker had tried to contest her superiority over him every year at the school, but with no luck. Osamu had tangled with Takada twice, ascribing his defeat the first time to the assistance of Butsu and the other fighters of the fourth-year A class. The second one, though, was a real duel and Saito had been forced to the bitter admission that Akira's clan skills were head and shoulders above his base tricks and her fury was in no way inferior to Osamu's venomous cruelty.

"I have only one question," said Hiro Sasaki, barreling right out the gate. "Are you protecting Genji Tanaka from the second-year D class?"

"Oh what, the cracked nut is looking for revenge?" Osamu Saito couldn't stop himself from teasing. The story of the "Ball Breaker" was still popular within Gakko Academy, and even, it was said, had started becoming famous in the neighboring schools, which must have incensed the proud Hiro.

"Shut your mouth!" Sasaki shouted, since the joke was in fact very insulting. "I have never yet fought with you, but maybe the time has come to find out which of us is the strongest?"

"I'm ready whenever, just don't forget your jockstrap," Saito said, not leaving it alone. He wouldn't be a general at Gakko if he couldn't respond immediately to threats.

"Hey! Hotheads! We are here to discuss

business. If you want to figure out what's going on between you two, do it somewhere else," Akira said, trying to cool things down. "Your men are watching you, and you're acting like children!"

"This snake started it!" Hiro said, justifiably upset.

"Don't be such a baby," Osamu said, mockingly. "I didn't say anything awful, just the truth. Maybe it was insulting, but it was true!"

"Guys, we are never going to agree on anything like this. Take a deep breath and let's talk calmly, without these back-and-forth jabs and insults," said the elder Takada, once again acting as the voice of reason.

"Fine," said Hiro, still upset, through clenched teeth.

"I'm not even that worked up," responded Saito, still mocking, but giving a little.

"Okay, boys, we need to end this cold war—" Akira continued, until rudely interrupted by Osamu Saito.

"What the hell is this? Are they not afraid at all?" The leader of the fourth-year C class frowned threateningly, staring at one of the entrances to the cafeteria. "Those nobodies are stepping in on us!"

"No fear at all," said Hiro Sasaki bleakly, supporting his enemy. When it came to Genji Tanaka those two were surprisingly supportive of each other.

"Calm down, the young ones also have the

right to eat." Takada smiled, being the only one there who didn't view the second-years coming in as a challenge.

"So you are protecting your younger sister and her boyfriend?" hissed Saito, forebodingly.

"You're too friendly to those upstarts," Hiro said right after.

"You lost your minds? You want to ask them why they came to eat here? It's your funeral, and I would love to see it!" Akira spat, angrily, not knowing what made her more upset. Was it the impudent arrival of Genji's gang that had her out of sorts, or was it the behavior of her overly anxious classmates?

Right then the second-years confidently set about getting their food, all the while freely and casually, as far as you could tell, talking and laughing with each other, unintentionally copying the upper-class gangs' behavior. Considering that Manabu still had an axe to grind for the second-year D and C classes, and Hiro Sakaki hated Genji Tanaka with all his heart, the number of angry looks and the amount of tension had risen significantly. The cafeteria was clearly about to turn into the scene of a massive battle.

But the nobodies had not come unprepared. And catching them off-guard or provoking them into an unfair battle would be no easy task. The Kato brothers and their fighters were carefully monitoring the situation, watching everyone around the tables taken by Genji's team. Kubo and Kodama's people were in charge of getting food to the table. Hideo Takayama along with his bruisers and Tomoko's nerds were in reserve.

The experienced veterans of school fights knew right away that they couldn't pull anything off extemporaneously. Any provocation, like trying to knock over a tray of food or hit on a pretty young girl, would be met with badass second-years unafraid to fight back. Tanaka had too many calm and collected guys at his back, they had too skillfully taken up posts in the school cafeteria.

They might beat them with experience and numbers, but victory would definitely not come easily. The arrogant kids were ready to fight back. But things were coming to a head. Osamu Saito and Hiro Sasaki's fighters were already starting to discuss things with one another, coming together in small, indignant bands, in groups of three or five.

Numerically the two gangs of the upperclassmen were one and a half times larger than Genji Tanaka's, and if you took into account their mastery of magic and hand-to-hand combat, they clearly had the advantage. Both sides could tell that a conflict was unavoidable. Genji's supporters knew that they would be crushed, but they were still ready to put up a decent resistance. The fighters of Hiro and Osamu's armies were not sure of each other, and looked on Akira's gang with trepidation. That led them to waste too much and miss out on the right moment for an attack.

All of a sudden Makise Abe's gang entered the cafeteria. It seemed like the third-year had somehow found a way to increase the number of fighters in his gang without taking over any classes. He had been joined by neutrals from the second, third, and even fourth years. Maybe those people's parents were in some way connect to the Abe clan. It was not a popular thing to do at Gakko, since those guys were taking a big risk, now surrounded in their own classrooms by enemies most of the time. But now Abe's gang was here, comparable in number with the forces of Hiro Sasaki. And Makise had clearly come to make a statement about himself and his people.

But the day's surprises did not stop there. Raiden Nakata entered the cafeteria, in person. The boy came up to Genji, surrounded by his own fighters from the second-year A class. And, seeing how the leaders and normal members of the second-year gangs were greeting each other warmly, it was clear that Tanaka, if he hadn't subjugated Raiden, had at least entered some sort of military alliance with the impulsive boy. Now the results of a confrontation were even more difficult to predict, since there were too many participants, with too many unknowns.

Gakko Academy

* * *

"Genji, my bro, I see that you decided to get some grub?" Raiden said, greeting me with a little joke, as if we hadn't met each other that morning.

"Yeah, I decided to stave off my hunger before our shared dinner, and also, I was afraid I would die of hunger before these never-ending lessons finally finished," I said, maintaining the joking tone of the leader of the second-year A class.

"This is a bit on an intense situation. You sure you're not gonna get indigestion?" Raiden was loudly trying to get their goat, showing off. The boy couldn't help but realize that every single one of his words would catch the ears of multiple members of the upper-class gangs.

"Nah, I'm a teenager, right now every calorie gets used. And this is pretty much normal. Can't I just eat at Gakko Academy?" I asked, not just to Nakata, but to everyone around.

"What's good, guys?" Makise approached, interrupting our conversation suddenly.

To tell the truth, I had noticed him coming a while back and was slightly tense. After all, our last meeting had ended with hospital visits on both sides.

"Whatever's good for you," answered Raiden, greeting him peacefully.

"Hey," I answered monosyllabically, not yet

knowing how to respond.

"Genji, you are a fine general at our school. I propose that we forget our previous disagreements," said the leader of the third-year B class, holding out his hand.

"Done," I said, firmly shaking his hand.

"Oh... right! You guys fought at the hospital, right?" Raiden Nakata said, butting right into our conversation. The guy seemed like a real busybody.

"Yeah, that happened," grumbled the Abe clan prodigy.

"Ah, but you see, Raiden, we are now good friends," I said, trying to shut the tactless Nakata up.

"Got it, awesome. So we should fight with you? Then all our classes can be friends?" Raiden joked again.

"What do we do now?" Makise asked, bringing to conversation back to serious topics.

"Eat?" I said, half rhetorically.

"Of course, that's personally what I came here for," broke in Nakata again. "I mean, we could fight the upperclassmen, but, whatever, not that important..."

Chapter 23

The Intense Lunch Break Continues

FOLLOWING THE PRECEDENT set by the leaders of the upper class gangs we all sat around one table, Genji, Makise Abe, and Raiden Nakata. Tanaka's allies from the second-year C and B classes were also supposed to sit near beside them, but they were in no hurry, knowing that today a seat at the leaders table might get you a beating. The guys had already basically accepted Genji's leadership. Since they allowed him to take responsibility for everyone this time, it would be easier for them to accept his as leader moving forward.

The leaders of the younger groups grabbed a mountain of food and began speaking formally with each other. At the same time, the second-year fighters and Abe's army set up a defensive ring around them. A fragile equilibrium once again reigned in the room. None of the groups had a decisive advantage over any of the others. Only if Akira Takada chose to support Saito and Hiro would the situation be any different.

But the girl had not yet decided what would be best for her. One possibility was for her to make an alliance with the younger classes and, at least for the rest of the year, rule over Gakko Academy. With the competition coming up that would be amazing. And if you considered the opposition from Okubo Academy, the fragile peace with Itigai, and the unclear intentions of the gangs from Gold Street and the Radaki region, then gaining control of the school was of utmost importance.

These young kids didn't yet understand that the bloody battles at the school were just child's play compared to what happened outside. The adolescent gangs fought with even more violence, and people could fan the flames of conflict between old academies. So leaders who couldn't get enough fighters under their control became easy prey for monsters like Noburo Surezawa.

Takada had been trying to impress the necessity of joining together onto the unstable Hiro Sasaki and the overly-ambitious Osamu Saito, but in vain. Those blockheaded idiots only thought about themselves. The first was obsessed with the idea of taking over all the D classes, the damned fool. While the second only thought about his own power and his disgusting activities destroyed any desire to work with him. That snake clearly didn't understand that soon even his own fighters would be jumping ship.

Given those circumstance, an alliance with Genji Tanaka was looking very attractive. Moreover, everything could be done within family affairs, as they say. Genji to Kiyoko to Akira, it was a logical chain. There was just one problem. As soon as Takada entered into an alliance with Genji, Hiro and Osamu, despite their mutual dislike for one another, could not fail to team up. There was nothing like an outside threat to unite enemies!

But, in light of the fact that the illustrious second-year had managed to attract Makise Abe and Raiden Nakata to his side, even a union of those old enemies seemed meager in comparison with the pair of Takada and Tanaka. Akira turned all those thoughts over in her mind, mechanically chewing and swallowing her food. What finally got her out of her deep thoughts was the terrible voice of Osamu Saito.

"So what, are we just going to live with the audacity of these upstarts?" he hissed. Ambition was literally choking the wicked leader of the fourth-year C class.

"What do you propose, then?" Akira was dissembling a little. Her head was still spinning with thoughts of a possible alliance. "You want a slaughter here, every man for himself?"

"Hmm... What for? You can join my side along with Hiro, and we will just wipe them out. There are more of us, and we are older," said Saito, with reason.

"But why?" asked the elder Takada, also with reason.

"They piss me off," answered Osamu immediately. These delinquents never needed a reason to beat someone up. They were just overjoyed at any opportunity to fight.

"Ha, what a great reason! If you couldn't tell, that was sarcasm. But I, unlike you, don't get into fights for no reason. But you're the only one who wants this pointless conflict!" Akira said, hammering home the point.

"I only want Genji Tanaka and his D class," Hiro Sasaki said, apropos of nothing. The boy was clearly a psychopath, the kind you could take advantage of for a while, but long-term cooperation was dangerous, like lighting a fire on a nuke to cook an omelet.

"Yeah, okay..." Akira didn't know what to say. And these were the guys who basically ran Gakko Academy. She definitely needed to make an alliance with the young Tanaka. He was the most decent one out of the three.

"Hiro, I have thirty guys and you have twenty. Nearly half of them are fourth-years, and the rest are one year younger. There are around forty second-years, and Makise has brought a little more than twenty fighters. Numerically we are practically the same, but we still have the advantage," Osamu Saito said, doing some simple calculations.

"Are you saying we should attack without Takada?" Sasaki asked, somewhat dismayed.

"Well, if Akira promises that neither she nor her people will interfere in the conflict," Saito said, prudently.

Now it was Akira's turn to give it some thought. If she really wanted an alliance with Genji, then she had to break with Osamu and Hiro right now. On the other hand, it was completely unclear how Makise Abe would react their possible cooperation, since he was still at loggerheads with Butsu. That wasn't even talking about Raiden, who, as far as anyone could tell, had no intention of being subordinate to anyone. There were too many things that weren't clear, so she couldn't make a reasoned decision, and her intuition, as if to spite her, was silent on the matter.

"Osamu, you are always trying to get something out of me." Since she hadn't decided anything, Akira tried to get out of the situation. "I don't owe you or your men anything. The upstarts don't bother me personally at all. Why should my army guarantee good conditions for your fight with them? What do I get out of it, except you two possibly get stronger?"

"Well, then join us!" Saito offered again.

"I don't want to fight," said Akira. "Why are you trying to draw me into your plan of action?"

"Hey! I'm giving you a lot of choices and you won't agree to any of them." Osamu, the hothead, was beginning to lose his cool.

"Yeah? You're only telling me to fight or scram. Should I just follow your lead, doing only what you allow me to? Why don't you go climb a mountain?" Akira was upset.

"Uhhh, why?" Saito couldn't understand.

"So you can scratch your balls!" snapped Akira, apparently comparing Saito to a subspecies of monkey that was always messing around in the national park.

"Hmm. That was kind of insulting. Fah, Akira, and they say your family—" Saito started responding to the jab.

"Shut your mouth, unless you want me to shove that joke right back down your trap." The girl's threat was ridiculous with her charming little fists. If you didn't know Takada then the threat would only make you laugh. But Osamu took it seriously. He remembered vividly how vicious the female leader of the strongest gang in school could be.

"Yeah, yeah, I'm done." Despite all his idiosyncrasies, Saito knew how to back down when he perceived a real threat.

"And I know how we can let off some steam without making a huge fight," Hiro butted in again. The man was clearly going crazy, like his brain was leaking onto the floor. "I will challenge Genji to a duel."

"Hmm. Makes sense. You can break his bones and finally calm down," stated Saito, not for one second doubting the outcome of the duel. "And I'll probably take on Raiden Nakata... Who else have they got?"

"Takayama, Kubo, Kodama, and the Kato brothers, who might be the strongest fighters in the second year," Akira said, casually recalling what her sister had said.

"True, but they are not sitting at the leaders table. Don't you want to get some revenge?" The spiteful Osamu was still needling Takada. "Don't you think Makise went too far with Butsu? He's definitely not respecting your gang, haha..."

"Goddamn manipulator!" Akira said to herself, but capitulated anyway. The honor of the gang had to be restored no matter what. "I will challenge Makise to a duel, even though there is little honor in fighting young kids."

"Yes, true, we are taking a big risk. Victory will bring no glory, and defeat will be remembered by everyone for a long time," answered Osamu Saito philosophically.

* * *

I ate, mechanically chewing my pieces of food. Maybe the decision to come here had been strategically viable, but being in this kind of environment was simply unbearable. My gut was screaming, "TROUBLE, TROUBLE!" But appearances had to be maintained. I was with some of the coolest guys at Gakko Academy, after all.

The prodigy of the Abe clan had taken the risk of continuing his education at the school, even after everybody in the district learned about him through my direct involvement. Now the boy was accompanied by a massive contingent of security every time he went to school and back home. He had to have balls of steel to keep studying in a public institution, and it was even more brave that he had maintained that decision in the face of his parents.

As for Raiden Nakata, he seemed to be the kind of person who didn't take anything seriously. He was smiling happily, gulping down massive portions of meat and vegetables in spite of his unimpressive frame. The boy was constantly looking around, hardly bothered at all by the angry glances of the upperclassmen. Jesus! I was even kind of jealous of his self-control and composure. He was either insanely brave or utterly stupid. But there was another possibility, that he was actually an amazing fighter. Time would tell.

As if to justify my fears, the trio of upper class leaders wiped their lips with pageantry, then, still chewing their food, started heading over to us. Ah, yeah, even an idiot could tell that trouble was on its way. And here I thought we might get out without a problem. I did not want to go back to the hospital, fuck!

Osamu Saito started talking first. He was walking a little ahead of the others since he had been sitting closest from the beginning.

"Which one of you is Raiden Nakata?" Saito asked, dispassionately, with his cold, terrifying, fish-like gaze, but it had no effect on the guys sitting at our table.

"That's me," Raiden answered calmly, continuing digging into his fried fish with a fork.

"It's impolite to eat when talking with an elder," Osamu said to Nakata, who was still chewing.

"Yeah, so what? It's impolite to interrupt someone's dinner when you don't even know them," Raiden responded, fighting back. "If you want to talk, wait. I'm not done eating."

"How uncivilized the youth are," Saito said, acting upset, looking for support from his companions, but they were stubbornly silent. "Maybe I should teach you some manners, Nakata?"

"What are you dicking for, Saito? I fought your captain and I'm not afraid to fight you!" Raiden responded flippantly and then, to make him mad, said, "But have the decency to let a guy finish eating."

"Oh, you cocksure whelp!" Osamu barely

kept himself from hitting the table, stopped in the nick of time by Akira. "Duel in the school arena, you and me, after lunch!"

"Done, right after I finish having a drink with my boys," answered Raiden boisterously, not showing the slightest worry about the upcoming fight.

"Don't be late," Saito said, getting in the last word.

There was a short pause. But I had no illusions that Akira Takada and Hiro Sasaki had come as seconds for Osamu Saito. The leaders were not close enough friends to do that kind of service for each other. Probably this whole deal with challenging the younger kids to duels was going to continue. And I didn't have to wait long.

Makise, did you think I would just let your fiasco with my captain go unpunished?" Akira began her part. It was to be expected. Hiro and I had a lot of unfinished business, and for Takada to fight with her sister's boyfriend would be utterly gauche. It would be one thing if I started it myself, but it would be a whole other thing if she herself challenged a second-year who had no beef with her. So Akira, as predicted, instead decided to take care of the one who had insulted her captain.

"Oh, so Butsu decided to hide behind your skirt?" Makise joked, predictably. And it was true, the fourth-year was not calling the clearly weaker opponent to a fight himself, but hiding in the shadow of the best fighter in the school.

"None of your damn business," answered Akira sharply and pronounced peremptorily, "I am a general of Gakko Academy, and I decide for myself who I will fight with and when."

"As you wish," sighed Makise theatrically, working the crowd. "The wish of a woman is my command!"

"We will go after these two." Akira nodded towards Saito and Nakata.

"Agreed." Makise smiled broadly, showing that he wasn't worried at all about the upcoming fight. You had to maintain appearances in front of your subordinates. Win or lose, Abe's authority would increase after the duel no matter what.

You didn't have to be a genius to guess that my turn was next. Unfortunately, I couldn't be as blasé as my companions. My opponent was undoubtedly a total psycho, as I realized in our first meeting. Or had he not gone completely crazy by then? Maybe my attack on his nuts was the straw that broke the camel's back for Hiro? You might laugh, but the guy scared me. Yeah, I might have been able to take him on once, but an insane person was always scary, not for their strength, but for their unpredictability.

Hiro Sasaki wound up like a cat before pouncing. He had obviously not been paying attention to the end of the conversation between Akira and Makise, just twitching like he was having a seizure. The guy clearly couldn't wait to get at me, and he took the conversation between Saito and Takada as a necessary, if annoying, hurdle to get past. As soon as the girl agreed to the duel he jumped right into the conversation without a pause.

"You, me, the arena, after them. No weapons!" The dumbass pointed at me with his finger and stuttered his conditions. I got the impression that he was so excited about the upcoming fight that he was barely unable to keep himself from drooling. Damn, it was like a cracked his nuts and broke his brain.

"Who are you to tell me the conditions of our duel?" I protested sensibly. "Personally, I plan on using everything I have against you. Including the flail that you know so well."

At those words the small metal ball on its chain flew out of my sleeve like I was waving a magic wand. Hiro Sasaki shuddered and unconsciously crossed his legs, covering his crotch. All this did not go unnoticed by the partisans of both my and the opposing side. The experience hooligans understood immediately, completely sympathizing with Sasaki's behavior.

Harsh laughter and whispers about "Ball Breakers" and omelets could be heard all around, and the women seemed to take joy in the possibility of Hiro's future impotence. All of that noise was going on in the background, but it was enough to enrage the hot-tempered Sasaki, since all he needed was the smallest reminder of that awful day when his ability to procreate was but in real danger.

"The gifted are not allowed to use things like that in a duel," Sasaki shouted, spraying saliva, losing face not only in front of my teammates, but also his own allies. He just took everything too emotionally.

"The key word there is, the gifted," I muttered calmly.

"What? What do you mean by that?!" the psychopath shouted in a fit of temper, but he was already started to get what I meant.

"Genji is saying that he is not a wizard, and so our rules do not apply to him," interjected Akira Takada.

I stared at my opponent in silence, trying to piss him off even more. I had no real reason to talk. I had said everything I wanted to say. If the upperclassmen believed that my weapons were breaking some written or unwritten rules, then it was up to them to do something about it. And this was not a friendly match like the one with Kodama and Kubo, but a serious duel between an ungifted second-year and one of the strongest fighters in the fourth-year.

"Fine," hissed Sasaki through his teeth, barely hiding his disappointment and even a hint of fear. "You can use your stupid things, they won't help you anyway!"

His false confidence wasn't fooling anyone. Despite his insanity, Hiro was clearly afraid. Was he afraid of the duel with me? Probably not. It was just the natural fear of all men who had been cracked in the nuts and were now in a similar situation. But for Hiro that phobia was exaggerated by his sick imagination, making the leader of the gang move awkwardly, blush, and lose his cool.

"Okay then," Akira Takada, the champion of the school, went over the rules, "the first fight is Raiden and Osamu, the second is Makise and I, and the third is Genji and Hiro!"

Chapter 24

Getting Ready for the Duels

THE SCHOOL ARENA WAS NOT as complicated as the one at ABS Club or as well-outfitted as in the professional duel halls. But it was clear that the equipment was not going unused. The worn out walls, the rickety stands for the audience, the dents in the firm mats the covered the floor of the arena, the cracked leather of the guards covering the steel slats, all of that gave support to the notion that the students of Gakko Academy spent nearly as much time dueling as they did studying math.

The opposing sides split up, going to two different changing rooms, the older students in the red one and the younger students in the blue one. How would Akira change in the presence of her ten fighters? Ah, there were probably completely separate rooms, even with individual showers. When it came to functionality everything was of the highest order, with clean washrooms, changing rooms scrubbed until they shone, no odious smells, a toilet, water coolers. They were all little things, but without them, trying to get ready for a duel and have a real fight would be much harder.

Only the fighters themselves and their closest seconds were in the changing rooms. I had Takeshi Kato and Taro Kodama with me, and Makise had one of the fourth-year neutrals with him. There were rumors that he was a strong fighter who just didn't like the company of people, otherwise he might have become one of the leaders of the school. Raiden Nakata was completely alone. His fighters and the members of my team and Abe's all offered to help him, but he stubbornly refused. It seemed like there was some family secret here, and I wasn't the only person who thought that. So nobody insisted too much.

Everyone else went to the viewing areas. Fighters needed a lot of air, quiet, and the chance to hype themselves up before a fight. I would be going last, so I had time to pep up and stretch my muscles. I did some work with strike pads that Takeshi was holding, but not really enthusiastically, just a bit of shadowboxing. Makise was doing the same, although he was also pretending to use magic. It was fascinating to watch, sometimes, at the right moments, his hands would flash like streetlights.

Raiden Nakata just locked himself in his own changing room and didn't come out into the main area. If this were Skayd, I would assume that he was pumping himself up with space marine stimulants. If I had just a couple tubes of those things I would absolutely crush any of the students here. But on Genji's world doping wasn't a big thing, since it was too weak. It did pump up the ungifted, of course, but not enough for them to beat a wizard. It could do something for wizards, but the comedown was awful, and the results were unpredictable. I mean, there were rumors about the new concoctions from the Biotech Corporation... But it's not like a student could use something like that. But then again, something in my memory was coming up about Raiden's parents, who were somehow connected to Biotech... But there was nothing to gain from wracking my brains over other people's secrets. I had enough of my own skeletons in the closet.

But I did need to try to remember something about that while using my rune of concentration. I, obviously, was far away from any scientific research like that, but everybody knew that the breakthrough in military stimulants came from the discovery of some fairly simple substance, by the standards of scientists of course. It wasn't the active ingredient either, but some kind of catalyst that increased the stimulating effect.

The substance had first been isolated from a wild animal specimen from one of the planets in the untamed cosmos. They had just fought too effectively, the small-looking predators, would could, terrifying to consider, tear apart the cyborg soldiers of the advanced reconnaissance. Just so you understand, these were the kinds of monster who would eat the local wizards for breakfast, one after another. Okay, I might be exaggerating a little, but there were no weaklings allowed in the advanced reconnaissance.

So, when this miracle medicine was synthesized, it surprised everyone how simple the formula was and how such a developed civilization had not yet made it themselves. The statements of expert researchers made it clear that even monkeys in the era before space travel could have made something similar. Something so simple, even in the technology needed. Damn, maybe if I tried real hard to remember my biology classes, I could make something similar in this world?

I mean, not me myself, but I had money, I could buy a lab. Thankfully the medical department in my holding company was one of the leading commercial ventures. I would just finance research in the right direction and voilà. Hmm. It was a good idea, but I had been a really dummy in biology and chemistry on Skayd. And it was pretty doubtful that anything like that remained in my mind, even subconsciously. Then again, a general biotech course with a specialization in human modification had been necessary for Psy masters. Clearly I needed to do some work with my memory.

Anyway, it was possible that something from vacuum work or discoveries in energy my come in handy later. I would first have to carefully study the accomplishments of local science and how it was helped by magic. Then I would have to compare it with the things that were considered common knowledge in the civilized cosmos. Sometimes, even if you don't know how, but just which way to go, you can strongly influence the final results. I had overlooked the rune of shadow, and there were probably thousands of things like that in science too.

These thoughts were running through my head, distracting me from the task at hand. Although I wasn't actually to worried about my upcoming fight with Hiro Sasaki. I had beat him once, I could do it again. My advantage was that I had all my weapons with me. That meant the long-range attack with the Gantan, the ruler and the flail at mid-range, and my tactical pens and my steel-toed boots in close quarters. Not too shabby.

It was just basic logic that worried me now. Hiro had too easily agreed to these conditions that were not very good for him. Just writing all off as him being a psycho would be too careless. Sasaki had been fighting in Gakko Academy for three years straight and had held his own against very many people, even if you considered that he wasn't trying to take over other classes.

A guy like could not be a terrible fighter. And that went not just for his physical condition, but his intellect too. Hiro could not be considered a tactician pure and simple. It wasn't so easy for him to get to strategy, probably, but to maintain his power he must have some sort of God-given talent for it. I couldn't relax. I had to be ready for anything. This time my opponent was ready and had a lot of time to think about how to beat me.

At the same time, the administration of the school was preparing everything for a grand series of duels, at least at the school level. Just the fact that three of the strongest fighters were going to fight in one day made today's event one of the most significant in the history of Gakko Academy. Moreover, today all the leaders of the educational institution were present at the arena, meaning that at least the whole school would be in the audience.

There were professional automatic cameras all around filming everything. The picture was sent to numerous monitors and screens. In the changing room where were getting ready for the fight, there were a total of three televisions showing the scene. We could watch everything that was happening from multiple angles and immerse ourselves in the atmosphere of the dueling arena without directly participating.

They said that especially interesting duels, chosen by the administration of the Ministry of Defense, were broadcast on an intramural network. As far as I knew it was so nobody could ever relax. That is, they showed these how these monsters acted in the academies of the country in real time. I got it. It was very stimulating, especially for those who were trying to climb to the top and thought they were the hottest shit. And now boom, you had yourself the spectacle of an awe-inspiring duel.

So, our fights had all possibility of becoming common knowledge, and not just because the strongest fighters in the school were taking part in them. There was also a societal factor at play here. The upperclassmen had taken it upon themselves to teach a lesson to the second-years, who were all interesting fighters in their own ways. The upperclassmen were already fairly well-known for their participation in numerous intramural competitions and just normal street brawls. But the younger ones were at best only slightly inferior to their opponents, which might make the fights more interesting.

Raiden Nakata was one of the few gifted who put stock in speed. And he also had some vague connection to the recently much talked-about Biotech Corporation. Makise was the prodigy of the Abe clan, and it was rare to see talents like that in a dueling arena, usually they were protected like special treasures. And then there was me, a true sensation. I was not a wizard, in a duel with one of the strongest fourth-years. If we won or even if it ended in a draw, that would turn the whole wizarding world on its head. I mean, we would be breaking the mold, at least.

The cameras first showed the as-yet empty arena, and then the spectators' stands, filled to capacity. I picked out Kiyoko and the Wada twins among my classmates. My girlfriend had two reasons to worry today. Both her sister and her young man were fighting today. So the girl was in a rough situation, but I wasn't worried about her. The Wada twins would keep her out of harm's way and console her if anything happened.

Dammit! As if on purpose the next scene showed me Tomoko Yasuda. What a bitch! She was staring like she was looking into my soul with her big round eyes. She was my age, but she carried herself like an experienced courtesan, a dangerously predatory and insanely sexy woman. Your tongue wouldn't even allow you to call her a girl. Hideo Takayama was hovering around her again, but she was keeping him at bay with a screen of nerds and clearly had eyes only for me. Damn, it was getting to me...

A loggia was set up for the teachers, separate from the students. The principal, as usual, was missing, but Ketsu Aoki was in his element. The all-powerful head teacher was giving orders, speaking on the telephone, agreeing to something, making arrangements. Basically, he was entirely in charge of the proceedings. There were a couple of assistants behind him, a few teachers, and some representatives of the security forces paying close attention to some instructions.

And slightly to left my favorite teacher had taken a spot. That was interesting... Mrs. Fumiko Ono, the object of my youthful desires, with whom I had almost gone all the way, was, for some reason, in the inner circle of the head teacher. Normal teachers both sit farther away and hear less, but Fumiko was, if not with them, at least very close. Why? Was the connection personal or professional? I would not be surprised if it was both.

In this world my amorous intentions towards the English teacher and her unexpected requiting of them would be seen in a completely different light. My father had told me multiple times that access to the school was forbidden to the clan's security forces and he had absolutely no control over what happened at Gakko, not even able to influence it indirectly. The fact that the Katos had made any sort of inroads there at all was a huge blunder on the part of the school, since such things were usually ruthlessly rooted out.

It was possible that I had become a pawn in one of Ketsu Aoki's games. And so Fumiko Ono was one of his means of influencing me, huh? So then why was he showing her off so casually? Maybe they were playing at sincerity? As if the spy had decided to play with her cards on the table, switching sides to the student? Love, schmove... But then again, nobody was pushing me to do anything. Strange!

Maybe I was just overthinking everything, though. I mean, it was a little too much for just a regular academy. Probably there just hadn't been any other seats, and so Fumiko sat in a free one, and Aoki didn't have anything he needed to hide, so there was no need to keep track of the closest ones so carefully. Two of her co-workers were sitting next to the teacher too, supporting that view. Fah, Jesus, I was would soon become paranoid, becoming just like my opponent Hiro Sasaki. One hit on the balls today and boom! Fah, fah, all this trash going through my head was going to jynx me.

Well, it seemed like things had started. A professional referee was walking out to the center of the arena, and two teams of professional medical professionals had taken up places that had been set out for them. Two wide passages split the room into equal halves. It so happened that the supporters of the upperclassmen were sitting on one side, and on the other were the teachers and students of the second-year, as well as Makise Abe's class. Hmm... Even the audience was divided at Gakko today.

Powerful security forces in their full kit

attentively watched the proceedings. It was not entirely impossible that the young wizards could lose it entirely and start a mass battle. In anticipation of just such a scenario, Ketsu Aoki had set up his reserve, nearly two dozen strong fighters. Adult men with composite armor, heads covered with spherical helmets with bulletproof glass, with short clubs and tasers as weapons.

However, even that force might not be enough to stop the teenage gangs. Just in case, then, two five-man school special forces units were lurking in the shadows around the arena. Neither I nor my recipient had actually seen those guys in real life. There were only vague rumors about them. It seemed like Ketsu Aoki had brought some of his fellow retired soldiers to the school. They were definitely badass warriors, the kind that, should anything happen, would flick us into the corners of the room.

The judges began slowing taking their seats. Usually there was only one arbiter on duty, whose job was to mark the end of the duel and determine the victor. Considering that nine out of ten duels ended with one of the sides being completely removed, and that there were no special rules in the arena, that was more than enough. But today was a special day, and all four sides were taken by judges, just in case. They were not professionals, but rather teachers of physical fitness, tactics, and other authorities in martial arts of the schools who were very familiar to the local duelists.

A table was set aside for three from the main commission. Those guys judged made the final evaluation of the corner judges' scores, making the final decision in the case of a contested outcome, and would announce the results. Jesus, everything was somehow so strict and official here. And the place for the second main arbiter was offered to Ketsu Aoki. To his left sat his secretary, his job being to gather the scores, pay attention to protocol, do the counting, and all other paperwork and red tape. And in the center an unknown man was perched imposingly.

As far as I could tell, he was not one of the teachers or workers at Gakko Academy. Did this guy come on purpose, or was he just drawn in by the scene? But the whispers that followed his arrival clearly showed that the man was well-known for something. But he was not within Genji's worldview, so it was another mystery.

"Makise, why are you all staring at the main judge?" I decided to get an answer to my question right away.

"What?" The Abe clan prodigy's eyes narrowed. "That is Mr. Tetsuya Matsumoto, the reigning champion of the games!"

"Damn, you're acting like he's a prince of the blood," I said, surprised at Makise's enthusiasm.

"Genji, are you high or something?" Abe asked, outrage for some incomprehensible reason. "What planet are you from, dude?"

"What? Did I say something wrong?"

"Tanaka, are you not looking at the screen? After the championship the imperial family officially recognized Tetsuya as an illegitimate son of the heir!" Makise's news hit me like a ton of bricks. How had I missed that? "He does not have the status of a prince, of course, and continues to have the surname of his patron, Matsumoto, but he is still recognized to have the blood of the royal dynasty in his veins!"

"Son of a bitch, what is a whole-ass prince doing at Gakko Academy?" Saying I was surprised would be a tremendous understatement.

"They say that he is an old friend of Ketsu Aoki's, and some think that our militant head teacher watched over him in the army. And they definitely got into some serious scrapes together. So it's a great honor for Tetsuya himself to judge us," Abe said, enlightening me once again.

Ah, yeah. How lucky for us. And here I thought all this pageantry with the preparations was in our honor. Fucking hell, a whole-ass prince on the jury, of course the administration was going to do their damnedest. Yeah, now they would be showing us on television, if not to the whole country, at least on the school network. God, I don't like that kind of attention. All of my tricks would be put under a microscope.

By the way the crowd was dying down, it was clear that the time had come. An assistant strode purposefully into the room and announced that we had five minutes to get ready. Raiden Nakata had to come out of his room and take a position by the door. Dammit! He didn't seem to be worked up at all. His breathing was regular, he wasn't sweating a drop... Either this dumbass was neglected even the most basic principles of preparing for a fight, or he was getting ready for the duel in an entirely different way.

Well, the arena would show us whose methods were better.

Chapter 25

The Duel

OSAMU CAME OUT of the red changing room to sparse applause from the upperclassmen. The leader of the fourth-year C class was unloved not only by the younger classes, but even his own supporters. But that barely registered to the cold and snake-like fighter, who was utterly self-controlled, focused, and ready for battle. You could fault the man for his incessant cruelty, violence, and disdain for people, but he was no slob, and not a self-important fool either.

His sister Naomi was his second. She was rumored to be the éminence grise of the third-year A class, meaning Saito's successes among the third-year classes were at least half due to his family ties. The boy was in his street clothes, having only removed his school jacket and rolled up the sleeves of his fancy shirt. This was a tradition at Gakko Academy and many other schools too.

He had no pads on his legs and he was wearing slippers, so if he fell it would hurt. Well, yeah, his hands were pumped up with magic, which was basically the same as protective gloves. His shoes weren't for increasing the power of his kicks like they were for me, since I had the steel toes. Most likely Osamu was used to wearing his semi-athletic moccasins, or just more comfortable.

Saito jumped in place a little, waved to his supporters perfunctorily, and then, crossing his arms over his chest, stood motionless in his corner of the arena.

Now it was Raiden's turn. Jesus, our ally hadn't even gotten around to taking off his jacket. But it wasn't at all standard issue, like mine, clothes made from that fabric wouldn't get in the way of his movement. The whole second-year class heartily supported the fighter and even the older students also shouted somewhat approvingly. As it later turned out, many of them hoped that Nakata would kick the annoying Osamu's ass.

Raiden was either truly overconfident or actually just that crazy, but the guy jumped in the air comically, cockily shot some punches and kicks into the air and as a finale masterfully flipped Saito a double bird. Nakata was on fire.

The vindictive Saito angrily narrowed his eyes, promising pain and suffering to the flippant fool with a single glance.

But Raiden, noticing none of that, continued showing off to the applause of the crowd. His antics with the fourth-year had not gone unnoticed and delighted the crowd even more. Moreover, the operators were, for some reason, showing his middle fingers in close-up on the television screens, adding a hundred points to the kid's reputation, and a full thousand to Osamu's hatred. Referees weren't allowed on to the arena, since a wizard duel could literally spell death for the judge, meaning that Ketsu Aoki announced the start of the duel himself, loudly shouting "FIGHT!" into a microphone.

The two guys slowly approached each other. Osamu, despite his clear superiority in weight, strength, and experience, was on the defensive for some reason, while Raiden walked like he had nothing at all to worry about. Freaking idiot, he wasn't even raising his hands. A few seconds later, and now the fighters were within striking distance. There was a short exchange of blows, and Saito suddenly fell back.

None of the audience members could catch anything, and even I, with my rune of concentration, hadn't been able to really see anything on the television screen. Just for one moment Raiden's arms had sped up enough to be blurry. But I had ascribed it to a bad connection or a fault in the electricity, since everything had gone back to normal in a second. But now Osamu had a cut on his forehead and a small blue bruise on his cheek. Did Raiden really manage to do that?

And now the room was filled with a joyous cry. It looked like the first confrontation was being played back in slow motion on the monitors. It was clearly visible with the cameras that Raiden had done two straight jabs, then, with incredible speed, a one-two punch. A short jab with the left and then a nearly instantaneous cross with the right. Goddamn! Osamu never even saw what hit him!

The overconfident Raiden could have ended the duel with that. He should have added either a left hook or repeated the right. With the speed the boy was dealing out hits, Saito would absolutely have hit the floor, and the just beat him out, an easy victory. The only thing was that Hakata's hits were not as powerful as most wizards'. It was clear that the magic was being spent on speed, and Raiden didn't have enough of the gift left for strength.

But his mass, multiplied by his unbelievable speed, had hardly a lesser effect. One big drawback was that Nakata was not particularly accurate. Wizards could smack you down with frightening power using their pumped-up fists, and no matter what you would get a strong hit, but without that advantage you would have to...

But Raiden, most likely, had been taught by wizards, who didn't seem to get the subtleties of normal boxers, or at least didn't care about them.

Nakata cockily circled around the outwardly confused Saito. The leader of the upperclassmen had still not come to his senses after that short attack. His eye was dripping with blood, and the threat of a lightning-quick attack from his opponent made him shy away from even the smallest hint of him closing the distance. That behavior drew laughter and booing from the crowd.

Our fool couldn't help but react. Nakata struck a pompous pose and started to comically accepting the crowd's admiration. He ever bowed, the idiot. Oh, dammit, I jinxed it! Raiden was actually starting to give the grandstand a bow. At first that tomfoolery was just driving Saito crazy, and he couldn't do anything, but when his opponent, paying no attention to safety, bent at the waist and let his opponent out of his sight, Osamu attacked.

Using your fists to attack downward was pretty awkward, but Saito, experienced in these matters, instead sent a bone-crushing kick towards his opponent's head. At first glance the hit seemed to have reached its target, since Nakata couldn't even manage to lift his stupid overconfident noggin. But after that punishing kick from the fourth-year Raiden was still on his feet, which would not have been possible after taking a blow like that.

The phenomenon had obviously intrigued the jury too, otherwise how would you explain the slow-motion playback of that awesome kick? If the screens weren't lying, at the very moment when Saito's shoe came in contact with Nakata's melon, he had managed, with a great effort, to speed up the raising of his head enough to actually avoid the powerful kick of his opponent. Not entirely, of course, a bit of the attack still caught him, but it was not nearly as deadly as it might have been.

Raiden was incredibly fast, and if he had taken the fight seriously, then that embarrassing blunder would never have occurred. Osamu tried to press the attack, developing on his success, but the somewhat staggered Nakata still managed to keep his distance fairly easily and maintained it for some time. The boy was definitely not faking it. The kick had gotten to him, and he was doing everything in his power to hold on until he recovered.

Osamu Saito also realize that, just as he realized that if he allowed Raiden to get his shit together, then the duel might end with an embarrassing defeat. So the leader of one of the strongest gangs in the school played his trump card. I had to admit that he chose exactly the right moment. Nakata was trying to stay at a distance, so when Saito suddenly increased it, my ally, rather than being careful, instead chose to relax. And that he would pay for.

The fourth-year masterfully demonstrated why older wizards so often had an advantage over newbroken ones. Osamu concentrated his raw power and sent out a small ball of magic which, covering the distance between the fighter, hit Raiden right in the chest. The effect was stunning. Nakata was dazed, losing his ability to figure out what was happening.

Saito dashed in close and amped up the situation, giving him a vicious one-two. The outcome of the fight was, for all the spectators, including myself, a foregone conclusion now. But Raiden had another idea. Rolling mindlessly to the side, the boy hit his opponent with a sprawling swing. The speed and power of the hit were so exceptional that Saito, already celebrating his victory, couldn't react correctly. Now both fighters were dazed. There were only two choices now. Keep your distance, or flail wildly.

A smart person would have chosen the first option, but those two had clearly left their brains at home. In the clinch, the boys started pummeling each other like simple street hooligans. Raiden would get in three or four hits by the time Saito could respond with one. But his attacks had much more weight to them and staggered Nakata, threatening each time to knock out the overly arrogant second-year.

For a moment the whole room stood still,

holding their breaths. Stunning blows rained down from both sides, blood flew in droplets throughout the arena, and the brawl, it seemed, had no end. And then, the more experienced Osamu, as if on cure, went down, avoiding the intended portion of quickened attacks, and, in turn, beat his opponent twice on the body.

It was like Raiden had been hit by a truck. Those fists, pumped up with magic, didn't encounter any resistance and broke his ribs, and the heavy penetrating blow obviously reached even to his internal organs. Nakata fell to the floor to a marionette with its strings cut, and it was clear to everyone that it was over. The medics, seconds, and judges all rushed to the arena.

But the vengeful beast, breaking all the unspoken rules, began beating his opponent, who had started writhing in pain. As if in a hurry to do as much damage as possible, Saito grabbed one of Raiden's arms and broke it with a sudden hit from his knee. But while that could be explained as coming from the heat of the battle and the desire to take out a dangerous opponent while it was still possible, the following kick to the head and punch down with a pumped-up fist were beyond the pale.

The people rushing in pushed the asshole away, but the bastard had finished his dirty business and smiled, self-satisfied. Even the scornful booing of the students couldn't wipe the joyous smile off the greasy face of Osamu Saito. The idiot could never understand that, although he officially had the victory, the hearts of the people had been won that day by the hilarious and unbelievably confident Raiden Nakata.

Nobody could hold us back in the changing room, and we rushed out like a crowd of well-wishers into the arena, but we could no longer see our friend. They had quickly moved him onto a stretcher and sent him to my hospital. I called Yuki Ueno and Yoshiko and asked them to let me know about Raiden as soon as they knew anything about his health. There was nothing else I could do, and I was only comforted by one fact, which was that Nakata was a wizard, so he would definitely get better soon.

* * *

All the while the organizers continued preparing for the next duel as if nothing had happened. Some of the woven mats, damaged in the course of the first duel, were replaced with new ones, and the protective barriers were checked to make sure they were still in working order. Although nothing serious had happened to the protective outline, the regulations still demanded that everything be rigorously tested before the next fight.

Gradually the incensed roar in the stands began to quiet down. Nobody there was against brutality, but the senseless sadism of Saito after he had already won stirred up a whirlwind of indignation. But you had to give Osamu his due. He acted like he couldn't hear the outcry at all. Having come out on top, the leader of the fourth-year C class calmly took his seat in the stand with his own fighters. The noise around him immediately died down, since nobody want to get attacked again, while the noise in the younger class stands, on the other hand, ramped up again.

Akira Takada and Makise Abe were still in the changing rooms. Makise had skillfully hyped himself up. The guy was clearly no stranger to getting ready physically. Of course, his flow and changing poses gave off a certain uncertainty in their incompleteness. Dammit! No, he was a wizard. Most likely, when I felt something didn't make sense, I had to first take into account the influence of the pumped-up magically hits, and only then technique. But that wasn't true either. Technique was beyond these students, only hits with raw energy. But even that wasn't too bad. They had sent me to the hospital for a long time in the past.

Wizards had to leave these flaws in their technique. This was a weakness of the gifted, that they hammered these perfected sets into their muscle memory, ones that were dependent on the use of techniques they didn't have yet, so they had to get by without them somehow. A sacrifice you made now so you could be perfect in the future. But it wasn't that big of a deal, since all the other wizards did the exact same thing.

However, when they had to deal with people like me or Noburo Surezawa from Okubo Academy, then it wasn't so easy for them. All of the flaws in their defense became obvious, which is how a weakling like Surezawa, who was the country's champion boxer, could trample weak schools under his feet and take out Akira Takada, the best fighter at Gakko, in a duel.

But today the fearsome girl only faced a fight with a regular fighter. Akira had experience, strength, and the techniques developed by the Takada clan over the years on her side. Makise's clan school was in no way worse. He was younger, yes, but that was made up for by him being a prodigy. Abe's potential was unbelievably high, and in the future he had every chance to become a Meijin. But talent was only ten percent of success, and the rest was work, work, and more work. That's why Makise should already be a highly-trained adolescent. And why it was so hard to predict who the favorite in today's battle should be.

As usual, the red corner was for the older ones, the blue for us. Akira came to the fight in a special outfit. As far as I knew, it was the standard uniform for real athletes, participants in the Games, both in individual duels as well as in team battles. But damn, even through the TV screen it was making a big impression on me…

Akira's uniform, form-fitting like a second skin, didn't leave any even an iota up to the imagination. The girl stood before the public practically naked. Okay, nanofabrics could be considered clothing, but they didn't cover anything at all, just the opposite. And the color scheme emphasized what it needed to. Jesus, I would lose to Akira in the first minutes of the fight, or bring it to parterre, even though Matvey Nikolaevich had strictly forbidden close contact with wizards.

Her well-developed breasts were emphasized by an intricate design. I thought I could even make out the nipples. Her flat stomach, round thighs, thick booty, and the triangle between her legs. Who the hell designed this costume?! The prevent didn't spare colors in specific places. I wasn't the only one drooling, by the way. The room was literally shaking with stomping, hooting, and whistling. The male half, as a whole, was expressing their approval.

Jesus, there should have been at least some shock absorbers, but Akira had probably taken them off on purpose. Of course, without them she could hit more. Makise lost his concentration completely in the first few seconds, looking like a man on the verge of being knocked out. How do you fight with such a beauty?! You had to be a consummate misogynist, a castrated eunuch, or just a woman to not be staggered by Takada's breathtaking outfit. Maybe I was too quick to choose my girlfriend... Or maybe I could be with both sisters...?

While I was drooling onto the floor, covetously staring at the charms of Kiyoko's older sister, the gong sounded and the fight started. Hmm. Makise was clearly no less impressed than I was, otherwise how could you explain why he had not yet even managed to raise his hands when he took a powerful direct jab to the face? There had been ten feet of space between them. He could have defended himself ten times over, but he did nothing of the sort!

Ah, yeah, would you have been able to? I completely understand my ally. When Akira started moving... Even adult men held their breath. It was some kind of magic! Her perfect round butt cheeks bounced in such a way that one of the operators stopped showing the fight, focusing only on them. Another one, very professionally, constantly filmed the heaving globes of her front half. Which meant, of the three screens I had in the changing room, only the one in the middle showed what was going on in the ring. But I was watching the side ones! And so was everyone else!

The room only came to its senses when Makise had gotten over the powerful blow and rebounded back to the opposite corner of the arena. That helped the boy a lot. It seemed like such a good clocking had cleaned out the guy's brain and returned his ability to think. The Abe heir jumped back up to his feet as a different person, meeting the flying Tanaka with a powerful one-two punch. Sure, it didn't go anywhere, but the tenor of the fight had changed. Otherwise the fight threatened to be over in a few seconds.

What followed was an exchange of insignificant blows that was rather disappointing for fight lovers. Although, while I don't know how the women saw it, the men were watching with their mouths wide open. It was understood that everyone later would confirm that they had never seen such artistry in fighting, but actually they were just staring at that goddamn beautiful figure.

Abe did not disappoint. Do not think that I am talking about how he fought. No! I am talking about him as a man. Understanding the complexities of the situation, Makise decided to do what every normal man longed to do. Despite the risk and the rain of heavy blows, he craved to grope the girl. At least three times the prodigy of the clan attempted to change the fight into something that was completely non-traditional for wizards. But clearly he himself could not use his legs or do throws. Or maybe the very experienced Takada simply knew how defend herself from those. One thing was sure. Makise was about the first person who ever made a duel like this, against all logic and good sense.

Gakko Academy

Everything ended with an insulting smack on the nose and follow-up flurry of blows to the body. Makise was, for a second time in the short fight, shaken up enough to completely clear his head. There are times when fighters are in a state where they all of a sudden began to see the whole picture of the fight and intuitively predict their opponent's next move. The young Abe was reeling from the attack, while Akira was preparing the finishing blow.

I felt it in my gut that my ally was preparing a trap. And when Takada dashed forward, Makise did the dumbest thing a fighter could do in the arena. Instead of a left hook to the liver or a devastating right jab to the jaw, he did something that immortalized him as a legend in Gakko Academy. Abe did the unthinkable, turning sharply and grabbing Akira's boob with one hand, placing the other one directly on both of her ass cheeks.

The crowd went wild! Both operators continued to give close-ups with the persistence of a madman, so I could see everything in the finest detail. The situation was now truly awkward. Takada, having failed in her finishing move, was now caught in the strong and somewhat embarrassing grip of Makise. But our fighter touched everything in his desire, and also soon put himself it an unwinnable situation. Doing a throw now would be too awkward and to land a punch he would have to put some distance between them, and nobody would be able to tear their hands away from that. So they were at a stalemate.

But then, the face of the third-year showed so much contentment that it was clear, he would hold on to what he had managed to grab, even at the price of defeat. Even the strict judges viewed this kind of fight with complete understanding. But that, it seemed, did not satisfy the elder Takada. She wrenched herself out of the strong embrace and slammed her elbow across Makise's head as hard as she could.

She followed it up with a knee hit and then a crowning one-two on the head. If I caught a series of hits like that, I would either be in a casket or the ICU. But Abe was an incredibly durable person, and maybe he had gotten charged up with Psy energy no less than I would from the girl's boobs and butt. In any case, Makise found the strength within himself to back off a little and repeat the trick he did with the magic cloud on me in the hospital, to everyone's surprise.

For the gifted Akira, who was also very familiar with this clan stuff, an attack like this could not be called devastating. She had something like a shield (or more precisely, just a magical reserve) around her, and that significantly reduced the damage. But it was still a pretty damn good hit. The girl was literally knocked to the ground, and now it was Makise's turn to try and end the duel in his own favor.

And he did not disappoint us. None of us, none of the guys. Abe threw himself straight forward and knocked the girl to the woven mat with a sweep. Then he perched on top of the fragile Akira with his whole body. The audience literally howled in excitement. Any normal member of the male sex would want to be in Makise's place right now.

But the boy clearly did not know what do next. Abe had zero grappling ability, and Takada's firm tits were pressing right up against his chest, drawing his attention. It was a good thing my ally had put on a jockstrap, but still, you had to look. In the end our pseudo-warrior could think of nothing better than to just keep lying there. To be honest, to a lot of people it seemed like his bumbling attempts at fighter seemed more like a desire to get Akira out of her snug outfit.

For the first time the rule worked, the one that the old Yakut had drilled into my head. The mass of the strong and stocky Makise pinned the skinny girl's body to the ground, where magic would be no help, because you couldn't argue with gravity. However, Akira, having calmed down and stopped panicking, collected her thoughts and pumped up her arms and her body with energy. Then she sharply lifted her opponent with her legs and the lower part of her body, moving her feet in a circle, she twisted suddenly and ended up in cowgirl position on top of Makise.

With her feet pressed under her opponent's hips, she squeezed his torso tightly with her thighs. This was actually just a clear victory. My ally had mere seconds to change the situation. He could have turned around suddenly, which would risk giving his back to Akira, although considering how prepared the gifted were, that wouldn't be too bad. He could have hit her right in the head and twisted suddenly to the side at the same time to get out from under the comparatively light Takada.

But right now he had to think quickly and clearly, putting his plan into effect in a flash. And my brat Makise did not disappoint the men in the room. Withstanding the powerful blows of the champion of Gakko Academy, he lifted himself up, grabbed the girl by her hips, and pressed his face right into her... sizable chest. Hot damn! A perfect, I am not ashamed to say, even genius way out of the situation. With her opponent's hand tightly gripping her ass, Akira had no chance to turn away, and the fact that he was pressed up so tightly against her, guaranteed that her hits couldn't reach his long-suffering face.

Now everyone truly believed that Makise was the prodigy of the Abe clan! How else could you explain his truly brilliant techniques? All the men in the room were truly shocked by the creativity and resourcefulness of the inexperienced third-year. I felt like many of them envied his position. To pull off a fight like that you really had to work at it. The slightly sweaty, delightful girl was writhing about in Abe's arms, exciting her opponent even more, along with the male half of the audience.

As Abe later admitted to me, if he hadn't had the strap where he did, he would have embarrassed himself about twenty time in front of the whole school. Akira Takada definitely had a terrifying weapon, the power to turn off the mind of even the most experienced fighter. Abe, trained by the most bloodthirsty in his clan, instead of making an effective decision in the fight saw only those moves that would lead him to a close embrace with the beautiful champion.

Everything ended rather badly for Makise in particular and the second year in general. Takada, livid, knowing that she was becoming a laughingstock in front of the whole school, yanked her opponent's head away from her breasts and with precise, sharp hits stunned the young Abe. At that time he nearly passed out, no longer able to keep the two ass cheeks he had come to love so much in his hands. The athlete's body fell to the mat, and Akira give him a few more violent sledgehammer hits to the head.

Her reward was Makise, falling unconscious, with his face covered in blood, but the boy looked at Akira not like a defeated opponent, rather smiling sweetly and even somewhat contentedly at the beautiful girl. Whatever you thought, and whatever was officially announced, the real winner was Abe. He had gotten what he wanted from the duel, even though he had to pay a terrible price.

Epilogue

AKIRA TAKADA'S VICTORY was announced and the medics hurriedly carried another duel victim away from the scene. But, just like last time, the sympathies of the audience were with the younger classes.

Osamu Saito had barely defeated the second-year Raiden Nakata, and if he hadn't been showing off and acting disappointingly stupid, then by all accounts the fourth-year, despised by so many, would be lying in the hospital instead.

In the same way, Akira's victory looked very meager. Makise had hardly fought at all, spending the whole fight trying to get his pervert hands on the girl's goods. And because of that he had made so many sacrifices that he had won the respect of a large portion of the audience. Even the women were thrilled by the single-mindedness and bravery of the Abe clan's prodigy. If a man was willing to go through that much for a woman, was he not an ideal life partner? Probably more than one girl in the room had asked herself that question.

A little later the following emotional conversation occurred in the head teacher's office.

"Ketsu, hahaha, what? What was that? You promised me sensational fights, but that, ha, ha, ha!" The bastard of the imperial family could not hold back his laughter.

"Your Highness—" began Aoki, the head teacher, but was interrupted by an authoritative gesture from his guest.

"Aoki, are you trying to insult me?" The aristocrat furrowed his brow. "Do you think that recognition has changed anything. Or have you forgotten how we fried rats, saving ourselves from the savages on Kalimantan?"

"I understand, brother, forgive me," Ketsu Aoki changed tone immediately. "Let me say that what happened, for me at least, was completely unexpected. You know that we have long been pushing the classes toward this massacre. Gakko has many new experiences ahead of it, which we have been preparing deep within the Ministry of Defense, as you know. And I thought that today's fights would spur the school gangs to action, to training, to mental activity..."

"They're just kids, Aoki," Matsumoto broke in politely.

"Yes, but believe me, I had prepared a real spectacle! The first boy is the son of the head of

Biotech!" said Ketsu excitedly.

"Oh yeah?!" Tetsuya was surprised.

"And there is some unsubstantiated evidence that some of their products have been tested by the father on his own child!" Aoki said, surprising him even more. "Did you see his speed? That is not magic. It's definitely something else!"

"Damn! And I was thinking about taking you out of the school. I thought you were losing your touch here, becoming some loser nerd..." The prince said, giving his plans away a little.

"Ha, lose my touch... And the second one? Did you see the second one? He is the prodigy, goddammit, of the Abe clan. How many prodigies have we had in this country recently?" The legate asked, heatedly.

"Basically none," Tetsuya answered dejectedly.

"Exactly. How often do you see in once place a wizard hopped up on Biotech stimulants and a prodigy from an ancient clan, and then they get into a fight with strong opponents?" asked Aoki.

"Prodigies? Never. They hole them up in clan schools until they reach the rank of Shihan. And the Biotech stimulants are still just a myth," Matsumoto answered, thinking it over.

"Right! I got it all ready, I waited. Getting all these monsters in one school, organizing battles for the whole school network... Shit! And instead Nakata put on a goddamn clown show and poured the whole duel down the toilet! But that piece of shit really could have been a sensation. It's like he lost on purpose!" The head teacher was clenching his fists in rage.

"Oh, you have even more intrigue going on here than at the ministry," Tetsuya said, supporting his old friend.

"And the goddamn Abe?! The whole fucking battle he's just groping the tits and ass of the school champion, one of the strongest fighters from the Takada clan!" said the head teacher, getting even more upset.

"Those ones, the outcasts?" asked the prince.

"Uh-huh," Ketsu answered gloomily.

"Then what, your plan didn't come off?" the prince asked, disheartened.

"Hmm.. I have not seen and did not show everybody what I wanted to show them, but the boys, no matter how much they tried to hide their potential, showed enough. We are going to work! In addition, I have saved the worst monster for last."

"Something even stronger than the first two?" The prince was doubtful.

"Much, much stronger. But I am not going to spoil the surprise. You will see for yourself!"

End of Book Two

Want to be the first to know about our latest LitRPG, sci fi and fantasy titles from your favorite authors?

Subscribe to our NEW RELEASES newsletter:
http://eepurl.com/b7niIL

Thank you for reading *Gakko Academy!*
If you like what you've read, check out other sci fi, fantasy and LitRPG novels published by Magic Dome Books:

NEW RELEASES!

Crossroads of Oblivion
a portal progression fantasy adventure series
by Dem Mikhailov

Gakko Academy
a portal progression fantasy adventure series
by Evgeny Alexeev

War Eternal
a military space adventure LitRPG series
by Yuri Vinokuroff

The Hunter's Code
a LitRPG series by Yuri Vinokuroff & Oleg Sapphire

I Will Be Emperor
a space adventure progression fantasy series
by Yuri Vinokuroff & Oleg Sapphire

An Ideal World for a Sociopath
a LitRPG series by Oleg Sapphire

The Healer's Way
a LitRPG series by Oleg Sapphire & Alexey Kovtunov

A Shelter in Spacetime
a LitRPG series by Dmitry Dornichev

Kill or Die
a LitRPG series by Alex Toxic

Living Ice
a portal progression alternative history series
by Dmitry Sheleg

Reality Benders
a LitRPG series by Michael Atamanov

The Dark Herbalist
a LitRPG series by Michael Atamanov

Perimeter Defense
a LitRPG series by Michael Atamanov

League of Losers
a LitRPG series by Michael Atamanov

Chaos' Game
a LitRPG series by Alexey Svadkovsky

The Way of the Shaman
a LitRPG series by Vasily Mahanenko

The Alchemist
a LitRPG series by Vasily Mahanenko

Dark Paladin
a LitRPG series by Vasily Mahanenko

Galactogon
a LitRPG series by Vasily Mahanenko

Invasion
a LitRPG series by Vasily Mahanenko

World of the Changed
a LitRPG series by Vasily Mahanenko

The Bear Clan
a LitRPG series by Vasily Mahanenko

Starting Point
a LitRPG series by Vasily Mahanenko

The Bard from Barliona
a LitRPG series
by Eugenia Dmitrieva and Vasily Mahanenko

Condemned
(Lord Valevsky: Last of The Line)
a Progression Fantasy series
by Vasily Mahanenko

Loner
a LitRPG series by Alex Kosh

A Buccaneer's Due
a LitRPG series by Igor Knox

A Student Wants to Live
a LitRPG series by Boris Romanovsky

The Goldenblood Heir
a LitRPG series by Boris Romanovsky

Level Up
a LitRPG series by Dan Sugralinov

Level Up: The Knockout
a LitRPG series by Dan Sugralinov and Max Lagno

Adam Online
a LitRPG Series by Max Lagno

World 99
a LitRPG series by Dan Sugralinov

Disgardium
a LitRPG series by Dan Sugralinov

Nullform
a RealRPG Series by Dem Mikhailov

Clan Dominance: The Sleepless Ones
a LitRPG series by Dem Mikhailov

Heroes of the Final Frontier
a LitRPG series by Dem Mikhailov

The Crow Cycle
a LitRPG series by Dem Mikhailov

Mirror World
a LitRPG series by Alexey Osadchuk

Underdog
a LitRPG series by Alexey Osadchuk

Last Life
a Progression Fantasy series by Alexey Osadchuk

Alpha Rome
a LitRPG series by Ros Per

An NPC's Path
a LitRPG series by Pavel Kornev

Fantasia
a LitRPG series by Simon Vale

The Sublime Electricity
a steampunk series by Pavel Kornev

Small Unit Tactics
a LitRPG series by Alexander Romanov

Black Centurion
a LitRPG standalone by Alexander Romanov

Rorkh
A LitRPG Series by Vova Bo

Thunder Rumbles Twice
A Wuxia Series by V. Kriptonov & M. Bachurova

Citadel World
a sci fi series by Kir Lukovkin

You're in Game!
LitRPG Stories from Our Bestselling Authors

You're in Game-2!
More LitRPG stories set in your favorite worlds

The Fairy Code
a Romantic Fantasy series by Kaitlyn Weiss

***The Charmed* Fjords**
a Romantic Fantasy series by Marina Surzhevskaya

More books and series are coming out soon!

In order to have new books of the series translated faster, we need your help and support! Please consider leaving a review or spread the word by recommending *Gakko Academy* to your friends and posting the link on social media. The more people buy the book, the sooner we'll be able to make new translations available.

Thank you!

Till next time!